AN AIR THAT KILLS

Books by Francis King

TO THE DARK TOWER

NEVER AGAIN

AN AIR THAT KILLS

THE DIVIDING STREAM

THE ROD OF INCANTATION (*poetry*)

THE DARK GLASSES

THE FIREWALKERS

THE WIDOW

THE MAN ON THE ROCK

SO HURT AND HUMILIATED (*stories*)

THE CUSTOM HOUSE

THE JAPANESE UMBRELLA (*stories*)

THE LAST OF THE PLEASURE GARDENS

THE WAVES BEHIND THE BOAT

THE BRIGHTON BELLE (*stories*)

A DOMESTIC ANIMAL

FLIGHTS (*two novellas*)

A GAME OF PATIENCE

THE NEEDLE

HARD FEELINGS (*stories*)

DANNY HILL: MEMOIRS OF A PROMINENT GENTLEMAN

THE ACTION

INDIRECT METHOD (*stories*)

ACT OF DARKNESS

VOICES IN AN EMPTY ROOM

ONE IS A WANDERER (*stories*)

FROZEN MUSIC (*novella*)

THE WOMAN WHO WAS GOD

PUNISHMENTS

VISITING CARDS

SECRET LIVES (*novella*)

THE ANT COLONY

YESTERDAY CAME SUDDENLY (*autobiography*)

THE ONE AND ONLY

ASH ON AN OLD MAN'S SLEEVE

A HAND AT THE SHUTTER (*stories*)

DEAD LETTERS

PRODIGIES

THE NICK OF TIME

THE SUNLIGHT ON THE GARDEN (*stories*)

WITH MY LITTLE EYE

AN AIR THAT KILLS

by

FRANCIS KING

with a new introduction by the author

Kansas City:
VALANCOURT BOOKS
2008

An Air That Kills by Francis King
First published by Home and Van Thal, 1948
First Valancourt Books edition, January 2008

An Air That Kills © 1948, 2008 by Francis King
Introduction © 2008 by Francis King

Library of Congress Cataloguing-in-Publication Data

King, Francis Henry.
An air that kills / by Francis King. – 1st Valancourt Books ed.
p. cm.
ISBN 1-934555-27-4
1. Uncles–Fiction. 2. Nephews–Fiction. 3. Manners and customs–
Fiction. 4. England–Fiction. 5. Authors–Fiction.
I. Title.
PR6061.I45A77 2008
823'.914–dc22

2007039269

Published by Valancourt Books
Kansas City, Missouri

Composition and design by James D. Jenkins
Set in Dante MT

10 9 8 7 6 5 4 3 2 1

INTRODUCTION

WHEN I was a child, living in India in a white house with a huge verandah and a multitude of servants, I already had only one answer to the common question put by adults to children: "What do you want to be when you grow up?" I wanted to be a dress-designer.

Squatting at my mother's feet, a box of crayons beside me and a pad of drawing-paper before me, I used to make sketch after sketch of frocks (in those days people like my parents rarely spoke of dresses) for her to wear to bridge parties, to the races, or to dances at Government House. From time to time my father would frown across at me and bite on his pipe. Before his premature death in his forties, he had risen to the rank of Deputy Director of the Intelligence Bureau in India. A brilliant shot and in his youth a hero of the hockey field, the last thing that he wanted was a son who carried on, as he put it, "as though he were a nancy boy" and might be destined to become, for God's sake, a dress designer. From time to time, exasperated beyond endurance by my behaviour, he would admonish me to take my hand off my hip or to "stop simpering and mincing."

"Mummy, mummy—look, look!" My mother would look down from whatever women's magazine had just arrived from England after a transit of several weeks by sea and would bestow on me a fleeting, indulgent glance and then a smile. "Oh, lovely, darling." She would tweak the sketch out of my hands, glance at it and then put it down on the table beside her. She was not a showily elegant woman but she always dressed smartly and "sensibly." Although she would frequently ask the *durzi* (tailor) to copy something for her from one those magazines sent out to her, she never asked him to do the same from my sketches. These ended up in the waste-paper basket. Nonetheless, evening after evening, as the punkah swayed above us or the lightning flashed and the thunder boomed around us, making my terrified mother cover her ears with her hands and squeeze her eyes shut, I used, totally absorbed, to continue with my work.

Then all that changed. Before I was nine, the separation took place not merely from my beloved mother but also from a beloved India of pony rides, games of pat-ball on the dried-up tennis lawn with the golden-haired son of our nearest neighbours, lavish fancy dress parties and obsequious, ever solicitous servants. No child of a respectable English family could possibly stay in the country after the age of nine, since otherwise… Since otherwise, what? I used to ask the question but never got an answer. I presume that it would have been: "Since otherwise you might go native." A friend of my mother, herself returning "home" (England was always "home" to the English expatriates, however humble they were and however many generations of their families had been resident in India) to be with a daughter stricken with tuberculosis in the sanatorium in which she hoped to be cured but in fact soon died, offered to take me with her. My last memory of my mother was of her running along the platform beside the train that, carrying me hundred of miles to a giant liner of the P & O company anchored in Bombay, remorselessly accelerated until she could no longer keep up with it and halted breathless, a hand pressed to her heart and the tears streaming down her cheeks, near the precipitous end of the platform.

England seemed a cold and indifferent place when finally I arrived there. My relatives were neither of those things; in fact they did everything in their power to make me feel welcome and happy. But, inevitably, the demands of their own children had precedence over any that I might make, and to those children they showed far more affection than they ever did to me. It was then that I found a new vocation that at once supplanted my previous one. I began to tell myself stories. I even began to write stories. Many years ago a master puppeteer told me how, even as a child, he had similarly adopted what was to become his lifelong vocation. Powerless to stop his father drinking or his mother from having a succession of lovers, he bought a puppet whenever he could save enough of his lavish pocket money to do so. By pulling the strings of these puppets, he had the power to make them behave exactly as he ordained. He was their absolute lord, putting them to death in their boxes and then jerking them back to life on a mere whim. For me it was the same. The imaginary characters to whom I spoke when alone and about whom I eventually came to write were entirely subservient to me. In this imaginary world I was, like the youthful puppeteer, the absolute lord. Often I could not easily differentiate between that imaginary world, always so vivid, and the drab reality around me. So it often is for me even now. After I have spent the best part of a day on the doings of my characters, they are for a time still far more solid and vivid for me than the vague shadows into which all the real people around me were transmuted while I was working.

Because I began to write so early in my life, I published early. In 1946, while I was still a twenty-three-year-old student at Oxford, my first book *To the Dark Tower* was published. My second *Never Again* appeared a year later. *An Air That Kills* appeared in 1948, when I was just about to take up my first job as a lecturer for the British Council at the British Institute in Florence. It was with a novel about Florentine life, *The Dividing Stream*, that I could be said to have "established" myself with literary editors and the reading public two years later. That I did so when so young has had the effect of making people suppose that I am even more ancient than I am. My friend for more than fifty years, Angus Wilson, was ten years older than myself. But my three first novels preceded his first book, a collection of short stories entitled *The Wrong Set* (1949) by three years. In fact, when he had suffered a nervous breakdown while working secretly on enemy ciphers at Bletchley during the War, I was one of those to suggest to this most brilliant of conversationalists that he should attempt a book as therapy. The result won him instant fame—and, significantly no further breakdown ever followed.

When, in order to write this introduction, I picked up *An Air That Kills* after so many years, I at once felt that I was reading a work entirely new to me by a writer of whom I had previously never even heard. Then, gradually, memories revived. The young Paul, painfully struggling to escape from the constriction of his teenage chrysalis in order to emerge into manhood was, for all the differences of psychology, upbringing and appearance, essentially myself. So too, paradoxically, was the older man, his uncle Mark, whom I had subconsciously created as myself in a still distant future. Although Mark is the narrator, I now feel, what I did not feel at the time of writing, that Paul is the more deeply imagined character of the two and so the one about whom at the close we there-fore know and understand far more than we do about his uncle.

The reason for this is now clear to me. In creating the two characters, I was hindered by the constraints that any writer of that time suffered when dealing with the still dangerous subject of homosexuality. When I was a student, I made no secret of my sex-ual inclinations. In contrast, many of my gay fellow students were careful to keep their sexual unorthodoxy discreetly concealed. Some of those friends now remark to me on my "courage"—or "recklessness," as one of them recently called it—in being so frank. Unfortunately this frankness could not extend to *An Air That Kills*, since if it had done so it might never have been published.

A recollection now returns to me of how, over lunch at his London club, the East India, my godfather, then a distinguished civil servant of the Raj, asked me what career I proposed to fol-low when I had graduated. I replied "Oh, I really want to be a writer. But until I begin to have some success at that, I'd like to be in the Foreign Service—if I can get in." He pondered. Then he turned his head to gaze intently at me with his piercing blue eyes. "Don't you think that you'd be a little too"—he hesitated—"un-conventional for that. I think that you might be better suited to the British Council. They do cultural and academic work abroad, you know. They don't demand the same standard of"—again he hesitated—"well, conventionality from their people. Yes, they're far more easy-going." A shrewd old chap, he of course knew the score. But at that period, it was better to be indirect about such a regrettable, albeit common, aberration, rather than openly to refer to it. So it was into the British Council that I went—an organisa-tion for which I can only be grateful for its tolerance and humanity in an age when most institutions were so intolerant and inhumane about the "illness" (as many people then saw it) from which I was suffering.

Had it not been so difficult to write freely and frankly about the love that even by then hardly dared to speak its name, Mark would, I now see, be a different character, and his obsessive attach-ment to his nephew an immediately more understandable one. I wanted it to be a sexual obsession, as well as a spiritual love, but it was impossible to make it so except by indirection of the kind that other writers whom I admired—James, Conrad, Forster—had adopted before me. Such novelists wrote in a code that they hoped that knowing and sympathetic readers would, like those clever cryptographers at Bletchley, be able to decipher. If a gay character was humorously presented as such an outrageously camp figure of fun as Evelyn Waugh's Basil Silk in *Put Out More Flags*, Christopher Isherwood's Mr. Norris in *Mr. Norris Changes Trains*, or the transvestite dame of traditional English pantomime, then that was all right. But if the reader was expected to take a gay character seriously, then he must be one of two things: either sinister and depraved, or so much racked with self-disgust and guilt that he ended up being murdered or killing himself.

My book was greatly influenced, in theme but not execution, by an Anglo-Irish writer, Forrest Reid, now sadly far too little read. Over and over again Reid returned to the same theme of an older man's love, not for someone in his late teens as in my book, but for a pre-pubescent boy. Remarkably but perhaps not surprisingly, there is never any suggestion of sexual activity between the couple, even though there are innumerable descriptions of the physical attributes and the charm of the youthful loved one. In my novel, the relationship is not dissimilar: Paul for Mark is the son that he never had, Mark for Paul is the caring father for whom he has always craved. Both are outraged when a malicious woman suggests that there is more to the relationship than just close friendship.

Rereading the book brought home to me how much England has changed in the course of my lifetime. Nowadays only the very rich have live-in servants and those servants are rarely English but usually from less prosperous foreign countries. The merely "comfortably off" make do with au pairs, educated girls who, eager to improve their English, are usually accepted as one of the family. Emotions were then kept sternly in check—the "stiff upper lip" always in place. This reticence is reflected in the dialogue of the novel, which may perhaps strike younger readers as at best formal and at worst stilted.

Some readers may find it improbable that Paul's rites of passage to manhood should take place when he is nearing his twenties. Nowadays in England both boys and girls all too often have their first sexual experience soon after they have entered their teens.

But, when I was incarcerated in a public (i.e., private, fee-paying) school, to which girls were never admitted as students and only rarely as visitors on special days, the sad truth is that, although there was everywhere a steamy atmosphere of testosterone, sexual activity was so much taboo that sex all too seldom took place. It was the same at Oxford. Most students, male and female, were still virgins when they arrived there and most of them remained so. A beautiful and intelligent girl, whom I had known for many years before we found ourselves up at the university simultaneously, committed the enormity, as it was then considered, of getting herself pregnant and was at once banished, never to return. One of the great academic figures of the time, Maurice Bowra, who was widely known to be gay, once remarked to me, "The trouble with this place is that it's all talk and no do." Paul in being so innocent was no exception from the norm of that period.

What do I think of the merits of the novel? As I have indicated already, I have read it after more than half a century as though it had been written by some other writer, whom I never knew and who died a long, long time ago. If I were to write on the same theme now, I should, as I have also already indicated, handle it with far more frankness—making it absolutely clear that Mark's obsession with Paul is as much one of overwhelming physical attraction as of paternal love.

On the positive side, I was surprised by the assurance with which, even at that comparatively early age, I created a variety of believable characters and kept the narrative constantly and irresistibly (I hope!) moving. The other potent influence on me at that time was Somerset Maugham. He was a writer the absolute opposite of Forrest Reid. Reid was a shy, socially awkward provincial, who left his native Belfast only to take part in croquet tournaments (he was a redoubtable player) the length and breadth of England during the summer months. He was totally unworldly, he had no celebrity friends other than E.M. Forster, and his style can best be compared to exquisite embroidery. In contrast, Maugham was a cosmopolitan, a ceaseless and adventurous traveller, host to famous politicians, painters and writers in his magnificent South of France Villa Mauresque, and a writer of remarkable range. Yet from this couple, totally different from each other, I learned equally valuable lessons in my youth.

What I chiefly learned from Reid was how to handle the English language. What I chiefly learned from Maugham was how to tell a story and to make the people in it credible. Maugham once told me that the most potent influences on him in his youth had been French, not English, authors. Interestingly, a reviewer, Jonathan Keates, of the most recent of my novels, *With My Little Eye*, in the *Times Literary Supplement*, wrote of me: "King's style, so acridly precise, so delicate in its manoeuvres, often seems more French than English in its emphasis on subtext and implication rather than on the concreteness of circumstance." That French influence on my work came to me, at one remove, from Maugham—a writer whom English and American critics still so often fail to acclaim him for what he is: the English Guy de Maupassant.

Francis King
London

September 15, 2007

An Air That Kills

IT was not a long attack.

When, some two hours later, my mother came into my room to find me sprawled face downwards on the rumpled bedspread, I was suffering from nothing worse than a feeling of clammy clothes swaddling clammy body and an intermittent hammering, like a chisel on rock, over my right eye.

"My dear!" She peered first at the trousers thrown over the back of a chair and then squinted at the tie hanging from the bedpost beside her. "Are you all right?"

"I was feeling rather groggy. But I'm better now. More myself."

"I'm sure you've a temperature. You look so flushed." Her hand went down to my forehead and I felt the hard, chill weight of the three rings on it. I nearly jerked away but then controlled my impatience. Above me her small, triangular, still pretty face had an expression of serenity not uncommon among the egotistical and complacent: never in her life had she worried deeply about anything but her own well-being, and since she had always possessed health, money and the attention and service that money buys, it was not surprising that there were less lines on her forehead than there were on my own. Her soft, billowy hair had been tinted a pale mauve—a fashion that repelled me no less than the crimson varnish on the nails of her wrinkled hands.

"You're burning! You must let me get the doctor."

"No, no. It's nothing. Off and on I get this fever."

"I know that you think that any doctor in a place as remote as this cannot be any good. But old Dr. McGregor is absolutely first-rate. He was a Harley Street gynæcologist—oh, very much in demand, world-famous in fact—before he retired to the island with that grim and gruesome wife of his."

"I don't need a gynæcologist, mother. And I'm sure that Dr. McGregor doesn't know as much about malaria as any half-reputable Indian doctor."

"As soon as I saw you I thought how ill you were looking. So yellow, so thin. I was terribly shocked. Did you notice?"

I shook my head.

"You never notice anything. Well, of course I tried not to show it. . . . But is there nothing else wrong with you? Is it only this wretched fever?"

"Oh, I'm run down of course." I was becoming impatient with so many questions about myself. "But it's hardly anything. I had a check-up at the School of Tropical Medicine. They said that there was nothing really serious the matter. I just had to go on taking the pills."

She sighed. "I suppose these doctors know what they're talking about. Did they tell you to rest?"

Involuntarily I grimaced. "Well, to take it easy."

"Then you've come to the right place. You have this year of sick leave. So don't even think of returning to India until that's over. And don't rush away back to England as you always do. Try to spend your whole leave here in Scotland—with us, on the island. The air here is marvellous, everyone's so healthy. You will do that for me, won't you? You'll stick it out here?"

"I'll see."

"No, I insist. Promise to stay for five or six months."

But I would not commit myself, and a glance at her watch had already told her that it was five minutes past tea-time. She disliked having to wait for anything, above all for meals.

Hurriedly she excused herself, adding: "I'll get the maid to bring your tea up to you."

"No. I'll come down."

"Oh! . . . In that case I'll leave you to follow. I expect you want to tidy up."

Looking in the mirror to straighten my tie, I realized how much of a shock my appearance must be to anyone who had not seen me for ten years. The skin of my face had a taut, stretched look as if it had been recently burnt; my eyes, blue-black at the centre but jaundiced at the whites, were sunk deep in their sockets. A nerve in my temple twitched uncontrollably. A shock. But did she really care? No. No more than I should care if she herself were ill. All sympathy was dead between us; if we ever thought with affection of each other, it was when we were apart—and then it was not really affection that we felt but only a nostalgia in which it was pleasant to indulge for a few moments when we had nothing else to do.

At the top of the stairs I had a brief spell of giddiness, and had to clutch the bannisters in order to prevent myself from plunging headlong downwards. I told myself how foolish I was not to have agreed to my mother's suggestion that the maid should bring my tea up to me. These days I could never make a decision without wishing at once to reverse it: and it was hard enough to make any decision at all.

"Ah, Mark! Come and be introduced to Miss Stott." My hand was wrung energetically by a tall, gauche girl in tweeds who smelled vaguely of dogs and stables. I noticed that as our fingers met, a blush, painful in its intensity, mounted from her throat to her forehead.

"Miss Stott and Paul went for a walk," my mother explained.

"And where is Paul?" The only other occupant of the room, my mother's companion Tilly, turned towards the girl.

"I don't know."

"Didn't you come back together?"

In her embarrassment the girl had stooped down and begun to play with one of my mother's Pekingeses, but it did not escape me that she was once more blushing. "No—no, we didn't."

My mother, busy pouring out the tea, exclaimed: "Now don't say you two have been quarrelling again!"

"Oh, we didn't quarrel. He wanted to go one way, I wanted to go the other. That's all."

"That's all," Tilly repeated with an upward inflexion—half question, half malicious comment. Then she turned to me, and it was extraordinary how both her face and voice softened: extraordinary after so many years. "Your mother tells me you're ill. I wish you'd take more care of yourself." She took my hand in her large, firm one and drew me towards the sofa where she herself was seated; it was a gesture at once proprietary and intimate. Yet the very touch of her cool flesh, the smell of her eau-de-Cologne, repelled me.

A door slammed down the passage, and at the sound the girl

who had the appearance of waiting for just this to happen, exclaimed: "That's him! He must be back!"

"I wonder if he knows that tea is ready," my mother murmured.

"Shall I go and tell him?"

"If you like. Yes, do. Tell him to come and meet his uncle."

I noticed that as the girl turned the handle of the door, her raw, big-boned hand trembled. When she was gone, my mother exclaimed: "Such a nice girl! I do wish Paul would be kinder to her. He's so boorish."

"I think it was disgraceful that he wouldn't come with us to meet you," Tilly put in.

"Oh, I don't know. I don't expect he finds a middle-aged uncle much of an attraction. I must admit I'm anxious to meet him, though." Yes, I *was* anxious: all at once I realized it. I had hardly given him a thought since my arrival, but now, as we waited for the girl to return with him, I felt an excitement, almost an apprehension. This would be our first encounter.

"Well, Betty?" The silence in which I had been thinking of my nephew—perhaps for the duration of a minute, perhaps only for a few seconds—was broken by the girl's return. Her freckled, horse-like face, with its long nose, pale auburn eyebrows and heavy jaws, blinked at us in dejection.

"The door's locked. He won't answer."

"Perhaps he isn't there," my mother suggested.

The girl shook her head. "I heard him moving about."

"Did you tell him his uncle was here?" Tilly asked.

"Yes."

"I can't understand it!" my mother exclaimed.

"Oh, you know he often does this sort of thing," Tilly retorted. She turned to me: "It's so difficult without a man in the house. He's more than we two women can manage between us."

"I expect he's working," Betty put in.

"Working! I'd like to know what work he does!" Asperity put an even sharper edge on to Tilly's voice. "It's so rude to his uncle."

"His window may be open," Betty suggested. "Shall I go round and see?"

The two women assented to this plan. "Put your head through and tell him to come at once—from me," my mother said.

"Oh, leave the boy! It doesn't matter. Anyway, it's raining and Miss Stott will get wet."

But they only shook their heads. Betty went, and we sat in silence listening to the argument that followed her departure.

"Go away!"

"Your grandmother says——"

"Oh, go away!"

"But your uncle's here."

"Damn my uncle."

"Please, Paul——"

"Can't you see I'm busy? I don't want tea. And I don't want to meet my uncle."

"Sh, Paul! He'll hear you."

The window slammed shut.

I could not repress a smile, but the two women, sitting in the long, low-ceilinged room, with the silver tea-things between them and the rain outside, had on their faces an expression of extreme disapproval. Betty returned, shrugging her shoulders: "He won't come." Her voice was only just under control, and I noticed that she went to a chair where she could sit with her face averted from us. For many minutes barely a word was uttered. There was an atmosphere of subdued tension which oppressed me—at that time it was part of the nature of my ill-health to be morbidly sensitive to such things. Then suddenly, inexplicably, it passed: the girl swung round in her chair and began to eat with a plodding thoroughness. Tilly produced some embroidery, my mother talked.

I had known that the two older women would sooner or later tell me of their war experiences, and after a few desultory remarks it was on to this subject that they both pounced. They were pathetically eager to impress on me that they, too, had had their share of hardship and sacrifice. Admittedly, the island had never been bombed; admittedly there had always been plenty of butter, meat and eggs. In many ways they had been more fortunate than others. But for five years they had been exiled on this remote outpost off the coast of Scotland; and on the one occasion when they had gone to the mainland—to Edinburgh—the Germans had made a raid on the city. "Tilly was so brave. But I cried. I just cried and cried. I couldn't help myself. It was so horrible. We returned the next day, and I vowed never to leave the island until the war was over."

I stared at the flickering reflection of the log-fire in the Georgian tea-things and tried to stop my eyelids from falling inexorably downwards; from a mile away, I could hear the melancholy swish and thud of water, a sound which recreated for me some part of the nostalgia I had that afternoon experienced before my bedroom window. Nearer at hand, and fading into it, were the voices of the two women and the chump-chump of Betty's jaws as she made her way through a slow, but comprehensive, meal.

Gradually, prematurely, the day faded; the room seemed to expand, I could no longer see the rain beyond the windows, and Tilly's face, heavily shadowed now, had acquired a peculiar, almost menacing strength. I knew that I should soon fall asleep.

"Any tea left?" The unexpected voice startled me out of my lassitude. There was, too, some familiarity of tone and inflexion which made me swing round as if expecting to see someone I had once known well. Our eyes met; I stared.

Tilly was saying something. He came towards me. I saw his hand extended; saw it, and after what must have been many seconds, shook it. But I could not take my eyes from his face.

I wondered if they all thought my behaviour odd, but I need not have worried. As he went to ring for some more hot water, Tilly whispered: "I'm glad you snubbed him. The way he came in as if butter wouldn't melt in his mouth!"

By then I had recovered. He sat down in a chair opposite me, and began to eat. Evidently my mother thought that he should be making some effort to talk to me—I, myself, felt that it would have been kinder—and she at once began: "Your uncle had a very tiring journey."

"Oh, yes."

"Very tiring. Didn't you, Mark?"

"Yes, it was rather tedious."

"Paul's a great walker. You both have that in common. You walk a lot, don't you, Paul?"

So she went on. But all her efforts at creating an artificial cordiality failed—for one insuperable reason: Paul would not respond. I was conventional enough to dislike him for withholding that response. I thought him ill-mannered. In fact, having once recovered from the helplessness into which his first appearance had stunned me, I decided that he was not worth bothering about. (Not worth bothering about? Had I really decided on that?) Soon Betty said that she must go; she turned to him: "It's stopped raining. You haven't seen the puppies yet. Why don't you walk back with me?"

He did not answer, but merely shrugged his shoulders.

"At any rate, you will see Betty out," Tilly commanded.

"How are the pups?" my mother asked.

At once the girl's face became radiant. "Oh, sweet! You must come and see them. They're spaniels, you know," she said, turning to me to address the first words that had passed between us other than formal greetings.

After they had gone, my mother once more exclaimed: "Such a nice girl! She does so love coming here. Often it's inconvenient, but I haven't the heart to send her away. I think the poor child looks upon me as a mother—she lost her own when she was born. So sad, I think. Oh, I do wish Paul wouldn't treat her so horribly. I think she'd like to be friends with him. I'm sure she would. You can see that, can't you? I do what I can for her, and I know she appreciates it. It's rather wonderful when one meets someone who's *really* grateful for all one does."

I let her run on, but I was not listening. Tilly was tugging at her embroidery—a knot had formed—tugging and tugging until the silk snapped: her eyes, burning with their unspoken devotion, rested on my face. I knew that I was waiting. A tread would sound in the passage, the door would open. I waited, and the seconds slipped away. . . .

At last I heard his footfalls. A door slammed. He had gone straight to his own room.

II

DURING the next two or three days I had no opportunity of becoming better acquainted with my nephew. I saw him at meals, but otherwise he seemed to carry on an existence independent of the rest of the household. From time to time I made desultory efforts at drawing him out but the nature of his response discouraged me. It was not that he was brusque or offensive in any way: but I had the feeling that if he was polite to me it was only from a sense of duty; in reality he found me a nuisance and a bore. Could I blame him?

At any other time, I might not have accepted defeat so easily. But in my state of physical debility I could persevere for only a short space of time. The slightest effort wearied me; I gave up. In any case, I seemed to have lost the faculty of caring about a thing sufficiently to exert myself over it. My vitality, once an inexhaustible source, had now to be conserved with the strictest of economy. My days were mostly spent in eating and sleeping: I would go down to the revolving summer-house at the far end of the garden, and there, within view of the sea, I would doze over some three-decker novel that I had found in the bookshelves of the house. I can remember nothing of those novels now: I suppose that at the time of their publication, each of them had its separate individuality, but the years had drawn them together and made them seem intolerably the same. Yet I went on reading them, one after the other, because the demands made by any other kind of book left me exhausted. I had hoped to do some work on my History of the Mogul Empire while I was on the island. For years I had been filling notebooks on the subject but had always lacked the time to sieve and arrange my mass of evidence. Now I had the time, but the inclination had left me. Upstairs in my room were fifteen volumes from the London Library, and I had looked at none of them.

Although my desire was only to be left in peace, I could not prevent my mother from badgering me for advice on the anxieties which from day to day beset her. She never followed my advice; but to ask for it only to reject it seemed to give her a sense of confidence. Inevitably, the topic of Paul must sooner or later be brought up.

One day she came down to the summer-house. "There's something that's been worrying me."

"Paul?"

"How did you guess?"

I shrugged my shoulders.

She wished to do her duty by him, she explained: she owed that to his poor dead father. But it was not easy. Paul was not an easy person. I listened to her, reclining on a wicker chaise-longue, my eyes closed. "No, he's not easy," she repeated. "He's not like other boys. He doesn't seem able to make up his mind about what he wants to do in life. I had hoped the Army might appeal to him—the uncles could have done so much to help. But his health prevented that. And it was the same with everything else that we suggested."

"Had he no ideas of his own?"

"None. Except the University."

"And what was wrong with that?"

"What was wrong with that? But, my dear Mark, if he'd got a scholarship, I'd have been only too glad. But otherwise, how could I afford it? How *could* I? Owing to this beastly war, my little income has dwindled to practically nothing. And, as you know, I've had to pay out for him for over six years now. His poor father left three hundred pounds, his mother even less. I feel I've done everything that could be expected of me. I paid for him to go to a good public school—admittedly they gave him a grant and he won a scholarship—and I'm keeping him now. But it can't go on, it just can't go on. I shall be ruined." I experienced a sardonic pleasure in hearing once more all this talk of a small income and financial disaster. I, too, had wanted to go to the University, over thirty years before, and since I, too, had failed to win a scholarship, I was told that it could not be afforded—a decision I might have borne with a greater equanimity if my mother had not, that same year, spent four months at Monte Carlo.

"Of course, I know it's not altogether his fault that he failed the scholarship," she went on. "It's unfortunate that he got this tubercular arm and was bed-ridden for nearly a whole year. But that, too, was a terrible expense to me—a terrible expense."

"I thought you wrote and told me he was in a public ward."

"So he was. But that doesn't mean that there weren't a hundred and one things to pay for. As for a private ward—we couldn't even consider it!" She paused for a moment's breath, and then continued: "Not that I grudge it, mind you. I'd do anything for poor darling Gilbert's child. But he's been living here since his last term at school—over eight months now—and he shows not the slightest sign of getting himself a job. It can't go on Mark. My income won't stand it. There are his clothes, his meals, his pocket-money——"

"His pocket-money? How much pocket-money?"

"Five shillings a week."

"Well, that won't break you."

"What do you expect me to give him?" she demanded indignantly. "Five pounds? That's enough and more than enough for a boy of eighteen."

I did no more than shrug my shoulder: but the gesture infuriated her.

"It's not as if he showed the least gratitude, or even tried to be pleasant towards one. You don't know. You haven't had to live with him for months on end. He's quite unlike any boy I've ever met."

"I can see for myself that he's something out of the ordinary."

"He can be so disagreeable and disobedient. He did quite well at school, but even they found him a handful."

"What is this work he's supposed to do when he locks himself up in his own room?"

"Heaven knows! He has some idea of being a writer, I think."

"Have you ever seen any of his writing?"

"Only once. He won't show one anything. But Tilly found a bit of a short story in his waste-paper basket. We couldn't make head or tail of it. Curious, morbid stuff."

"H'm. . . . I think he should have his chance. I think you should let him go to Oxford."

"But I've already told you——"

For a time we argued. Then, suddenly, as would often happen in those days, a profound lassitude overcame me; I no longer cared. I felt ashamed at not persevering and yet—what could I accomplish even by perseverance? Never, in my whole life, had I persuaded my mother to do anything she did not wish to do.

As I went in to lunch some minutes later I passed Tilly and my nephew in the hall. I glanced at him with a new sympathy. My own adolescence had passed in something of the same atmosphere of revolt and misunderstanding. I heard him ask Tilly if, on the motor trip which she had just made down to the town, some two miles away, she had remembered to pick up a book that he had ordered. I winced at her contemptuous retort: "No. I was too busy. I suggest you walk down."

III

THAT afternoon I happened to stroll down to the town and picked up the book for Paul.

He did not at first seem to understand when I handed the parcel to him. "I overheard you ask Tilly about it. As I was down in the town, I thought I might as well pick it up for you."

"Thank you," he stammered. He was seated out in the garden with a pad and pencil. "I don't know why you bothered. Thank you very much." I felt that his gratitude was no less sincere for being so gauche.

"What is the book?"

"Kierkegaard. . . . He was a Danish philosopher."

"Yes, I did know."

I had not intended to snub him, but my words had that effect. "I'm sorry. I didn't mean to—to——"

"Why be sorry?"

"I thought you might imagine. . . . After all, it was rather patronizing of me."

"Of course not. I'm not as sensitive as all that. May I sit down?"

He moved farther up the seat to make room for me, but said nothing.

"I'm not disturbing you?" I asked.

"No, rather not."

There was a silence, in which he fiddled with the pad, and I watched him. He was small and he looked much younger than his eighteen years. His dark curly hair fitted him like a cap—there was no parting, and I imagine that he seldom brushed it. He was dressed in a worn-out pair of corduroys and a tweed jacket. The sun had caught him, though it was still early summer, and the flesh of his throat seemed curiously brown against the white of his open shirt. From his fidgeting and from the conversation we had just started I realized that when he had previously seemed to be rude and arrogant, he had been suffering from acute shyness.

"Your grandmother was telling me that you'd like to go to the University."

"Yes." He spoke in a flat voice, little more than a whisper.

"I imagine you find life here rather dull."

"Oh, I don't know."

"Have you many friends?"

He muttered something with his face averted, so that I could not hear him. Evidently he did not wish to discuss his own affairs. I realized then that it would not be easy to win his confidence, and with that realization came the uprush of excitement that one experiences when one is about to embark on some arduous under- taking in which there is no certainty of success.

"I see you read a lot. I have a subscription to the London Library, so I can get you any book that you may want."

"Thank you."

"Let me have a list, and I'll see what I can do about it."

"Thank you."

Apparently I should achieve no more that day. But I was not discouraged: I knew that the paralysing effect of shyness lasts long after one has ceased to feel shy. I got up. "Well, I must go and wash my hands before tea."

When I entered the house, I looked back at him from the hall window. He was gazing outwards into space; on his features was a smile of almost childish pleasure. He had not smiled once while I was talking to him.

IV

AFTER this encounter, I found myself looking forward to the same evening when there might perhaps be a further chance of talking to him. But as soon as dinner was over and we had drunk our cof- fee, he got up and left us without a word: I knew that he must have gone down the drive towards the town—I had heard his whistle fading gradually on the still evening air. Tilly and I were now left *tête-à-tête*, my mother having gone for the weekend to one of the neighbouring islands.

"Bézique?" Tilly suggested.

"If you like."

"But you never did enjoy card games."

"They're a way of wasting time. I used to think it wicked to waste time. Now I have more time on my hands than I know what to do with."

"I'm afraid you must find life rather boring here."

"Boredom usually comes from within oneself—not from outside circumstances. It does in my case."

"I think you're one of those people who are fated to be unhappy."

I did not answer, and we began our game. Tilly played with an eager concentration, and I knew that I should lose to her. An utter weariness descended on me. "I wonder where Paul went."

"To the town, I suppose. Up to some mischief or other."

"You're rather hard on him."

"Oh, at that age, you know——" Had I imagined it or was there a peculiar, heavy suggestiveness in the way she spoke the words? Our eyes met, and I quickly looked away. Suddenly I had become aware of her physical presence—the nearness of our two bodies with only the card-table between us, the flesh of her arms and throat under the grey voile of her dinner-dress, our knees almost brushing each other; once again I was experiencing the shame with which she would always be associated for me—the shame of one's first carnal act.

I knew that, as we pored over our cards, we were both gazing back over the years at that incident, she with longing, I with disgust. Tilly had first come to my mother's house as maidservant, when she was sixteen years of age and I four years younger. I still find it difficult to believe in the transformation of that clumsy, mute animal into the woman who was to become my mother's inseparable friend. Her ascent was slow. She became my mother's personal maid; and then, when my mother had a bout of ill health, accompanied her as nurse-companion to the French Riviera. Between them there sprang up one of those passionately spiritual

friendships so common among women, so rare among men. My
father was already dead. In spite of differences of age—my mother
was nearly twenty years senior to her—class and temperament,
the relationship endured. Tilly had a remarkable aptitude for ab-
sorbing the manners of a society that was by birth alien to her:
perfectly, unobtrusively, she extricated herself from one milieu and
fitted herself into another.

It was strange, for the Tilly who had first come to us had
seemed like any other of the girls who worked in the house, but
for her strength and remarkable, if sullen, good looks. Tall and
big-boned, with thick, straight fair hair coiled in a plait round and
round her head, she approximated closer to the ideal of that period
than of our own. She spoke little, seldom smiled, but her efficiency
was a wonder to us.

At first, I had taken no particular notice of her; I joked with
her, teased her and behaved (as one was brought up to behave towards servants) as if she were no more than a useful household
pet. As a person I did not become aware of her until after my third
half at Eton. I had come home with an invitation from a school-
friend to spend a fortnight at his house in London; my mother
had questioned me about this boy, and then inexplicably—perhaps
because she mistrusted my affection for him, perhaps because his
parents were divorced—had refused to give permission for the
visit. In chagrin, I rushed up to my room, threw myself on my bed
and burst into tears.

Tilly, entering to turn down my bed, found me there in the dim
half-light. She crossed the room to me and asked me what was the
matter: but I would not answer. Then she sat down on the bed and
said one or two words of comfort. I felt, irresistibly, that I needed
someone's protection and love, and sitting up on the bed, I buried
my face in her lap. She let me lie there for a while, stroking my head
with one of her large hands. "Oh, Tilly, I'm so unhappy!" I cried.
She made me an inarticulate, animal noise of sympathy and drew
my head on to her breast: I rested there, trembling not only with
grief but a new, strange awareness. I pressed my cheek against hers,
I touched her hair; and she in turn began to caress me, running her
hands down my arms and back. At each touch sobs, of pleasure
now, not of disappointment, issued from my lips.

So it began; and though that day we went no further than I have just described, I began to crave more and more to be near her, to touch her and to feel her hair brushing my own cheeks. I do not believe that she deliberately set about corrupting me; but slowly this innocent play of ours degenerated until it was carried into a region unknown and terrifying to me. Never again was I to experience a remorse so profound. But, having once made that journey with her, I could not be still until our next return: and so, from time to time over a period of four years, we enjoyed an intimacy which I was so often to repudiate with shame, so often to renew with pleasure.

Now, some twenty-five years later, the memory of these events swept over me. Here we were, playing cards together; I looked at her, with hate, with repulsion and—I must be honest—with a vague lust that was part recollection, part reality. I felt, irresistibly, that I must get away from her. But how? What could I say?

"You're thinking of something else."

"What makes you say that?"

"You've missed endless chances. Perhaps you're tired."

"Yes, I suppose I am, really."

We spoke with the careful politeness of those who have between them some topic which they know they must not mention.

"Shall we stop playing, then?"

"After this game."

When the game was over, she put away the cards while I folded the card-table. There was a silence. She picked up her needlework; and then, as though at last giving way to an agony she could no more withstand, she broke out: "It's strange, isn't it? I believe that after all these years I—I still love you." Her eyes were fixed on me; her face, usually so strong, now seemed fragile and defenceless. I did not answer and she repeated: "Yes, I still love you. I suppose I always shall." Suddenly, with tremulous panic, she got up and began, with short, jerky movements, to push away her needlework. "I don't know what made me say that. I couldn't help it. I think I'll go upstairs now." I saw that there were tears trickling down her face. She went out quietly, shutting the door behind her.

The strain was over. I had felt ashamed and shocked while she had still been with me: but now there was nothing but a profound, irrational joy. I rose and walked two or three times up and down the room, clasping and unclasping my hands. I picked up a book only to put it down again. I stared at my reflection in the long, gilt-framed mirror that hung in one corner: my cheeks were flushed, my eyes shining as though at some good news.

At last, I went to the grand piano, raised the lid and began to play. The keys were stiff and dusty, and it was obvious that the instrument had not been tuned for a long time. I played from memory some of the pieces that I had long ago learnt in this same house, and the sound filled the room with ghosts, not of the dead—they did not trouble me—but of the living. A sadness, calm and without any tinge of bitterness, descended on my spirit.

After many minutes, I realized that there was someone else in the room with me, but at first I did not look round. When I did, at the end of one piece, I saw a figure, which I knew to be Paul's, standing in the shadows outside the french windows. He was perfectly still, and I could not see his face. "Go on," he whispered. "It's so long since we had any music in this house."

"But I can't play properly——"

"Go on," he repeated.

So I went on. All vexation, all weariness, all regret—they were stilled. It was strange how much of the music I could remember after so long a time. The thin, tinny sound of the piano brought a strangeness to all I played, imbuing even the gayest piece with a peculiar melancholy. At last I turned.

"Thank you." I saw his face for a moment as it moved out of the shadows; I rose to ask him in. But with a swift good night, he had already gone. I went out in the garden, and looked to left and right. The light burned from his bedroom window; he must have climbed in. A moment later I saw him jerk the blinds across. But for a long time I remained there, waiting—for what? I stared into the darkness. A moth blundered against my face, and fell to the ground. From the hillside above the house, a sheep coughed. It was getting cold and I went back into the darkened room.

V

THE next morning I made a visit to the kitchen to see Florence, the cook, who had been with my mother even longer than Tilly had. A Cockney, she had married one of the labourers on the estate and now lived with a large family at the lodge gates. She and I had always been good friends. She was a large, placid woman whose only fault was her love of a grievance: she never wearied of complaining to me about Tilly and my mother, though, for all her evident dislike of them, she had given her whole adult life to their service.

As I came into the kitchen, I was astonished to find Paul there, sitting on the table and helping himself from a box of dried figs. He and Florence were in conversation.

"Hullo, Paul! What are you doing here?"

"Oh, Master Paul often comes down here for a chat. Now just you lay off them figs. I don't know what your grandma will say when she sees how they've shrunk."

She walked over to the dresser, and with much blowing, began to lift down a bin of flour: Paul immediately leapt up to help her. "There's a gentleman for you, Mr. Mark. I don't seem to get my breath right these days. And my back! It's my waterworks, I shouldn't wonder."

While Florence made her pastry, we all talked. We discussed her health, her children and the food situation. Paul seemed more at ease than I had ever known him before. I had been afraid that he had no sense of humour, but he made us laugh with his good-natured gossip. His face, which had once struck me as being morose, now seemed frank and open. He kindled in me a gaiety that matched his own.

Then, suddenly, he jumped to his feet. "Oh, Lord! What time is it? Half-past ten! I was supposed to meet Betty at ten to play a game of tennis. Damn, damn, damn! I must fly."

"Oh, Master Paul! You really are too forgetful," Florence scolded him as he rushed out of the door. Then she smiled, in indulgence, as she turned to me: "He's a nice boy, that."

"I'm glad to hear you say so. From what Tilly and my mother led me to think——"

"Oh, don't you pay any attention to them. Tilly's got her knife into him—why, I don't rightly know. And, of course, she's made your mother feel likewise. They don't give him a chance now. Mind you, he's high-spirited and he doesn't always think of others. But he's a good boy at heart." She sighed. "I often wonder what'll become of him."

Her words might well be no indication of his true character; she was a kind, perhaps sentimental, woman who gave her affection indiscriminately to anyone who seemed to be in need of it. But on this occasion I was inclined to believe all she said.

"I've never had much to complain of about him. He's always been kind and civil to me. Those two never cease to declare how disobedient and rude he is. Well, if he's rude to them, I can only say they deserve it. After all, he's only a kid, isn't he? And look at the way they go on at him!"

Through this warm, unsubtle creature I was beginning to understand something of Paul's life. I let her run on, for by now I was interested in him and welcomed any information, however trite. Among other things, she told me how Tilly had deliberately created mischief between Paul and my mother, giving to some hasty words of the boy a meaning that was quite alien to them.

When I left Florence, I went down to the summer-house. I did not read, but lay on the wicker chair, looking out towards the sea, my mind full of Paul. I wished I could somehow help him. I decided that as soon as my mother returned, I should speak to her, explaining that what Paul most needed now was her affection. Like most adolescents he craved for stability; love would have given it to him but he had been denied love. In default, he had begun to invoke the authority of Tilly and my mother by countless small misdemeanours, since it was only in that way he could prove to himself that he 'belonged'. What terrifies an adolescent is the sense of being let loose, without ties, in a strange and hostile world: that someone should care about him was essential to Paul, even if to be cared about meant only to be nagged and snubbed.

Thinking of Paul's problem, I grew sleepy. The night before I had lain awake for many hours in a state of morbid turmoil. A thousand obsessive fears had weighed on me. I wondered if I should ever regain my health; if I should ever find existence anything but a tedious and irksome business; above all, if I should experience the joys of reciprocal love once more. Since May had left me, life had become no more than a preparation for the death which, in my vitiated state, filled me with innumerable vague terrors.

I must have dozed for several minutes. Looking at my watch, I saw that it was nearly twelve. Paul would probably have returned by now, and since his presence could usually lift the black cloud that weighed on me, I walked back to the house with the intention of seeking him out. I found him on the terrace, still in his white flannels, a book in his hand: he seemed absorbed.

"Well, did you have a good game?"

He started when he heard my voice, and as he turned to answer, I noticed how he slipped the book away from him so that a cushion half concealed it.

"Yes, thank you. I'm rather a rabbit, I'm afraid. I've only just started playing. All the time my arm was bad I wasn't allowed to."

I sat down beside him: our eyes met and he smiled. His flannels were grubby and his shoes needed cleaning, but in his open-necked shirt he had the attraction which exists wherever there is youth and health.

"What are you reading?" I drew out the book that he had been at pains to conceal.

He reddened. "Your book."

"I feel honoured. Is this the first time?"

"Yes. . . . I knew you'd written a book about India, but it never occurred to me that it could possibly be at all interesting. It's so unlike what I'd expected. I do like it."

"What made you start to read it?"

"Oh, meeting you, of course. And you're unlike what I'd imagined, too—thank goodness!"

"What had you imagined?" I asked, amused by his ingenuousness.

"I suppose the typical Indian civil servant. You look like that, you know. When I first met you, I said to myself, 'Just as I imagined.'" He broke off. "Am I being awfully rude?"

"Of course not. I'm interested. But tell me why I look like the typical Indian civil servant."

"It's not only looks. Your voice, too. Clipped and rather abrupt. . . . Oh, I shouldn't be telling you this."

"I'd no idea I betrayed my origins quite so plainly."

"But in your case appearances are just a blind. You're really utterly different."

"And is that a good thing?"

"Of course. For me, it is."

I was glad to have him speak without any shyness or restraint. I was glad, too, that he had felt me to be 'different' and sympathetic to his own way of thinking.

"Why have you never written another book? This was published in 1923, wasn't it?"

"Yes. Nearly twenty-five years ago. I wrote it after I had been in India for just over a year. It had no successor because the man who wrote it had, in a sense, died."

"Died?"

I paused a moment, wondering whether to go on or not: then I realized that if I wished to win his confidence I must give him my own. "I didn't want to go out to India," I continued. "Like you, I wanted to go to the University. Like you, I was told I couldn't go. They badgered me, and in the end I gave in. I wasn't suited for the life of a colonial administrator—I was studious and shy, and only books really interested me. For a while I was a hopeless misfit. You can probably see that from the book. I was naturally sympathetic towards the Indians—they were impractical, muddled and lazy as I myself was—and I was naturally out of sympathy with my fellow countrymen. But within a year or two the crooked pin had been straightened." I sighed. "It was a painful process. And when it was over——"

For a while we both sat silent, then he gave a slight involuntary shiver. "I hope they don't do that to me."

"You mustn't let them."

At that moment Tilly came up the garden path. Her face clouded when she first saw us, then she forced herself to smile.

"What on earth have you two found to talk about?"

"Oh, nothing much."

We went in to lunch.

VI

THAT afternoon, when I set forth on my usual walk, Paul ran out to join me. "May I come with you?"

"Of course."

"Are you sure you don't mind?"

"Why should I mind?"

"You might find it rather a bore having to trail around with me."

"I was thinking exactly the reverse—*you* might be bored with *me*."

"No chance of that!"

Paul strode ahead and I attempted to keep up with him; but in my state of health I soon became exhausted. He stopped in horror: "I'm so sorry, I've been unforgivably selfish. Why didn't you say I was going too fast for you?"

"Perhaps I felt ashamed."

"Oh, rot!"

But at that moment I despised myself for my feebleness; in his eyes, I must be unmistakably 'elderly'. I felt sad and discouraged.

Perhaps he realized this, for as we began to climb upwards, he slipped his arm into mine, quite naturally, as if to reassure me. "There's something I've been meaning to ask you."

"Yes?"

"When you first met me—do you remember?—at tea that afternoon——"

"Yes. I remember."

"Well—why did you look so astonished when I came into the room? As—as if I were a ghost!"

"So you were—in a sense."

"How do you mean?"

"You looked like someone of whom I used to be very fond."

He turned eagerly. "My father, you mean?"

"No. Your mother."

"Oh." For a moment a look of disappointment passed across his face. "Don't I look at all like my father?"

"A little."

"But I'm really like my mother."

"Yes, extraordinarily so."

He began to trudge on and I followed him.

"You're disappointed."

"No. What makes you think so?" He spoke sharply.

We continued in silence until we came to a small valley high up among bald, treeless hills. It was here that our ewes were penned before the lambing season. Paul greeted the shepherd, a boy of about sixteen years of age.

"This is my uncle, Angus. Angus helps Mr. McBryde with the sheep."

The boy touched his cap, obviously ill at ease in my presence. But Paul continued to talk to him—it was evident that he and the boy were old friends.

"What are you doing next Saturday, Angus? Come to the cinema with me."

The boy was uncertain what to answer, but in the end muttered his assent. He was a sturdy, good-looking youth with feet in large boots and hands whose nails were black with grime. He seemed a strange companion for Paul.

For a while longer we chatted and then said good-bye. "Angus is a great film fan," Paul explained.

"Do you often go to the cinema with him?"

"Quite often." He was immediately on the defensive. "I suppose that shocks you."

"Of course not. I just wondered what you two had in common."

"Nothing," he said with a sudden bitter emphasis. "I don't know why he puts up with me."

"Oh, he probably thinks it a fine thing to be seen around with one of the gentry." But as soon as I had spoken I regretted this cynicism.

"Angus is not like that," Paul said quietly. "He hasn't become my friend for anything he can get out of it—money, or kudos, or anything else."

"No, I'm sure he hasn't. I'm sorry I said that."

"He's the only real friend I have here. Granny and Tilly don't know about him. You won't tell them, will you?"

"Of course not."

"Somehow, I don't think they'd approve. They'd be sure to try to put a stop to it. They did once before."

"How was that?"

"Oh, there was the son of one of the tradespeople in the village. He was quite different from Angus. He won a scholarship to Glasgow, in the end. Grandmother and Tilly hated him—chiefly because one day he came to the front door and asked for me. They thought he should have gone to the back." He gave a short laugh. "Funny, wasn't it? But now you see why I don't want them to know about Angus. He might get the sack or something."

I hesitated to ask the next question, but at last I gathered courage: "Are you very lonely here?"

"Yes." There was no expression in his voice as he spoke the monosyllable.

"Aren't there any other boys of your own age—I mean, boys with whom you might have more in common?"

"Oh, there are plenty of boys of my own class, if that's what you mean. Grandmother spends her whole time trying to fit me in with them."

"But you don't fit?"

"No. I suppose I'm—peculiar."

We were descending a steep path, and all at once he began to run, loose pebbles cascading after him. He waited for me at the bottom, and then we walked slowly on: but I guessed that when he had careered down the path, he had wanted to escape from any further questions about himself.

VII

ON the homeward journey, we passed a house of grey brick, standing exposed to all winds on a jutting spur of hillside. There was about it an air of general dereliction. "That's where Betty lives," Paul said.

As he spoke, a touring car chugged up the rough road towards us and came to a halt; Betty herself was driving, with her father beside her. "Oh, Paul!" she shouted. "Have you no memory? I reminded you only this morning."

"Reminded me? What of?"

"The lecture, of course. I waited and waited for you."

Paul struck his head and groaned; he ran up to the car and began to make clumsy apologies. "Damned casual," Betty's father muttered; he glared at us.

"Oh, daddy—you haven't met Mr. Langworthy—Paul's uncle."

"How d'you do." He sniffed and looked away from me with a rudeness that embarrassed Betty far more than it did myself. Then, as Betty was still in conversation with Paul, he rapped out: "Come on, come on, woman! We can't wait about all day, y'know."

"Just a moment, daddy." She said a few more hurried words, and they drove off.

"That was awful," Paul said.

"Does he always treat her like that?"

"Oh, I didn't mean him—though God knows he's bad enough. Not quite right in the upper storey. He was always a bit strange, and then they interned him when the war broke out—he's a fascist, you know. That just finished him off. It's no fun for her. No, but it was awful of me to forget all about the lecture. I keep on doing that sort of thing with her. It's not that I don't want to remember; I just can't."

"Oh, it's quite a common psychological failing. I don't suppose you had any desire to go and so—quite unconsciously of course—you put it right out of your mind."

He pondered for a moment, and then laughed. "Well, perhaps that is the answer. I certainly had no wish to hear Canon something-or-the-other talk about lepers in the Church Hall. And I'd no wish to see Betty. But I could kick myself for letting her down like that."

"She rather gets on your nerves, doesn't she?"

"You've noticed that? Yes, I suppose she does. I find myself in a perpetual state of irritation when we're together. Yet, fundamentally, I think I'm fond of her and want to be nice."

I nodded. "There's nothing more irritating than to have some-one care for one far more than one can ever care back. I think devotion which one can't return is the most cruel of all human afflictions."

"That sounds rather cynical."

"I know that from experience. But I've always been at the oth-er end, so to speak. The adorer, who maddens the adored with his perpetual whining."

"I suppose Betty *is* fond of me."

"Of course she is."

"I wonder."

It seemed to me incredible that he should doubt it. Evidently, he was not vain, which surprised me, in view of his considerable personal charm. One day, I supposed that he would become aware of that charm—inevitably; and with that awareness, some part of it would at the same moment vanish.

VIII

THE next day, I had one of my attacks. I had somehow dragged myself upstairs and thrown myself on to my bed, without any-one knowing that I was ill. I disliked being treated as an invalid, ill health never having had the slightest attraction for me.

Some minutes later, there was a knock at the door and Paul entered. "I thought you must be up here. I came to ask you——" He broke off. "Oh, I say! Aren't you feeling well?"

"Just one of my attacks. Nothing to worry about." As I spoke to him, my jaw chattered idiotically and it was all I could do to get out my words. "In my suitcase—there are some pills. Perhaps you'd get me two. With a glass of water. Not that they help much."

"Well, of course."

He hurried to the suitcase, but brought me the wrong bottle.

"No, not these. These are sleeping tablets. The others are flat discs. . . . I'm being an awful nuisance."

"Of course not. Do you often have to take the sleeping tab-lets?" He was again rummaging in my case.

"No more often than I can help. I've been sleeping better here.

It's a curse not being able to sleep, so the doctor gave that dope to me."

"I suppose you have to be careful not to take too many."

"Yes. I've often been tempted to exceed the dose. Can't you find the others?"

"They're not here."

"Try the drawer."

He pulled open the drawer, and gave a short exclamation of surprise: for a moment he remained with his back to me, curiously stiff and still. Then he turned, the bottle of tablets in his hand. "Here they are." He gave a forced, nervous smile.

I wondered what had happened; then, with a shock, I realized. "The photograph? Yes, I've carried that about with me for the past twenty-five years. You recognize who it is?"

"Yes." He held out the bottle of tablets to me. I could not even guess what he was thinking.

"I suppose it seems strange to you. But—I don't see why I shouldn't tell you this now—we were once engaged to each other."

"You were engaged——!"

"Didn't she ever tell you? Yes, we were engaged for nearly four years. Then she married my brother—your father."

"But—but why? Why didn't she marry you?"

"I suppose because she cared for him more," I said with a lightness that I did not feel. "We became engaged just before I went out to India for the first time. It seemed best to wait until I'd settled down in my new life. Then I came home again and it was all arranged. She had been seeing quite a lot of your father in my absence and a few days before the wedding she broke it off. They got married almost immediately. She was already expecting you."

His next words amazed me. "Oh, how typical!" he exclaimed contemptuously. Of all the reactions he might have shown, this was the least expected. I stared at him in incredulity until he began to smile: "You're shocked at my saying that. You are, aren't you?"

"Yes, I am—frankly."

"I don't see any use in pretending to feelings that just don't exist—or in hiding feelings that do exist. Mother was like that. I know."

For a moment, I felt as if the whole scene were some illusory part of my fever. "I can't understand how you can speak of her in that way."

"Can't you?"

"I never for one moment blamed her. Why should I? After all, it's a thing that often happens. One loves a person, one falls out of love. Separations do that to one—one can't help it. No, I never had any animosity against her—or my brother."

"Oh, I don't suppose *he* wanted to do it. But she would twist anyone around her fingers." He must have seen the look of horror on my face, for his next words were curiously gentle: "I think you and I knew different people. Don't let's go into it all. There's no point."

"We must go into it. I must know. I can't understand you. Didn't you—didn't you like your mother?"

"Oh, for heaven's sake let's leave the subject!"

"No. Tell me."

There was a moment's pause; then he said quietly: "I hated her. You wanted to know—now I've told you. I hated her."

"But why? Why? What could you find to hate in her?" At that moment I realized that the cherished image was about to be struck into a thousand fragments.

"She behaved so badly to father. She ought never to have left him."

"But that was quite impossible. He was almost off his head."

"He needed her. Oh, but that wasn't all. It was one thing to stop living with him. It was another to behave as she behaved—shamelessly—openly—with anyone who took her fancy."

"You don't know what you're saying. All this has only happened in your imagination."

"It's true. And now I've hurt and horrified you. You made me tell you." I think he intended to leave it at that. But, even had I allowed him to keep silent, the urge to unburden himself of his full bitterness had become too strong. "Oh, she never cared about anyone except herself—certainly not about me. You've probably heard Tilly and grandmother say that I was dragged up anyhow. Well—it happens to be true. She never gave a moment's thought to me—never! And the things I had to witness when I was still quite a child—shameless, appalling things! We moved up and down the Riviera, from hotel to hotel; and mother always had her 'friend'—not always the same friend—close at hand. I came to despise her, and then to loathe her. I wanted to go and live with father, but of course that was impossible. I thought of him often. He was the only person I cared for. And then one day she told me he was dead—oh, quite casually, just like that. It was only long after that I learnt *how* he had died—in the bedroom of an Earl's Court boarding-house, the gas turned full on." He had spoken most of this in a jerky, abrupt fashion, without emotion: but at those last few words his voice sank to a tragic whisper.

"I never realized that your childhood had been so unhappy."

He left my words unheeded: all that now mattered to him was to go on, to tell all. "And when mother was killed—I can remember it so vividly. I had been ill, and I suffered from dreadful nightmares—you know how children do. She was motoring over to Monte Carlo for the evening—a rich South American had asked her, and she seemed very thrilled. I begged her not to go. I told her how frightened I was of being left all alone in that great hotel. She only said: 'Now don't be a silly boy.' And when I cried, she went out and locked the door on me. When they told me of the car crash, there was only one phrase running through my head: I'm glad, I'm glad, I'm glad."

The sharp, glittering fragments lay about us; there was no more to say. We looked at each other, appalled by the havoc we had ourselves created.

It was I who spoke first. "Perhaps if you understood her, you might forgive her. I don't think you can ever have properly understood her."

Hurriedly, like the workers who come out with spades and shovels after a bomb has fallen, I set about retrieving what I could from the disaster. The illusion of the girl whom I had long ago loved must somehow be built up anew. "You mustn't forget that she had lived seven years of absolute hell with your father. And she was a person who needed to be loved. She was high-spirited and she wanted to enjoy herself. Perhaps she went about it in the wrong way. And perhaps, in seeking the happiness which had for so long been withheld from her, she made you suffer. That doesn't make her wholly bad." But as I spoke, my mind was saying: "She had lovers. But she never turned to you. In all her unhappiness, she never turned to you."

He was looking at me with compassion. "I shouldn't have told you. I can't forgive myself. I see I've made you suffer."

"No, no. No harm ever came of telling the truth." (Did I really believe that?)

"I *have* made you suffer. I'm sorry. . . . And you're not well."

No, I was not well: but beyond all temporary aches and fevers, beyond the shivering of my body and sweat of my forehead, beyond all this there lay a black, profound despair. What she had done did not matter—I forgave that. But she was dead; I wanted her. I wanted her as I had never wanted her before. Beside that longing, all her faults and failings were of no account.

I lay with my head turned sideways, hot cheek against cold pillows.

"Is there anything I can get you?"

"No, thank you." I did not turn my head to say the words.

"I'm sorry."

He stood for a moment in the doorway, and then went out.

IX

THE memory of this scene, though it embarrassed us at our next encounter, could make no difference to our friendship. There was no reason why it should. 'I think you and I knew different people.' In those words of Paul I saw the key, not only to this particular situation, but to the whole complex business of human relationships. He had his memory, I had mine: each was true—within its limits.

We were never again to refer to what had passed: but an occasional oblique reference would remind me that he had not forgotten. For example, we had been discussing Tilly. Paul had complained of her attitude towards him: "She hates me. I can't think why. I've tried so hard to be friends with her."

"Poor Tilly! She's never forgiven you for being your mother's son."

"What do you mean?"

"Oh, just that she hated your mother."

Paul questioned me further, and in the end I had to confess to him about myself and Tilly. "She was rather keen on me, you see. And then when I became engaged to your mother, she was frantically jealous. And when the engagement was broken off she made no attempt to hide her exultation."

"I've noticed her protective attitude towards you."

"Yes, it's never altered."

"Strange. . . . All the time our lives are diverted by things we don't know about. Because she was once fond of you, Tilly hates me. And perhaps"—he coloured—"you would never have become friendly with me, if it hadn't been for——" He broke off.

Yes, it was strange. The woman whom he so much loathed had brought us both together. In him, I found her.

Meanwhile we were seeing more and more of each other. We went for long walks; he persuaded me to go riding with him—it was years since I had given up this sport; we had intimate conversations. My memories of that time are all bathed in sunlight. I suppose it must have rained; I suppose we were often confined to the house. But now, looking back, I can recall nothing but that beautiful, barren countryside as the background to all we said and did; the thought of it at this moment fills me with a desolating sense of loss.

When he asked me to look at a novel he had written, it seemed that I had finally and completely won his confidence. "You won't laugh at it, will you?"

"I'll try not to."

"I do so badly need someone's advice. You're the only person. Betty tries to be sympathetic and interested, but she doesn't really know."

"I'm not sure that I 'know'. But I promise an honest opinion."

I spent the best part of a night reading the book. I was absorbed; but whether someone who did not know Paul as I knew him would find an equal interest, I rather doubted. It was so essentially the work of an amateur; and like most first novels, it was crammed with everything the writer had ever thought or felt, regardless of its relevance to the theme.

The next morning I spoke to him about it: "I've read your book."

"Have you? What do you think of it?"

"I said at the beginning that I'd be perfectly truthful about it. You want that, don't you?"

"Of course."

I had felt that the whole story (its title was *A Beginning*) was no more than a day-dream of what Paul would like his own future to be. A young man leaves his home on a remote Scottish island to go to London; for a while he struggles, then he becomes famous as an artist (writer to artist is the usual transference in this kind of book); he falls in love with a woman who is no more than a vaporous ideal—sweetness and light, with not a redeeming shadow of character. Their love for each other is expressed in terms of a highly-coloured prose, half Wilde, half Pater; apparently it is a relationship devoid of all physical passion. . . .

It is easy enough to make fun of this kind of novel: but to make fun of it was the last thing that I wished to do. It seemed to me then, as it seems to me now, that though much of the book was valueless, yet it was full of a promise which I still hope to see fulfilled. When he was not trying to create a 'style', he wrote simply, clearly and euphoniously; there were one or two admirable situations; and at least half a dozen of the minor characters were drawn with insight. No, he must not be discouraged.

I began by gently drawing a parallel between his novel and *The Young Visiters*. "Both books create their own world. Your London has never existed except in your own mind. For example, this Mayfair dance. A hundred things make it quite unreal. The Club scene, too—and the scene at the Regimental dinner. You've had to imagine everything—it's just a dream."

"Yes, I know. I've never been to a Mayfair dance, or a Club, or a Regimental dinner. That's the trouble."

"I think you should stick to the things you're really familiar with—the life on this island, for example, your childhood, your schooldays——"

"Oh, no!" he exclaimed. "Haven't you noticed how many English writers there are who can write quite wonderfully about childhood? But if they try anything else, they fail. I don't want to be like that. I want to write about adults, the world, everything."

"So you must. But not yet. Wait till the experiences come to you."

"Wait!" His mouth sagged. "That's what's so difficult. Oh, how I wish I could get away from here. I want to see things. I want to meet people. Then I really will be able to write. I'll write something worth while—not this sort of drivel."

"It's not drivel. There are things in it I like enormously. I don't think you should try to publish it—frankly, I don't think it would stand a very great chance. But you must go on."

He was not listening to me. He stood at the window looking out, his hands in his pockets. "I suppose I shall get away some day or other."

His despair touched me, and I went across to him. "Of course you will. You're still very young."

"You don't know how much I envy you."

"Envy me?"

"You've done everything, and you've seen everything. You've travelled; you've been married; you've written a book which people go on reading."

"And what have I done with all my experience? Nothing. The material is there, but the creative gift is dead."

It is seldom that one can comfort another by a recital of one's own woes: nor could I, on this occasion.

"It's awful to feel that one's life is just drifting past. Time's so precious."

I let him unburden himself of the full measure of his gloom. I knew I could not comfort him, and to listen sympathetically seemed the next best thing. Everything in him was reaching out to the life of which he dreamed: he wanted to see pictures, hear music, and above all, to meet people with whom he could exchange the ideas that at that moment teemed within his mind. There was something tragic in his frustration.

X

I MUST help him; but in what way I was not then decided. It was not until the next day that a plan came to me.

We had gone for a ride together, taking a picnic lunch with us. It was fresh when we set out, after an early breakfast, and the wind chilled me through my aertex shirt.

"It's going to be a wonderful day," Paul exclaimed. He began to whistle 'Over the hills and far away.' He was riding a little ahead of me, in shorts, his legs bare. He looked over his shoulder: "All right?"

"Rather cold."

"Let's have a gallop then. I'll race you. To that spinney."

Of course, he won. As I galloped up to join him, he put out a hand and caught my horse's bridle. He was laughing, and I began to laugh, too.

"What's the joke?" he asked.

"I might as well ask you that."

"There is no joke. Just happiness."

We walked our horses on, our reins slack. I remarked: "Strange how much pleasure one can get out of the physical act of sitting astride an animal when it's in motion."

We were now riding along a cliff path, and far below us the Atlantic thudded and hissed, hurling its waves inwards like burnished knives. The wind was high here, and it kept blowing Paul's hair into his eyes, so that he had to brush it back with one hand. "How warm the sea looks," he called. "Let's bathe."

"I haven't brought my costume—or a towel."

"Doesn't matter. No one ever comes here. And the sun will dry you in absolutely no time."

"All right. But not now. A little later."

As I write these words, I can so vividly see Paul: his legs and arms are sunburned, his hair is in disorder; he has a jagged tear in the back of his shirt where he has ridden beneath some brambles. Behind him the sea falls and rises, tremulously rises and falls. A gull hangs overhead. He is there and will be there, forever. . . .

At last we came to a place where the land curved gently down until it reached the shingle, and we dismounted. "Where shall we tie the horses?"

"Oh, leave them loose. They won't go far." We took off the saddles and bridles and the horses cantered away from us, whinnying and sniffing the salt-laden breeze. Then one of them began to roll. Again we both laughed.

"I love to see them do that," Paul said. He began to take off his clothes and I took off mine.

"I'm not really supposed to bathe," I said. "The doctor would have a fit."

He looked concerned. "In that case, do you really think you ought to?"

"Oh, damn the doctor. Race you to the water!"

The first shock winded me but, after that, it was wonderful. Paul tried to duck me; we splashed each other, shouted, laughed and swallowed great quantities of water. The sun shone down out of one of those green-blue skies so common in that latitude.

"I'm hungry," I said at last.

"So am I. Let's eat."

We scrambled out, and lay down on a rock for the sun to dry us. Paul undid the saddle-bag in which he had brought our lunch, and offered me a sandwich and a hard-boiled egg. "That was good," he said.

"Yes, wasn't it?"

We munched in silence, our eyes closed against the glare that beat down upon our naked bodies. "I can't understand why you want to exchange all this for life in England," I said at last.

"Oh, when one has someone to share it with, it *is* wonderful. But alone . . . it doesn't seem the same. And then the winter—that's horrible. It'll be awful when you go."

"It's nice of you to say that."

"I mean it. You've been so kind to me. I think we have an awful lot in common."

"I think so, too. That's why I don't want you to make all the mistakes that I did. It's silly I know, but I feel—oh, well, that in you I'm having a sort of second chance. You know, I always wanted to have children—a son." I was telling him something I had breathed to no one else.

"When will you be going away again?"

"I don't know. I don't *want* to leave the island. But I have business in London, and old friends to see. My former wife has asked me to go and stay with her. Anyway, Tilly and mother are beginning to get on my nerves. I never could stand them for long."

"There's no definite date fixed for your going, is there?"

"No. Within the next two or three weeks."

He was sitting up now, his legs crossed, one hand flicking pebbles into the water. "I shall miss you," he said in a small melancholy voice.

As casually as I could, I replied: "Why don't you come with me?"

"To London?"

"Yes."

"But I couldn't possibly afford——"

"You don't have to afford it. Come as my guest."

"Oh, it would be wonderful! Do you really mean it?"

"Certainly, I mean it."

"But grandmother—and Tilly. . . . What will they say?"

"They can say anything they damn well please. I don't care."

He laughed; then his face went grave. "But you might get bored with me."

"I don't think that likely."

"You're very kind. I wish there was some way I could repay you."

"Your company repays me. You remember what I said about always missing a son?"

He started slightly, then looked at me, with what seemed to be an unspoken dedication.

I felt embarrassed. "Have another sandwich?"

Paul was full of questions and plans. When should we go? What should we do? How should we travel? I answered him as best I could, and at last he seemed satisfied. "Let's go in again," he suggested.

"No. I feel too sleepy. You go in and I'll take forty winks."

"Lazy!"

"You forget that I'm twenty-six years older than you are."
(Twenty-six years! Suddenly, the thought of that vast gulf oppressed me.)

"Oh, all right!"

I lay and watched him through half-closed eyes. He swam out
a long way, and then turned and waved to me. I waved back. I felt
glad that I had made him happy, and glad, too, on my own account. I shut my eyes altogether, yawned, and fell asleep.

I awoke with a slight shiver; the sun had gone behind a small
cloud. And where was Paul? Anxiously, my eyes raked the view.
Then, at last, I saw him; he stood with his back to me on a strip
of shingle which pointed, finger-wise, towards the mainland. The
outgoing tide must have exposed it while I slept. 'And the waters
were divided,' I repeated to myself, 'and the children of Israel
walked on dry land.'

The sun shone out again: I gazed to where Paul stood, his body
lucent in its slanting rays. He seemed to reach, ardent and quest-
ing, towards the mainland—the Land of Promise. I felt that all of
him—every thought, nerve and sinew—at that moment strained
to part the waters. An inexplicable foreboding seized me. I had accepted so great a responsibility, and should I prove myself worthy
of it?

At that moment Paul turned and waved to me. I waved back.
Vision, fear, presage—whatever it was—was forgotten.

XI

I KNEW that there were two people whom my invitation to Paul
would especially concern—Tilly and Betty. That same evening I
had told my mother of my plan; she had argued with me, but with
no real enthusiasm—she couldn't understand why I should wish to
saddle myself with the boy, and she was certain that I should regret
it. But secretly, I knew that she was glad to have Paul taken off her
hands. We parted amicably and I went to bed.

Half an hour later there was a knock at my door. It was Tilly.

"I saw that your light was still on, so I thought I'd come and speak to you straight away. Your mother's just told me." She spoke under the stress of an agitation which she could not conceal. "You're not seriously intending to do this?"

"To do what?"

"To take Paul away with you."

"Yes."

"But it's mad! It's absolutely mad!" She came to the side of my bed, clasping and unclasping her large hands.

"Why is it mad? You must allow me to be the judge of that."

"You've no idea of the sort of person he is. I know that you're taken with him. But you'll see. You'll regret it in a week or two. He's just out for what he can get from you. There's not an ounce of affection or gratitude in him. I know!" I had realized that she disliked Paul and was jealous of my friendship with him; but this implacable malice horrified me. She was laying bare the secret places of her heart to me; and if there was to be found there nothing but sand, stones and the husks of dead hopes, was I not myself in part to blame? "Tilly," I got in at last, "I think I know what I'm doing. I know that for some reason you hate Paul. But I like him. And I want to help him, if I can."

"Of course you do," she retorted with a curiously vulgar sarcasm. "Of course you do. He's making a fool of you just as she did. It's just the same."

"Tilly!"

"He's so like his mother. And he's got you where he wants you. I tried to save you then, I'm trying to save you now. Oh, don't take him away with you. It'll be a mistake. I know it'll be a mistake."

"I'm not a child."

"You said that then, too." All at once she spoke with a mournful resignation: "And I was right, wasn't I?"

"I want to go to sleep. I don't think there's any point in continuing with this argument."

"Yes, I was right. You know I was. And I'm right now. But you won't be persuaded. . . . So it's all fixed? When do you leave?"

"In a week or two."

"If you only knew—what it is—to have loved someone—year in, year out—for a lifetime——" Her face was contorted with anguish. "And for nothing! Nothing!" She turned and went out of the room, and I was left staring after her. Her outburst unnerved me. I told myself that she was a bitter and vengeful old maid and that I should take no notice of her. But an uneasiness still remained with me. The foreboding of that afternoon revived. I read for a long time and then switched out the light, but could not get to sleep.

XII

THE day before we were due to leave, I met Betty shopping in the town. She looked ill and unattractive—her forehead covered in a rash of small pimples, her hair scurfy.

"I hear that you're leaving us tomorrow," she said. "And Paul's going with you." When she spoke to someone she did not know well, she always kept her eyes lowered.

"Yes, I thought it was time for him to see something of the wide world."

"I don't expect we'll know him when he comes back. If he ever comes back." She shifted from one to the other of her large feet.

"Oh, he'll come back all right."

She did not answer, and we remained facing each other for what was becoming an uncomfortable silence. I was about to turn away, when she said:

"I'm glad for his sake. I don't think he's been happy for some time."

"Yes, I suppose he has felt rather frustrated here." I tried to say something that would cheer her, and eventually got out: "It's lucky he had you. I know what your friendship has meant to him."

"Oh, I don't think I've been much help," she said in a dry, constricted voice.

"I'm sure you have. Paul doesn't show things—you know that yourself. But it's easy to see——"

"Has he ever said anything?" she asked with a sudden eagerness.

"Not in so many words. But he always speaks of you with—with so much affection."

"Perhaps he does like me," she said at last, with what seemed to me a pathetic hopefulness. "I shall miss him." She turned away. "I'd better say good-bye now. I hope you have a good crossing."

"Won't you be coming to the quay tomorrow?"

"No. I don't think so. I've a lot to do tomorrow. I've things to do for father. Good-bye, Mr. Langworthy." She held out her hand, and I took it; it was strangely hot and moist. For the first time during that interview, her eyes sought mine, betraying the grief which she attempted to conceal. "Take care of him," she whispered. "Please take care of him." Then she broke away and was gone.

XIII

WHEN I told Paul of this interview, he was unhappy. "What can I do?" he asked. "What *can* I do? I like her, I'm sorry for her. But there's nothing more. I wish she wasn't so fond of me." Then he told me of a scene which had taken place the day before.

He and Betty had been playing tennis. For nearly all that week it had been raining on the island, and as they ran about the court, the mud squelched beneath them, their shoes became soaked and the water whisked off their rackets. The balls, dappled with green, barely rose from the ground.

"You're not trying," Betty complained after a quarter of an hour. They had already argued about playing at all under such conditions.

Paul banged a ball viciously into the net. "Oh, what's the good!"

"I do think you might make an effort. I know you think I'm such a rotten player that I'm not worth bothering about."

"It's not that. You know it's not that. Oh, damn!" a ball had landed in the laurels. "Now I shall have to get soaked."

"Oh, I'll get it!" She pushed her way angrily into the dense bushes and returned, her clothes and hair dripping. "There you are!" She flung it to him.

"You could have left it," he expostulated.

"That's how we always lose balls." They banged about for a little longer until suddenly she shouted: "I'm not going to play any more."

"Why?"

"Oh, because you won't try—and you don't want to play, anyway."

It was true, but he argued with her. "Come on! Now that we have started——"

But she was already in the summer-house, pulling off her tennis shoes and lacing up her others. He sat down beside her. "Oh, hell!" The lace of one of her brogues snapped as she tugged at it. She began to make a knot. "This is the last game we shall play together. Why did you have to spoil it all?"

"I didn't spoil it all. The rain did."

"I know I irritate you. But you might at least try to be polite to me."

"Oh, I'm sorry, I'm sorry! I can't say more." She did not answer, her face averted from him, and he repeated: "I've said I'm sorry."

"It doesn't matter," she sighed. "You don't know how unhappy I feel." She was shivering in her light tennis clothes; with repulsion he noticed the goose-flesh on her arms and legs. "I shall miss you, Paul."

"I shall miss you," he said with conventional politeness.

She shook her head. "This is different. You don't understand. I can't explain."

I have spoken already of Paul's complete lack of vanity; and at that moment he had no inkling of what would follow. It seemed to him that Betty was making rather a fuss over this parting; but he had long since decided that she was 'hysterical'—in his view, women so often were.

She clasped her hands between her large, bony knees. She sat hunched. Suddenly she turned: "*Do* you understand? Haven't you guessed?"

"Guessed what?"

"Oh, Paul, Paul, Paul!" She threw herself on his shoulder, her whole body shaking. "Hold me, comfort me, comfort me!" Her hands clutched at him; her hair, moist and vaguely unpleasant, brushed against his lips.

He was appalled. "Betty . . . What's the matter? What's happened?"

She raised her face, and then pressed her lips against his right temple, as though sucking from there invisible solace for her hurt. "I love you. I want you. I can't let you go."

He stammered his amazement: and almost immediately she, who had been pressing her whole body against his, began to push him away from her. They were both horribly embarrassed.

"I don't know what I'm doing. Forgive me. I couldn't help it." She picked up her racket, her shoes and her cardigan. "I don't think I'd better see you again," she said, suddenly composed.

"But you'll come to say good-bye——?"

She shook her head. "I'd rather not. It'll be easier." With a tragic intensity she added: "Perhaps I shall never see you again."

"Of course you will. Don't be absurd."

"That's what I feel. I can't help it. I've felt it for a long time now. Even before your uncle came. . . . Oh, Paul, what's to become of me? How can I live without seeing you?"

Suddenly, she stooped down and took his face in her hands. Her lips met his. Then, with a sob, she broke away and ran from him down the path which led to the drive. He called her name; he almost followed her. When one is young, it is easy to confuse pity with love and the thought came to him: perhaps I love her. His compassion and the vague lust aroused by her kiss blended together and for a moment deceived him. But later, as he recounted the incident to me, he saw things as they really were.

"How frightening it is to be loved like that! I hope I never suffer as she must be suffering."

XIV

"GOOD-BYE! Good-bye!" Paul cried joyfully. He turned to me: "Oh, it's so wonderful to see the last of the island." He looked back and his face became grave: "And yet there's a sort of sadness, too. Strange how one feels the jolt even when one leaves a place where one has been unhappy . . . I hope I never have to go back."

"Do you really feel that?"

"Oh, perhaps if you come with me," he corrected. "But not

alone. The island looks so beautiful from out at sea. Don't you think so?"

I nodded my head. "Perfect."

"Yes, you know I shall have to go back. When I see it like that—distant and shimmering through the haze—it almost makes me want to change my mind. Oh, not really, of course! But you understand what I mean."

"Yes, I understand. What one has one doesn't want. But when one can no longer have it . . . Isn't that what you mean?"

"Well—not exactly——" he deprecated.

"It's what I suffer from—and it's the most terrible of all spiritual maladies. To want only what one cannot have. Beware of that."

He laughed. "You say that with so much seriousness!"

"I mean it seriously. You know, I don't believe I've ever been really contented in my whole life. And why? Simply because I never want the things that I achieve. And so life becomes no more than a series of disappointments."

"You're trying to depress me. But I can't feel depressed."

"Perhaps it's just the sea-sickness that makes one so bitter."

"Are you feeling sea-sick?"

"Yes—aren't you?" I spoke with the resentfulness that is usual on such occasions.

"Good God, no!"

"Well, I think I'll go down to the cabin."

Ten minutes later he came to see how I was.

"Feeling better?"

"No—bloody."

"Is there anything I can do for you?"

"No. Just let me die in peace."

He was standing at the porthole, and shouted excitedly: "Oh, look, look! Land ahead!"

My only response was to lean out of the bunk and vomit.

XV

WHEN we arrived in London, we moved straight into a furnished flat that I had rented from some friends. "It must be terribly expensive," Paul commented.

"Well, furnished flats aren't exactly cheap these days. Still, it won't break me."

The next few days passed in an excited bustle: we went to concerts and art galleries, the South Kensington Museums, St. Paul's and Hampton Court. It was strange how my former lethargy had disappeared; I was feeling immeasurably better.

One of my first tasks was to introduce Paul to my tailor. I am a conventional person, and it embarrassed me that he had nothing better to wear to the theatre or a West End restaurant than corduroy trousers and a shabby tweed jacket. He, himself, felt no such embarrassment. He was quite unconscious of his appearance, and dressed with an untidiness which survived no matter what clothes I bought or lent him. For example, though I told him that he could borrow any of my ties that he wished, he invariably wore the same green woollen tie, pulled into a tight, ungainly knot. He never gave his shoes to Mrs. Bridge, our help, to clean, and often would walk about with one sole flapping loose. His hair remained as it had always been, unparted and unbrushed.

All these are small details, and no doubt it was foolish of me to be worried by them. But I have always found social faults much harder to forgive than moral ones. I told myself that it was unimportant if Paul met me for tea in Gunters in an open-necked shirt, and yet I had to remonstrate with him. He, in turn, sulked.

Tilly and my mother had never wearied of saying that he had no manners, and I now saw how right they were. He had been 'dragged up'—that had been his own phrase—and how could I blame him? But this lack of manners, which I had so easily dismissed on the island, was now a source of acute discomfort. On his second day in London I took him to my Club: it was unfortunate that we should run into an old friend of mine, a retired General whom I had known in India. He suggested that we lunch

together. An amiable bore, he attempted to chaff Paul, talked of
his own schooldays and told a number of scabrous stories. Paul,
with a sincerity that I myself lacked, made no attempt to conceal
his boredom—yawning openly, staring into space with his head
propped on his hand, and failing even to smile at the improprieties.
Worse, two of his fly-buttons were undone. I knew that my old
friend was not impressed.

Gradually, I tried to educate Paul, but it was a task calling for
a tact and delicacy in which I was too often to be proved wanting.
His sensitivity was extreme, and if I alluded too openly to some
social misdemeanour he would either make the heated retort, "If
you feel so ashamed of me, give me my fare home," or he would
be plunged in a depression from which he would not emerge for
several hours. My tongue is sharp, and often I would be tempted
to lash out at him, only to regret it when I saw how easily he was
hurt. I would find that he had borrowed my latch-key and then
lost it, had spotted ink on his bedroom carpet or had failed to give
me a telephone message: and on each of these occasions I had to
exercise a deliberate self-restraint. Moreover, Mrs. Bridge perpetually complained about the state in which he left his room; fortunately, she liked him—servants always did—or she might perhaps
have been driven to give notice. Paul suffered from the misappre-
hension that the proper place for clothes was on the floor; going
into his room, one stumbled over soiled linen, crumpled flannels,
shoes, books and letters. It was his natural instinct to drop anything for which he had no immediate use, and no complaints from
Mrs. Bridge or pleas from me could alter it. What I have written
here of the faults in Paul's upbringing may suggest that his company was beginning to pall on me. But, through all differences, my
affection for him remained untouched. I was enjoying what is one
of the greatest pleasures of old age—the possession of a disciple. I
suppose it was foolish of me to be so delighted at having my advice
sought on every conceivable subject. I was able to transmit to him
all my own personal tastes and prejudices. Philosophy, music, art,
literature, food, clothes: it is with a wry amusement that I now
recall our conversations on each of these subjects. No doubt I derived a sense of self-importance from playing Socrates to his eager
neophyte. But there was a satisfaction more profound. To arouse

the potentialities dormant in another is, perhaps, in itself an act of creation; and in creation the human soul knows its greatest joy.

XVI

IT had long since been arranged that I should spend a weekend with my former wife and her husband in the country. I did not know if Paul would wish to accompany me. "Be frank. If you'd like to come with me, come. She may even have some interesting guests. She rather likes to gather celebrities about her. What do you say?"

"I'd like to come. There's—there's just one thing, though." He coloured. "What—well, what exactly is my relationship to your— to May?"

I laughed. "I really don't know. Ex-nephew, I suppose. But don't let that worry you. May's the easiest person in the world to get on with."

"It seems funny——" he began, and then broke off.

"What seems funny?"

"Oh, nothing."

"You mean that I should go and spend the weekend with my former wife?"

"Well—yes. Though it's really quite sensible, I suppose."

"May and I are still very good friends. Why shouldn't we see something of each other? Her husband doesn't mind."

"I don't think I could do it. I mean, if I'd loved a woman. But— but perhaps you didn't."

"Didn't love her? I think I love her now. Though when we part-ed, it seemed entirely finished between us."

We said no more on the subject: but when I was next alone, I went over the conversation in my own mind. Did I really still love May? Certainly I had missed her when we parted; and I wanted her now—with a physical longing that I had never known when we had been together. Perhaps it was the old story of wanting what I could not have. For the five years of our life together, we had bickered endlessly; I had been convinced that I had made a mis-take in marrying her, and when she had left me, my first thought had been, "Thank God." Who could have seen the despair that was so soon to overwhelm me? In the months that followed, I sought all the conventional solaces for a broken heart: I worked without intermission; I drank; I even despatched my bearer on a few unrewarding occasions to fetch me a native woman from the bazaar. I told myself that I should never get over it.

But was my love for May anything but an illusion? I had loved Paul's mother, and when I lost her, I sought out the first person who reminded me of her. The resemblance between Carol and May was wholly superficial—they spoke alike, they did their hair in the same way, they had the same taste in clothes—but any approximation to the loved image was then enough to satisfy me. Through the years, that first resemblance lost nothing of its power; and when Paul and I set out a week later, I was as excited as on my wedding day.

XVII

SOME part of that excitement evaporated as soon as I saw her. "Oh, I am glad to see you, Mark!" she cried out. "Do you think I may be allowed to kiss you after all this time?" She turned to her husband: "Neil, may I kiss him?"

The famous smile revealed the no less famous teeth. "Of course." It was the first time that I had met Neil McClintock, though of course I had often seen him on the screen.

She put an arm round me and kissed me full on the lips. "There!" Neil and I glanced at each other in embarrassment. "You don't look well," she announced. "You look years and years older. But it's wonderful to have you here. Do you think I've aged at all?"

"Not a bit." I could answer with perfect sincerity.

"It's nice of you to say so."

She still looked girlish, with her small pouting mouth, her closely-curled hair (surely it was tinted?), and her beautiful figure. She and Neil, as they stood arm-in-arm, were a magnificent couple. I hastened to introduce Paul. "He's rather worried about what he should call you. The question is—are you an aunt or not?"

"Oh, no, please! He mustn't call me Auntie May. I must either be Mrs. McClintock or May." She looked at him and smiled: "I think May. Don't you?"

He gave a short laugh and then blushed. "Yes, I think so."

"Good. Now let me show you to your rooms before tea. I've some people for you to meet. Do you know George Wandle?"

"The critic? No. That's more in Paul's line. He writes."

"Is George Wandle here?" Paul asked incredulously.

"He is."

"Gosh! That's exciting."

May winked at me, but I could see that she was pleased. We were by now ascending the staircase and Neil had left us: "Well—what do you think of the husband?" May asked.

"I haven't had a chance to get to know him."

"Don't be silly, dear. There's nothing to get to know. Either you think him beautiful, or you don't."

"Oh, he's beautiful, all right."

"I still can't believe that he really exists. I have to pinch myself to make sure I'm not dreaming."

Paul and I had rooms next to each other, with communicating door; as soon as May had gone, he came into mine. "You never told me that your wife had married Neil McClintock."

"Didn't I? I suppose I didn't think you'd be interested."

"Not be interested! You know, I never for a moment imagined that we should be staying in an enormous house like this, with all these celebrities. There's a swimming-bath outside my window." He came across to me: "I don't believe you're in the least bit thrilled."

"Not really."

"But why not?"

"I suppose because I'm twenty-six years older than you are."

"What difference does that make?"

"I seem to have lost the capacity for being impressed by famous people. That tends to happen with age, you know."

"Oh, I know I seem childish to you," he said good-humouredly.

"Anyway, I like it."

When we came down, May introduced us to the other guests.

There was Monica Dean, a large, blowsy girl with a mass of coarse black hair, thick lips and a skin that was greasy and covered in small blemishes. Her brother John, a young man with a sad, prim face and a barely perceptible lisp, extended to me a hand that was strangely limp and cold. It was, I realized later, a symptom of the incurable malady of which he was even then dying. I remembered having seen some of his poetry in one of the 'little reviews' with which Paul littered the flat.

The only other guest was an awkward boy, in a crumpled grey flannel suit which he had obviously outgrown. "George Wandle is lying down," May told us. "He's got one of his attacks of asthma—he suffers terribly from it. But this is his secretary—Tom, Tom, Tom. . . . Oh, dear, I can never remember your name."

"Badson."

"Badson. Of course. I must try and remember that. Badson. Badson." She repeated the name with a faint grimace.

"Pleased to meet you." The unfortunate youth wrung my hand clumsily, and then turned to Paul. With his tow-coloured hair and large, bovine features he seemed to me fairly amiable. There was a Cockney twang to his voice. I think he was glad to find in Paul someone as strange to this world as he himself was. He immediately began to talk to him, dragging him headlong into a discussion of French literature. He spoke so loudly, stammering and contorting himself in his effort to express his by no means intelligible views, that the rest of us could do no more than listen to him. May's eyes met mine, and her eyebrows shot up in a way with which I had long since grown familiar. "Well, really!" I seemed to hear her exclaim.

Neil attended punctiliously to our wants. He was dressed with the excessive care that immediately makes me distrust a man. His hair flowed back in regular waves from his wide, unlined forehead. He wore brown-and-white suede shoes and a blazer with the crest of a minor public school on it. I noticed how, as he stopped before each of us with a plate, his face automatically assumed its brilliant smile.

One of the maids came in: "Mr. Wandle says will Mr. Badson come up to his room at once."

"Tell him he's having tea," May ordered. "He'll be along in a moment."

But the youth leapt to his feet. "No, don't say that. I'll go now. If you'll excuse me, that is." He gobbled what was left of his cake and hurried out.

Monica Dean tittered. She turned to her brother: "What does Wandle see in him?"

"Oh, George was telling me he's most intelligent," May put in. "In fact I'm beginning to wonder if he doesn't write George's articles for him. Yes, most intelligent." The emphasis she gave to this last word made it seem wholly derogatory.

I glanced at Paul, wondering how he was reacting to the whole scene. His eyes moved from one speaker to the other with the greatest interest; he was as absorbed as a child at its first play. Then I realized that someone else was watching him, apart from myself. Every now and then Monica Dean gave him a swift glance. She was fiddling with the clumsy gold bracelet that she wore on her wrist—I had seen many such bracelets in Indian bazaars—and suddenly she exclaimed: "Oh, damn! I can't get this catch to meet." She rose and crossed to Paul, though her brother was placed much nearer to her. "I wonder if you'd mind. . . . One really needs two hands. You see how it goes?" She sat down on the sofa beside him, resting her arm across his knees.

Paul fumbled and at last succeeded in making the catch meet. "Oh, wonderful," Monica exclaimed. "That is clever of you!"

"I hope I didn't hurt you," Paul muttered.

"No, not a bit!" She leant across to take a sandwich from a table on his left: "Excuse me." They were in complete physical proximity. Then she drew back with a little laugh. She straightened out the fingers of one of Paul's hands, and scrutinized it: "Ever had your fortune told?"

"No. . . . Please don't!" He pulled his hand away from her.

"Don't you believe in fortune-telling?"

"I don't know if I believe or not. But I'd rather not have it done."

"What a shame! Even that one glance told me there were all sorts of exciting things in store for you."

"Oh, nonsense, Monica!" her brother put in. He slouched, weary and ill, in an armchair under the window. He had neither spoken nor eaten since we had entered.

"It's not nonsense. Still, if you don't want it——" She closed the fingers of Paul's hand, with a slow, lingering movement.

Her behaviour seemed to me pathetic in its transparency. I already knew exactly what kind of woman she was; indeed, I had guessed as soon as I saw the provocative way in which she sat with her skirt rucked several inches above her knees. Anyone of the slightest experience would see through her after a minute of her company. But I wondered about Paul. He had come to London intoxicated with the dream of meeting people of a surpassing goodness, beauty and intelligence: he was prepared to dedicate himself to those qualities wherever he might find them. I saw a grave danger that he might find them where they did not exist.

But as soon as we were alone together, he showed me that he had not been deceived. He used only one word to describe Monica; it is unnecessary for me to write it here.

XVIII

AFTER dinner Monica suggested that we should all drive over to a road-house a few miles away. I immediately excused myself and May decided that she would keep me company: "It's so long since Mark and I last saw each other. Besides, I don't like road-houses. If I'm going to get drunk, I like to get drunk at home."

Monica turned to Paul: "What about you?"

"Oh, I think I'll stick here."

"Nonsense! You don't want to play gooseberry to your uncle and May. You come with us."

Paul looked questioningly at me. "Why not go?" I said. "You'll probably enjoy it."

"Of course you will," Monica put in. "That makes three men and one little me. A bit awkward if we want to dance." (George Wandle was still confined to his room; Tom was with him.)

"Why not pick up the Booth girls from down the road?" May suggested.

"That's an idea. We'll pick up the Booth girls."

"You'd better take both cars."

Neil, who had been paying no attention to what had so far

been said, gave a start: "Oh, no," he intervened hastily. "We can all get into the Buick. Why waste petrol?"

"Six of you in the Buick!" May exclaimed. "You'll be packed like sardines."

Monica gave Paul a glance. "All the more fun," she murmured.

"What time will you be back?" May asked. "I'll have some sandwiches left out for you."

"Oh, before midnight," Neil answered hurriedly. "We won't be making an evening of it."

"Won't we?" Monica pulled a face.

"Neil mustn't miss his beauty sleep," May explained.

"It's not a case of beauty sleep." His conventionally handsome face became petulant. "It's just that I don't like late nights. They don't agree with me."

"I was only joking," May placated him, slipping an arm through his. Her attitude, firm yet good-natured, was that of a nanny towards a refractory child.

After we had watched the others drive off—Paul, the two Booth girls and Monica crammed into the back, Neil and John in front—she turned: "Well?" She smiled at me. "What would you like to do? Shall we go for a walk in the garden?"

"Why not?"

It was the first time that we had been completely alone together. We moved down the stone staircase and out on to the lawn. "Poor Neil!" she exclaimed. "He was so afraid that he would have to use both cars."

"Afraid?"

"My dear, think of the waste of petrol!"

"Is he mean then?"

"Mean! He'd think twice about giving anyone a cold. Is it wrong of me to talk about him like this to you? I'm really very fond of him. And when one's fond of a person, meanness—a vice I find harder to forgive than almost any other—seems just an endearing trait. The trouble is that he's never really got used to the idea of being rich. He's not vain, you see, and it seems to him just a matter of luck that he should be drawing one of the absurd salaries that are paid to film stars. It's luck, and luck can change. Nothing can convince him that it *won't* change. So he's very, *very* careful. Oh, but it doesn't really worry me in the least. I spend what I want to spend, and he scolds me—and I go on spending. I'm happy with him, you know."

"Yes. I can see that."

"There's little passion, but a great deal of tenderness. It's funny—people think Neil must be a great Don Juan. He's not. He's as near to being sexless as a man with natural instincts can be. He's a fearful prude. I mother him—how you used to hate to be mothered!—and I help him in his work. He's ambitious, which you never were, and I like that. All my life I've felt that I ought to have had a career, and the next best thing is to share someone else's. You loathed that sort of interference. He loves it. He's immensely hard-working and eager to improve himself; he knows his looks will go, and he wants something to offer in their place. He usen't to be able to act, but he can now—just. That's my doing. You probably heard about his Romeo last year—the critics were really very kind. I don't suppose any of them realized what hours and hours of hard work had gone into that part. We slaved at it for nearly two months—I knew it all by heart before we finished. I had to teach him nearly every inflection. He's got no ear, poor darling, and it was slow, deadly slow. But we succeeded; he earned the right to be considered as something more than just a matinee idol. Next year he wants to do Macbeth—after his Hollywood film. It's easy to laugh at him, but one can't help admiring him for his tenacity. There he is, one of Britain's most popular film stars, and he's going to go a long way yet. And how did it all start? Simply because a rural dean had a son who was remarkably good-looking. But for those good looks, he would probably now be working in a bank. That's what I think he means by luck. Let's sit down." She drew me on to a bench in the ha-ha through which we were now walking; the air was heavy with the scents of June. "It's all wrong of me to be talking about one husband to the other." She laughed. "Let's forget Neil, for a moment. Tell me about yourself." Gently she took my hand in hers. "Have you got that liaison job yet?"

"Not yet."

"But you will get it?" I shrugged my shoulders and she

exclaimed: "Oh, you're impossible. What have you done about getting it? Have you seen anyone since you came home?"

"Now that we're no longer husband and wife, you've no right to nag me," I reminded her.

"But it's so absurd. You're obviously cut out for the job; you have far more intelligence than anyone else in the whole service. Have you no ambition?"

"Even less than ever."

In exasperation she exclaimed: "I know what'll happen! You'll just be passed over."

"I don't really care. Anyway, I'm not sure that I'm going to return to India."

"What!"

"I have more than enough money to live on. I feel so utterly sick of the whole business—the country, the Indians, the English, the work. I just want to crawl into a hole and die." When I was with May, I tended to indulge in this extravagant kind of self-pity; her character, maternal and possessive, seemed to provoke it.

"Oh, my dear Mark! You've become so old, all of a sudden."

"There's no need to rub it in."

"That's what I always dreaded, you know. It happens so easily to childless couples. One must be with young people to keep young. Look at me! But for Neil, I should probably now be a sour old woman. Not that Neil's really so young—only a year less than I am."

"I don't believe it!"

"It's true. *And* how he works for it. No, I suppose in his case the youth is only an illusion. But even the illusion is enough. It does for me."

"I don't much like the idea of the old living as parasites on the young."

"But it's what's always happening. Everywhere you look, you see it. Youth *is* the sacred fount. Just you try it. Find someone young—love and be loved. It works, I promise.... You know, I feel so strongly that if we'd had a child, or adopted a child, we should still now be married."

"Whose fault was that?"

"Now, no reproaches! I know I was foolish about it. I was such an awful coward. I still am. Oh, Mark, what a pity it was! What a pity!"

"*You* say that!"

"I said no reproaches! Have you missed me at all?"

"Of course."

"Really missed me?"

"What do you think?"

But all this had now led to the only possible climax; a climax which I think we had both anticipated from the very beginning. In that hushed and dimming corner of the garden, two ageing people enacted a scene which might have seemed either distasteful or ludicrous to an onlooker. In my arms I held someone whom I had once loved—May, or Paul's mother, or someone even more remote in place and time.

"Come to my room," she whispered. "Not here, Mark! Not here. . . ."

XIX

"My dear, how naughty we've been! If Neil knew!" She sat at her dressing-table, coaxing her hair into place. "Do you regret it?"

"Of course not."

She sighed. "I'm afraid I'm a very wicked woman. Of the world, worldly. Sometimes, I ask myself: what real difference is there between myself and a woman like Monica Dean. She's a little more blatant, that's all." I was silent, and she exclaimed: "Oh, contradict me, Mark! What's the matter with you?"

"Nothing. Omne animal. . . ."

"I don't believe that—never have." She stretched and yawned with extravagant pleasure. "Dear old Marie Lloyd was right. A little bit of what you fancy does you good." Humming, she began to make up her face, while I watched her.

Enjoyment had given her a new prettiness; her cheeks were flushed, her eyes shone; under her wrap her breasts were still small and firm. But as I stood beside her, I could feel nothing but disgust. It seemed impossible that so short a time ago I had lavished on her the desire of ten years. Was this the woman—kind, sensual, stupid—who had obsessed me, no matter what I did? Was this her? Was it for this that I had suffered?

She rose and put out a hand. "Let's go down. The others will be home soon." But I could not bring myself to touch her. I opened the door for her and then followed.

XX

"You're back earlier than I thought!" May exclaimed, as the others trooped into the drawing-room at a few minutes past eleven.

Monica flopped into a chair. "Neil wouldn't stay any longer. And things were just beginning to warm up, too!" Pettishly she began to slap a cushion and then thrust it behind her head.

"I said I should have to get back early," Neil reminded her. He went across to May, and kissed her on the cheek. "I think I shall turn in straight away."

"Oh, wait a minute, dear. Your milk is just being warmed. Help yourselves, won't you?" She indicated the plate of sandwiches. "Neil, will you see to the drinks?"

"Does anyone want a drink? We put away pints and pints between dances."

"I should like a little drinkie, please." Monica was now sprawled full length, her hands clasped over her stomach.

"Of course. What would you like? Gin and lime? Whisky?" Neil smiled as he asked her. But as soon as he turned away, I noticed how his face hardened into a sharp displeasure.

We must have sat down there for some twenty minutes. Monica, May and John did all the talking. Neil was glancing through *Punch* as he sipped at his milk; I noticed that he never once smiled. Paul, who sat away from us at the window, I could only see in profile. He seemed curiously remote, his face in the shadows, his eyes on the dim world outside. I felt the urge to say something that would rouse him from his day-dream.

I glanced back at Neil. May had spoken of his youth, and in doing so, had acknowledged that it was no more than an illusion. It may have been that the light beneath which he sat was unkind to him, but even the illusion had now been destroyed. He looked what he was: middle-aged. It was pathetic that even while he was relaxing in his own home, he should keep his chin tilted at that absurd angle; for the first time, I noticed how his hair was trained to conceal a bald patch the size of a florin. I felt depressed, and hurriedly looked away once more. Of all the pretences in which we indulge, the pretence of youth seems to me the most pathetic. I was ashamed at having so completely caught him out.

Paul had not moved since I had last watched him; he still sat with his eyes on the garden. Untidy and unkempt, he obviously did not care what impression he might make on us. There could be no harsher contrast. May had spoken of the sacred fount, and if it existed anywhere, it existed in him. It existed, and he was unaware of its existence. Suddenly, our eyes met, and he smiled at me.

XXI

WHEN we had gone upstairs, he opened the communicating doors and came in, in his pyjamas, to talk to me. "What sort of evening did you have?" I had only just begun to take off my clothes; a methodical dresser, I was always astonished by the speed with which Paul got in and out of his.

"Oh, quite amusing." He sat down on my bed. For a moment he ruminated, then he gave a short laugh: "That girl Monica!"

"I thought you'd have trouble from her."

"I've never met anyone like that before."

"Haven't you? You'll meet plenty before long. How far did you go with her?"

He blushed. "Oh, we didn't do anything." My frankness could still embarrass him on occasions. He seemed undecided whether to go on or not; I thought it wiser not to prompt him. At last he said: "As soon as we got into the car, she began—well—to play footy-footy. I didn't do anything, and then she took my hand. She began to squeeze it, and—well—I was afraid she'd think me an awful stick, so I just *had* to squeeze it back. Of course that was a mistake," he went on. "I suppose she thought I liked it, and—and—and she just got worse and worse."

"Well, and *didn't* you like it?"

"No!" For a moment he was put out by my frivolity. "At least . . . Well, there *is* something attractive about her. Attractive in an odd, rather unpleasant kind of way. I can't explain."

"I know exactly what you mean."

"You do?"

"Well, of course."

"She kept on making me dance with her. I didn't want to really. I felt such a fool—she kept so close to me, and her cheek was right against mine. Everyone was staring at us."

"I don't expect they really were."

"They were, I could see them! I had drunk quite a lot by then—she made me drink each time she drank—and after a time I just didn't care if we *were* being stared at! I felt wonderfully happy, and she seemed quite nice all of a sudden. . . . When we sat out the next dance, she said I must come and stay with them—her and her brother—at their flat in Hampstead. I said yes, though of course it's the last thing I want to do. A little later, she said it was getting stuffy and how about some air. We went out, and she walked straight up to the car and got in. I said, 'What are you doing? I thought you wanted some air,' but she just laughed. 'Hop in.' So I got in, and she nestled close up to me. 'You are quaint!' she exclaimed. Oh, nothing much happened, and soon I began to feel sick—I suppose it was all the drinks. In the end I had to go and *be* sick, and I ran into John, her brother, in the gentlemen's lavatory. He wasn't feeling too good either, but in his case it wasn't the drink. Or so he told me. Apparently he gets fainting attacks. Not that he wasn't pretty pickled. He'd been drinking steadily the whole evening. 'I heard Monica ask you to stay with us.' I said yes, she had. He took my arm, and in the way people speak when they are drunk, he said: 'I like you. You're a nice lad. So I'm going to give you some advice. Don't come. Whatever you do, don't come. She's not nice to know.' Well, by that time I didn't need *his* warning. We left soon after, and I took jolly good care to have one of the Booth girls between her and me. I think she was awfully angry."

"She seemed rather peevish when you all came in."

He frowned down at the carpet. I took off my dressing-gown and got into bed. "I only hope——" he began, and then broke off.

"Yes?"

"Oh, it's just . . . I must have seemed an awful fool to her, mustn't I? It was the first time anything like that had ever happened to me."

"I shouldn't worry about being *that* sort of a fool."

"I'm so horribly inexperienced."

"Well, don't be ashamed about it! So you ought to be. I often think worldly wisdom is more of a penalty than a benefit. You mustn't hasten to grow up."

"But it's so impossible just at present. I'm neither one thing nor the other. I don't know what I feel, or—or ought to feel. I don't know what I want or ought to want. I know nothing." Suddenly he turned to me: "But for you, I can't think how I should manage. You give me a sense of confidence and—and safety. I think I came just in the nick of time. It's awful to be alone when one really needs someone. Oh, you must think me sloppy to go on like this." He got off my bed. "I'm keeping you awake."

"No, I don't think you sloppy. I'm glad you've said all that. I feel touched that you think I can help you. I want to help you."

"Thank you." He had said more than he had intended to say, and since, like most Englishmen of his class, he had been trained from childhood to hide his feelings, embarrassment now overwhelmed him. He hesitated for a while, fiddling with the top button of his pyjama jacket. Standing there, his cheeks flushed, his hair tousled, his feet without slippers, he looked no more than a child. Then he made for his room.

"It's so hot. Shall I leave the door open?"

"Yes, do."

"Good night."

"Good night, Paul."

It was a slightly unsatisfactory conclusion. But at any rate for a few seconds the restraints of upbringing had been set aside; he had asked me for my help, and I had promised it to him. That much had been achieved. I found that I could so easily put myself in his position; I could understand the difficulties, many of them imaginary, which now obsessed him. I was anxious for him as for my own son.

XXII

I SPOKE to George Wandle for the first time—introductions apart—when I went into the library after breakfast. My initial impression was of a great red-headed she-ape. His hands, with their tiny palms and disproportionately long fingers, dangled near his knees. He had a flat, wide-nostrilled nose, high cheek-bones, and eyes which he used with an extraordinary expressiveness. He rolled them, glanced at one from under long-lashed, fluttering lids, and at the same time skilfully manipulated the monocle that dangled from his neck on a thick black ribbon.

When I entered, he was sitting at the writing-desk with Tom Badson standing near him. A typescript was in his hand. "Oh, fool, fool, fool!" he exclaimed. "How do you spell 'psychology'? Not the first time you've dropped an aitch."

Tom blushed hotly.

"I hope we won't disturb you." Wandle turned to me. His voice, which had been over-precise and cutting while he spoke to his secretary, now became feminine in its suavity.

"Oh, no. I'm just browsing."

"How fortunate you are. I wish I had time to browse. That's the penalty of making a business out of one's pleasures." He glanced over his shoulder at Tom, and then thrust the typescript back at him: "You'll have to do it again. It's just a mass of corrections. I don't know what's the matter with you."

"I'm terribly sorry." Tom's face glistened with perspiration.

"My dear boy, apologies never excuse inefficiency. You seem to imagine that you can be as careless as you please, provided you say how sorry you are. I've stood it quite long enough."

"Well, I can't help it. I did my best," came the by now tearful retort.

"Then all I can say is that your best isn't good enough. Come on, take it!" Wandle shook the typescript at him. "I can't hold it out all day for you."

Tom took it and made for the door. His stupid, handsome

face was contorted in what might either be rage or anguish. But Wandle had not done with him. As the boy turned to shut the door, the infuriatingly calm voice pursued him: "Oh, Tom—one other thing. If you must go about without a tie on, do learn not to wear the collar of your shirt outside your jacket. It's just not done."

The door slammed shut, the expressive eyebrows leapt up-wards. "Oh, that boy! Never have I come across such a bovine, inept dunderhead! I try to be patient with him, but really——!" At that word 'really', Wandle's voice, usually baritone, shot into the treble register.

I did not answer, but continued to browse among the books. May had told me they had been bought with the house: "A library looks so bare otherwise. They're just trash, you know, but they do fill up space." They certainly were trash, but of a kind that has always interested me—bound volumes of magazines, Victorian novels, and books of reference long since out of date.

"Is that boy some relative of yours?" Wandle suddenly asked, without looking up from the pages on which he was engaged.

"Who—Paul? Yes, he's my nephew."

"Looks intelligent."

"Yes, he is intelligent."

"How old is he? Sixteen? Seventeen?" His pen still raced over paper.

"Eighteen."

"Really! I thought he looked much younger. What does he do? Still at school, I suppose."

"No. He's left school."

"At the University?"

"No. He's having a holiday with me just at present." I was beginning to resent this interrogation, and no doubt the tone of my answers had made this clear to Wandle. At any rate, he said no more on the subject. Instead, he began energetically to blot a sheet of paper, exclaiming: "What a week! Monday, I had to have two reviews ready neither of which was written. Tuesday, a talk for the B.B.C. Wednesday, Thursday and Friday, work on an article, a Forces Brain Trust—not a cent paid of course—poor old Rackham's funeral, two dinners—and on top of that, the first proofs of my new book! Saturday I came down here to work, as I hoped. But I got one of my wretched attacks of asthma. Now I have to make up for lost time on this beautiful Sunday morning."

I guessed that all this had been said with only one purpose: to impress. I had had the same feeling while Tom was being castigated. "I really oughtn't to be wasting your precious minutes," I put in. "I'd no idea you were so busy."

"Oh, that's all right," Wandle hastened to assure me. "My mind functions best when I'm talking. I can always write and talk at the same time"—he smiled modestly—"like old G.K. Chesterton."

"I can't believe you're not just being polite." I slipped my book on to the shelves. "I'd better leave you to it."

"Oh, no, don't do that."

"But of course."

XXIII

"I HAVE a feeling that Wandle will be seeking you out soon."

"What makes you think that?"

"Oh, I don't know. Just a hunch."

"But what on earth would he want me for?"

I shrugged my shoulders.

After lunch that same day, Wandle approached Paul: what follows is the account that Paul himself gave me. He was sitting alone on the terrace, reading, when he heard someone behind him. Then next moment Wandle was looking over his shoulder:

"*The Castle!*" he exclaimed. "How on earth did you get hold of that?"

"My uncle lent it to me——" Paul began, but Wandle, who was in the habit of asking questions to which he expected no answer, interrupted, "What do you think of it?" Again before Paul could give any opinion, Wandle ran on: "Did you see my article on Kafka in *Perspective*—about four months ago? No? Well, I think it might help you with your difficulties." (Paul had mentioned no difficulties). "Yes, I think you'd find it interesting. Remind me to lend it to you." He tapped with his malacca walking-stick on the stone paving: "I'm just going for a little stroll. Perhaps you'd accompany me?"

Paul rose with alacrity.

"Just one moment." Wandle produced a pair of sunglasses, with white rims over an inch thick. "This glare seems to bring on my asthma. I should have met you much earlier if it hadn't been for an attack. Yes, all yesterday—wasn't it too wretched? You've no idea how many doctors I've seen about it. Some say nerves, some say diet, some say. . . ." He continued to discuss his health, until they passed beneath a window at which Tom was standing. Paul had hardly noticed him, before Wandle broke off and shouted: "What are you staring at? Are you trying to spy on me? Have you finished that work I gave you? What? Don't mumble when I speak to you!" In a few seconds he had worked himself into a rage.

Tom's frightened face disappeared, but Wandle continued to mutter for some time: "Imbecile! Imbecile! Imbecile!" Soon he became calm enough to remark: "That youth ought to be serving behind the counter in a drapery store. Or hawking toothpaste at the back doors of council houses. He calls himself a secretary—a secretary!" He gave a snort.

By that time they had come to the stables where a few horses looked out over the doors of their loose-boxes. Paul went up to one and patted it: "Nice boy."

"That animal is a mare," Wandle said crushingly. Paul peered into the darkness and saw that he was right. "And she's really not very nice. Look at her hindquarters." He began to enumerate all her failings, the groom, who had just arrived, listening to him with a sour contempt. By the time he had finished, Wandle had become quite genial: "I bet that surprised you!" he chuckled. "You didn't expect a highbrow like me to know anything about horses. Now be frank. You didn't, did you?" The groom cleared his throat and spat outwards, and at the same time Paul realized that Wandle was no more than an egotistical bore.

"Do you like my suit?" Wandle asked as they walked away. After lunch he had changed into a white tropical suit, with a bow tie. "It's rather pleasing, isn't it?"

Paul had been so irritated by Wandle's treatment of his secretary and then by the disquisition in the stables, that he felt the desire to be rude at any cost: "No, I don't like it," he retorted.

Wandle's smile went rigid. His monocle leapt downwards. He

stopped and faced Paul: "You don't like it?" he asked incredulously. "Why? Why not?"

"I think it looks silly."

"Silly!"

"It makes you look like a tea-planter."

"A tea-planter!" He shrilled out the two words. "A tea-planter!" For a moment his face worked in a paroxysm of wrath and wounded vanity. Then with a calm, steely insolence he said: "You haven't any taste. When I first set eyes on you I didn't think you had any. Otherwise you wouldn't wear that atrocious check coat—off the peg, I imagine?—nor that grubby bit of cloth which I take to be a tie. And incidentally, though I am delighted to see that you are making some effort to tame your hair, I suggest you use a hair-oil less reminiscent of the kind of scent used by house-maids. Eastern Poppy, I think."

Wandle seemed to be disappointed that Paul made no reply to this outburst, and as if to goad him further, he suddenly asked as they made their way back to the house: "Do you write?"

"Yes."

"I thought you must. What's your line?"

"I sent you some of my poems a month or two back."

"Well, you really can't expect me to remember them. We get sent an average of thirty poems a day. And twenty-nine of them are complete bosh. Did we return yours?"

"Yes."

"Thirty poems a day," Wandle repeated. He sighed. "You know it's rather sad to think of all those young men—and old men—and women, too, of course—typing out their muck, and addressing their envelopes, and scurrying to catch the post—only to have it all bunged back at them, in the end. The world's so full of unsuccessful writers who would be far more usefully employed washing dishes."

"That could also be said of a number of successful writers."

Paul left Wandle and came upstairs to find me. "I shall never be published in *Perspective*," he exclaimed. "What an absolute toad that man is! I never want to see him again." He looked rueful; then he let out a laugh. "But he's so comic."

"What happened?"

Paul told me. "So now you see why he will never publish me," he concluded.

"Does that matter?"

"Oh, not really. Except that *Perspective* is about the best magazine in which one can appear. I should have buttered him up, and let him go on thinking what a wonderful man he is."

"I'll see what I can do."

"You? But what can you do?"

"I don't know. Something, I hope." I laughed. "When a man is as vain as George Wandle, it's not hard to get round him. You wait."

XXIV

I AGAIN found Wandle writing in the library. "I'm afraid I'm going to disturb you once more. I left a book here. I'm so sorry."

"No need to apologize." He swung round on the swivel chair. "I don't know why you disappeared last time. I meant it when I said I could write and talk at one and the same time."

"I only wish I could! I find it hard enough to concentrate on one job, without undertaking two."

"Oh, it's just a knack, you know. Just a knack."

"You must teach me sometime."

Wandle was flattered. "I suppose that's how I can do so much. People are always rather astonished at the number of my activities. Do sit down." He produced a gold cigarette-case and held it out to me; then taking a cigarette himself, he gently eased it into a thin holder.

"My nephew tells me that he's just spent a most instructive half-hour with you. I'd no idea you were an authority on horses."

Wandle, who had been reclining negligently, stiffened at my words. "To be frank with you, I think your nephew is rather ill-mannered."

"Oh, yes, he's that all right!" I admitted with a laugh. "But it's not entirely his fault." As persuasively as possible I gave some indication of Paul's upbringing. "He says things that sound rude, but he never really means them. He told me he was afraid that he might have annoyed you. As a matter of fact, he was in rather a state about it."

"Was he?" Wandle leant forward eagerly. "Oh, I wasn't really annoyed." He was wearing a rose in his buttonhole and as he spoke he kept smelling it, the nostrils of his flat nose dilating with each sniff. "I know he's only a boy. I didn't take him too seriously. Was he—was he really upset?"

"Yes, terribly. You see, you've always been one of his literary idols, and he was so excited at your taking notice of him. After all, it *was* rather a privilege."

"Well, I like to help any young man of talent. I—I suppose he must have read one or two of my books?"

"One or two! He's just about read the lot. He has copies of all the novels."

"The novels! Does he like my novels?" Wandle had written five novels of an inordinate length and dullness; each of them had been reviewed with the peculiar deference shown by critics to books that are unreadable, but none had sold. Wandle, himself, rejecting his fame as editor and critic, was tormented by the desire to win for them the popularity he alone believed them to deserve. But for this ambition he would have been a happy man; as it was, he was fretted by an intolerable chagrin.

"He thinks they're wonderful. He says there's been nothing like them since the later Henry James." I derived a certain pleasure from offering this two-edged compliment.

"How astute of him! I've always admired James, and I think I must have been influenced by him."

"Paul wants to be a novelist, too." I sighed. "I'm afraid he's still got an awful lot to learn."

"Oh, I don't know. He seems to have the root in him. The rest will come with time. I was rather impressed with some stuff he sent me a month or two back. Adolescent, you know—I couldn't take it—but promising, *very* promising. I should like to see some more of his work."

"Would you? Would you really?"

"Why not?" He smiled magnanimously.

"Well, it's awfully kind of you to say so. If you could find time. . . . I know how busy you are."

"I'm never too busy to look at good writing."

"Thank you so much. I'll tell Paul."

"That's all right." His nostrils again dilated over the pale rose. "As a matter of fact, I'll have a word with him myself."

XXV

DURING this interview Paul had been having a bathe with Tom. "I like him," he told me. "I wish Wandle didn't treat him so badly. And yet Tom seems to be devoted to the old brute. I can't understand it. I made some remark about him and Tom immediately jumped down my throat. He writes, you know, and as soon as I told him that I wrote myself, he wanted me to look at some of his stuff. I didn't know what to say, it was all so awful. Not even bad in an interesting way, but just dull, dull, dull. He's ambitious, too, which makes it all the more pathetic. Though I don't know why I should call him pathetic when I'm in the same boat myself," he added with a rueful candour.

"Oh, but you forget that the great Wandle is interested in you!"

"I'm awfully grateful to you for speaking to him."

"I enjoyed it," I could say with perfect truth.

A little later Wandle appeared and suggested that Paul take another stroll with him. On this occasion Paul behaved with exemplary politeness, and but for one incident at the end of their interview, nothing went amiss. There was a heavy storm later that evening, and as the two of them were wandering through the garden, thunder suddenly rumbled in the far distance.

Wandle halted. "Was that thunder?"

"I think so," said Paul carelessly. Again there was a rumble. Seeing the look of consternation on the older man's face, he suggested: "Let's wait in this summer-house, if you think it's going to rain."

Wandle gave one glance to the thatched roof, and exclaimed: "No, no! Not in there! We must make for the house."

He began to scuttle breathlessly across the lawn with Paul in pursuit. When they were no more than a hundred yards from the house, there was a flash of lightning, followed almost immediately by a crash. Wandle grabbed Paul's arm, gasping and cowering against him. In the weird light of the impending storm, his face, drained of colour, was a vivid green. "Quick! The house! The house!" Paul half carried, half dragged him inside. Wandle collapsed on to a chair.

"Aren't you well?" Paul asked anxiously.

"I'm—all right—now," he gasped. He pulled the silk handkerchief out of his breast pocket and mopped his face. "Yes, I'm quite all right," he said. "Quite all right," he repeated in a firmer voice, glaring at Paul as if he had asked some insulting question. "I think I'll go upstairs and find Tom."

As he mounted the stairs, there was a distant crackle of thunder which made him pause for a moment and then swoop on, his head lowered.

"I suppose he must have had some sort of an attack," Paul said when he recounted this incident to me.

"Nonsense! George Wandle is obviously terrified of thunder."

Paul looked at me in incredulity. "Do you mean to say. . . ?" I thought he would burst out laughing, but his face became grave. "Poor devil," he murmured compassionately. "I'd no idea."

XXVI

WHILE Paul and Wandle had been strolling together, I myself had been in conversation with Neil McClintock. Though it was obvious to me that he had deliberately sought me out, he tried to make it appear the most casual of encounters. Coming into the drawing-room he exclaimed: "Hello! You there! Muggy, isn't it?" He went to the french windows and pushed them open. "That's better. I'm sweating like a pig. What are you up to? *Times* Crossword? Hope I'm not disturbing you."

"Of course not."

"Smoke?" I shook my head, and he began to fiddle with a pipe. He had short, stubby fingers, stained with nicotine; his teeth, biting on the pipe stem, were a dazzling white. "It's been nice seeing you," he got out at last, between puffs of smoke.

"Yes. I've enjoyed the visit."

He went to the french windows and stood looking out. "Glad you don't bear any grudge against me."

"Why should I?"

"Oh, you know. . . ." He made some incoherent noises and then gave me his empty, brilliant smile. "I think you've been jolly decent about it all—putting yourself in the wrong to begin with and—and all that. We're—we're very grateful to you, old chap."

"Provided May's happy, that's all I care about. And I can see that she *is* happy."

"She's a grand girl. But I don't have to tell *you* that! I'm just—sorry—that our happiness should have—have had to be at your. . . . Oh, you know what I mean!"

"I know. You don't have to be sorry about it."

"It's grand of you to say that." He came up to me and wrung my hand.

Yes, he was nice, I decided. I liked him. He reminded me of one of those show dogs at Cruft's, who in spite of all the petting, pampering and admiration they receive, still retain their natural qualities. Success had not touched him. I hoped I should never have to see him again.

XXVII

WE were to leave the next morning, and though May urged us to stay a few days, we kept to this plan.

Wandle and Tom drove off before we did. Wandle's last words to Paul were: "Now don't forget to let me have some of your stuff. You know my address—why don't you bring it round personally? Have a drink or something." Tom stood a few yards away from us; his handsome face looked grey and strained. It was not until Wandle had finished saying good-bye that he himself came forward. Then he squeezed my hand in a grip that was at once firm and clammy: "Good-bye," he muttered hoarsely. He turned to Paul. "I hope I shall see you again some time."

"I hope so. You've got my address."

"Are you sure you'd like to see me?" he blurted out.

"Of course I'm sure," Paul said in surprise.

"Come along, Tom!" At the summons, the boy grabbed Paul's hand. Then he broke away. He picked up the three suitcases, and hurried after Wandle who was already strolling, unhampered by any luggage, towards the car. A strange couple, I thought, watching Tom open the back door for Wandle, arrange the luggage and then himself climb into the driver's seat.

May drew me to one side. The evening before she had whispered to me: "Again?"

I had shaken my head.

"Neil will be out."

"No, no."

"Oh, you and that ridiculous conscience of yours!" I did not tell her the real reason for my refusal: she would hardly have regarded it as complimentary.

I wondered now if she was angry with me, but she only said gently: "I'm rather unhappy about you, Mark."

"Oh! Why?"

She smiled. "I suppose because I haven't stopped regarding you as my own particular property. I hate to think of you all on your own."

"I'm perfectly all right."

"As if you'd tell me if you weren't!" She slipped an arm through mine. "The horrible thing is that I can't help feeling glad that you miss me. Beastly, isn't it? But I should have hated it if you had found someone else."

"You're being frank."

"Anyway, you've got Paul. I'm glad of that. You're not quite alone. He seems quite a nice boy. But——" She broke off.

"Yes?"

"I was going to say—be careful."

"Careful? Of what?"

"Oh, it's just that you're one of those people who are always being let down. Inevitably. You're not ambitious in other ways, but where friendship is concerned you have such impossibly high standards. People fail you—they can't help it—and then that makes you miserable. Try to learn not to give yourself quite so completely to other people. You don't mind my saying this?"

"Of course not. But in this case, I don't think the advice is necessary."

"I don't know."

"An intuition?"

"Oh, you always laugh at my intuitions. But they're usually right, aren't they? Not that I feel anything definite. . . . Still, I think you should take care. You've been let down so often—I've let you down. I shouldn't like to see it happen again."

"No fear of that."

I felt irritated with her, and rejoined the others. But in my mind she had cast the shadow of a vague unease.

XXVIII

As our car drew out, Monica threw an envelope into Paul's lap. "My address!" she shouted.

He looked at it for a moment, made as if to tear it up and then changed his mind; it was placed in his wallet.

I looked at him enquiringly. "You never know, it may come in useful," he said with a laugh. "Not that I ever want to see Monica again—or any of them for that matter. Except May," he added hurriedly—I imagine out of deference to my feelings.

"I'm sorry you feel so disillusioned."

"I'm not in the least disillusioned—in the conventional sense. No one was what I expected, but I don't feel bitter about it."

"That's the right kind of disillusion. The search for truth seems to me one of the most important things in life. One should never be afraid of losing an illusion, provided one doesn't substitute another in its place. The substitution of one illusion for another—that's cynicism."

"I feel that, too—about the search for truth, I mean. It seems to me that if only I can make myself see things as they really are, then I may at last begin to be a writer."

"You may also begin to suffer."

"But the suffering's worth while!" he exclaimed. He looked at me for confirmation. "Isn't it? Isn't it?"

"I think it is."

At the time, this conversation merged into the many other conversations we had on serious themes; it is only now, in the light of all subsequent happenings, that I remember it with a profound sense of irony. Life is so full of hints which we do not hear until it is too late.

We did not hasten back to London. We stopped the car in Oxford, had lunch, and wandered over the University. I showed Paul the college to which I had once hoped to go: "Balliol is not comely. The best thing that has been said about it is that it looks nice by moonlight." We went to the Ashmolean and wandered among the hideous casts of Greek statues in an atmosphere thick with dust. "Imagine someone who knew nothing of Greece and Rome being confronted with these specimens of classical culture." Our merriment scandalized the art students whose easels littered the place.

It was late evening as we drove into London. After the heat of the day, everything seemed to relax once more. The light was kind. While we had been in Oxford we had joked and fooled about like a couple of undergraduates; but now, as we passed through the dimming streets, we said nothing. A serene and abounding happiness filled my heart.

Suddenly I felt Paul's head drop on to my shoulder.

I looked down, expecting to see him asleep. But his eyes were open. He glanced up and smiled.

I remember that moment now with a queer, palpitating vividness. We were driving through a street of squat, ugly, smoke-grimed houses; some children played before a cinema, barging in and out of the crowds around it; in the distance I could hear a Salvation Army band.

It seems to me that the young go through life seeking their spiritual fathers and mothers, the old their spiritual heirs. In that quest we had both for a while been satisfied.

XXIX

A FEW days later Paul received a letter from the island, with the address written in a round, childish script. He scowled as he read it, and then held it out to me.

"From Betty."

That letter with its pathetic, broken, ill-spelled phrases, I shall not reproduce; as I read it, I was overwhelmed with embarrassment and shame. Never before had the recesses of a woman's heart been revealed to me with so piercing a candour. I could guess from what immeasurable despair and longing each of those sentences had been wrung. I returned the letter to Paul without a comment.

"What am I to do?" he asked. "It's not even the first I've had from her."

This surprised me. "Have there been others?"

"One other."

"You answered it?"

He shook his head. "I didn't know what to say. It was even worse than this. What *can* one say?"

I had no advice for him. I guessed that this second letter would also remain unanswered. Or perhaps Paul would force himself to write a few stiff, conventional lines which would hurt far more than any silence. I thought sadly of the plain, lumpish girl, alone with her father. But what could Paul do? How could he—or anyone—help her?

In the same post there was a letter for me from May. One phrase arrested my attention: "I do hope Paul enjoyed his visit."

I looked up. "I suppose you sent May a bread-and-butter letter?"

"A bread-and-butter letter?" Obviously he had never heard of such a thing.

"A thank-you letter," I explained.

"No. Should I have?"

"Well, of course. It really is too casual of you."

"I'm sorry. I didn't realize . . ." I had expected him to sulk, as he usually did when I reproached him with anything; I was pleasantly surprised. "I'll write straight away." He smiled engagingly. "It does rather take the gilt off the gingerbread, doesn't it? Like having to write thank-you letters after a birthday. After-all I *did* thank May when I said good-bye to her."

I laughed: "It's just another convention you must learn."

I was becoming indulgent to his social misdemeanours; they no longer irritated me as they once did. Paul, in turn, was learning to accept my corrections with equanimity. On one occasion, when I had said something in reproach, I asked: "Do you mind my speaking like this to you?"

"Not now."

"You did once."

"Yes. But since then I've learnt to feel safe with you. I no longer mind." He hesitated for a moment and then went on: "You know, you're just about the first grown-up with whom I've ever felt safe."

London had become insufferably hot since our return, and soon I suggested a move into the country. "Be quite frank. If you'd rather stay on in town, say so."

"I'm willing to do anything you want."

"That's just the answer I hoped you wouldn't give."

"Well, it's true. I don't care a damn. Why should I?"

"After all, I did bring you here to see life. Won't the country bore you?"

"Listen," he retorted with good-humoured exasperation, "I've told you a thousand times. I didn't leave the island because I preferred to live in a town. That wasn't the point. I wanted—companionship. I have it now. I don't mind what happens so long as I stay with you."

After this confession, I had no qualms about booking rooms for ourselves in a Sussex farmhouse. I arranged to sub-let the flat, at a nominal rent, to some friends of mine who would be away at all weekends; in this way, Paul and I could return for a day or two if we wished.

"It's quite wonderful," Paul exclaimed, leaning out of my bedroom window on the day of our arrival. We were perched on the edge of the downs with the sea only two miles away. He turned: "I feel we're going to be very happy here."

"And not in the least bored?"

"Of course not! We can ride, and swim, and go for long walks, and be just lazy. I shall start to write something—a novel perhaps—and you"—the thought only at that moment came to him—"you must begin a book."

"No, thank you." I shook my head decisively.

"Yes, you must. I shall make you. For two hours every morning we shall both sit down and write." He returned to the window; a breeze stirred his hair and the open collar of his shirt. "The sea looks perfect. You can see some sheep from here. The farmhouse is a gem. It is, isn't it?" Suddenly his face became grave: "I'm sure it must all be horribly expensive for you."

I laughed. "We won't discuss that."

"You are good to me," he said simply.

So our holiday began. The weather was fine, we liked the place, and we liked each other. We did all the things mentioned by Paul in that first enthusiasm of his. We rode, we bathed, we walked and we lay in the sun. We even sat for two hours a day, he writing and I pretending to write. I must have scribbled something, for at the end of every morning we had to read out what each of us had done. My manuscript I destroyed within a few weeks; it was intended to be a historical novel of India in the sixteenth century. Paul was writing a long short-story. He worked with extreme care, producing only one or two hundred words a day. What I saw impressed me.

The serene happiness of those days returns to me like the memory of a landscape one can never again revisit. Only one small incident for a moment troubled me; it sprang from a remark made by our landlady, Mrs. Hackhurst. She was a small, neat, kindly woman who treated us with extreme deference.

She showed us up to our rooms, and then as she was about to leave us, murmured: "I hope you and your son will like it here."

"Not my son," I corrected her with a laugh. "My nephew."

"Your nephew!" she exclaimed. "Well, fancy that now! I was certain he was your son. He takes after you so. He's the very image of you."

"Funny her saying that," Paul remarked when she had gone. "It's not the first time, either. People seem to guess."

Guess? Guess what? For a moment, the fantastic notion came to me that Paul actually thought he *was* my son. Could it be possible? As far as I remembered, I had never said anything that might, however remotely, suggest such a thing. To question him would be to cause the most acute embarrassment both to him and to myself. I told myself that my suspicion was absurd; I put the thought out of my mind. But a faint disquiet remained.

XXX

SOME four miles from the farmhouse there was a small seaside resort down to which Paul and I often strolled. We did our shopping there, had coffee or tea in one of the innumerable cafés, and sometimes even visited the cinema. On one of these expeditions I suggested that we should go on to the pier.

Paul groaned. He had a sore heel and he was feeling peevish. "I loathe piers. Anyway, that's such a silly little one. It's not even serious about going into the water."

By an irony which I later came to appreciate, I continued to urge him until he gave in with a grumpy: "Oh, very well!"

Paul had been right; it was a silly little pier, shaky and with a general air of dereliction. I pushed a penny into a slot machine and nothing happened. Paul quarrelled with the attendant at the shooting-gallery. Everywhere there was a smell of tar and stale urine.

Suddenly I noticed two women, one seated in a bath-chair, the other behind her. They were watching a stunted urchin, his hair shaved for ringworm, who had slipped a coin into a machine labelled "What the Butler Saw" and was now standing on tiptoe in order to get his money's worth. For a few seconds he was entranced; then, in outraged disappointment, he began to kick at the machine and punch it with his fists.

The woman in the bathchair was convulsed with laughter. She was enormously fat, with gleaming black eyes, black hair and one of the most humorous faces I have ever seen. Her taste in jewellery was exotic. Earrings of beaten gold dragged the lobes of her ears downwards; a string of jade beads, the size of pigeon eggs, circled her massive throat; her hands, plump and white, were covered in a variety of rings.

The girl who stood behind her gazed out to sea with dark, heavy-lidded eyes. Entirely detached from her companion, she did not share her amusement with even so much as a smile. She was dressed entirely in black, and it may have been this that made her complexion seem so peculiarly pale. I immediately recognized her.

"Quick!" I whispered. I caught Paul's arm, swivelled him round and without any further words, hustled him off the pier.

When we were well away, I explained to him. "I saw someone I didn't much want to meet."

"Who? Not the woman in the bathchair?"

"No. The girl with her. She was out in India."

"What? That girl with the wonderful tragic face? I was just going to point her out to you."

"Yes, that girl. She used to be an actress."

"Why on earth didn't you want to meet her?"

"Because I don't like her."

"What's wrong with her?"

I shrugged my shoulders. "She's one of those people who confuse life with the theatre. I can't stand them."

"How do you mean?"

"Oh, just that with them everything—every human experience—is no more than an act."

"But she didn't look in the least like that."

"People don't *look* like that," I said irritably. I felt that he was being stupid. "You hardly saw her. How on earth can you have any idea of what she's like?"

"Well, I liked what I saw," he said defiantly.

"Anyway, I'm not going to go back and speak to her, if that's what you want."

"I never asked you to."

We both stopped, appalled. For the first time since we had come to the farm, we were on the verge of a quarrel. We walked on in silence until we reached home.

XXXI

IN a place so small it was inevitable that we should again meet the two women. Less than a week later we were confronted by them as we entered a tea-shop.

"Hullo." There was no trace of surprise in Anne Wetherby's voice. She did not attempt to shake hands with me, but continued to grip the back of the bathchair in which her companion sat.

"Fancy seeing you here!" I exclaimed.

She gave a slight smile, lowered her eyes and then looked up again. "Why did you cut me on the pier?"

For a moment I could say nothing. "But I didn't realize——
How on earth——"

"I could see you in the glass panelling of the machine that little boy was working."

"Then I might repeat the question. Why did *you* cut me?"

She dismissed the matter with no more than a shrug of her shoulders. "I don't believe you've met Mrs. Patton." We said how d'you do, and I introduced Paul.

Mrs. Patton had an alert, humorous face and a rich contralto voice. She was very friendly, asking us how long we had been in the place and whether we liked it; she punctuated our answers with a laughter so natural that each time we could almost believe we had said something witty. Anne ventured nothing further, but remained gazing into space. Her indifference made me feel uncomfortable; I felt that we bored her and were not sufficiently important for her to conceal the fact. She could never be called a beautiful woman; but with her long nose, her erect carriage and her tragic eyes, she would always be a striking one. Her lips were too thick and protuberant, and this, with her black hair and sallow complexion had often made me wonder about her ancestry.

"You must come to tea with us," Mrs. Patton was saying.

"We should like to very much. But are you sure it won't be troublesome for you?"

"Troublesome? Of course not! Good gracious me, we always

welcome a new arrival. The local people are such bores. So stuffy! You've no idea. Let's fix a date."

A date was fixed and we said good-bye. Anne murmured the word listlessly; then, without smiling, she turned the bathchair and wheeled it up the street.

"Well?" I said to Paul.

"She's—interesting."

"But not in the least interested in us."

"I'm glad we're going to tea with them. I feel she might be worth getting to know. That sort of person fascinates me. There's something remote and mysterious about her."

"How pleased she'd be to hear you say that!"

"I think you must have a grudge against her."

"No, strangely, I haven't. But I much prefer her companion."

"Oh, she's all right," Paul conceded. "But she's not in the least out of the ordinary as Mrs. Wetherby is."

"At any rate she's genuine."

We continued to discuss the two women until we reached home, and even then Paul was reluctant to let the matter drop. He was convinced that I had been maligning Mrs. Wetherby, and championed her with a stubbornness so irritating that in the end I burst out angrily: "Oh, don't be ridiculous. You don't know her at all. You don't know anything about her. Wait until you've seen some more of her."

"Very well. I will wait."

Smarting under my rebuke, he remained cool and unfriendly through the whole of dinner. But while we were drinking our coffee, he caught my eye and smiled at me: "Uncle Mark?"

"Yes?"

"You won't be angry if I ask you something?"

"That depends on what it is."

"It's about——" He broke off, and grinned sheepishly. "May I mention her?"

"I never forbade you to."

"I've been thinking about her all through dinner."

"So that's why you were so silent."

"I'm sorry," he said humbly. "I know you're sick to death of the subject—but I should like you to tell me. . . . well, what's her story, exactly?"

"Story?"

"Oh, she must have a story," he replied naïvely.

"She's that kind of a woman, you feel? Yes, she certainly carries her story round with her."

From the way in which his mouth hardened, I knew that my disparagement was annoying him. For some reason his interest in this woman filled me with so ungovernable an irritation that I was driven to speak of her with a hostility far greater than I should normally have shown.

He continued to coax me until I gave in to him and told him what I knew.

XXXII

Anne Wetherby, or Anne Preest as she then was, first came out to India with a travelling theatrical company; she could not have been more than seventeen at the time. Professional actors are rare in India, and the company enjoyed a certain popularity. I suppose the plays they produced—*Marigold*, *A Little Bit of Fluff*, *While Parents Sleep*, are some of the titles that return to me—will remain with us so long as the word repertory remains; even at that time they were hardly fresh, but we enjoyed them.

Anne played juvenile lead, and it was at once apparent to the spectator that hers was a gift of a different kind from that possessed by the rest of the cast. It was not a comic gift, and in the farces in which she played it made one feel excessively uncomfortable. These light-hearted pranks in and about a double-bed took on a portentous significance as soon as she appeared: all at once they seemed indecent.

With her vibrant, almost harsh voice and her strained intensity, she obviously had in her the makings of a great tragedienne. But she still had much to learn. She moved clumsily; her gestures were no more than sketches of what they ought to have been; she spoke with a diction so mannered that it became absurd.

Sandy Wetherby, the man who was to marry her, was a Scottish engineer in charge of canals. He was a slow giant with red hair and a magnificent physique. At the age of thirty-six he was still unmarried; women appeared not to interest him. He and I shared a bungalow after May had left me, and though I was often exasperated by the ponderous, unhurried way he did things, I did not take long to recognize his abundant qualities; he was naïvely simple, kind and staunch. 'Steady' and 'reliable' people are not usually among those I choose for my friends; I am a gambler where friendship is concerned, and prefer the long odds, either utterly ruinous or utterly rewarding, which temperament and mobility offer to one. But I came to care for Sandy because of the characteristics I so despised in others: after May had gone, I had felt an overwhelming need for stability in personal relationships, and I was glad to anchor on the rock of his patient dullness.

I think he fell in love with Anne as soon as he saw her. We had gone to the theatre together, and I remember how I had been irritated by his guffaws at the heavily suggestive way in which the cast delivered all their witticisms: nothing was left to the imagination. But as soon as Anne appeared he became silent; he watched her, breathing heavily, with so rapt an expression that one could follow the whole action of the play merely by looking at him. When Anne left the stage, he caught my eye and grinned sheepishly: "God, she's wonderful!" he whispered.

He asked me to arrange a meeting with her; I helped him to choose presents; I was forced to join them when they went out together. "You must come, old man," he used to urge me, if I suggested that it would be more appropriate for him to entertain her tête-à-tête. "I never know what to do when we are alone. I just dry up." One night he proposed to her, and she accepted him: I had never supposed that she would. It had always seemed to me that she was laughing at him without his realizing it; she would make a fool of him before me and often there was an irony in the answers she gave to his questions. Moreover, there was a difference of nearly fifteen years between their ages, and a difference of religion: Sandy was a Catholic. I doubt if she loved him even then. He was earning a large salary, and to be his wife was a position of some importance: in any case, she had often told me how weary she was of the perpetual travelling from one town to another, playing the same sad trifles over and over again to indiscriminately appreciative audiences. Probably, too, she experienced a sexual passion for Sandy: tall, deep-chested, with a tanned face and great physical strength, he possessed a virility that was likely to appeal to a woman of her nature.

They were married and I was his best man. I remember one incident from the day of their wedding: some facetious guest had tied a variety of domestic utensils on to the back of their car, so that as they drove off there was a perpetual clank and rattle from behind. They drew up at the gate, and Sandy got out: he was grinning, as he roared: "Whoever put those damned things on can damn well untie them." When the youth came forward, he made as if to punch him on the chin, but instead pushed him backwards with a gesture of rough affection. Then, suddenly, Anne got out: she was in a cold fury. "Do hurry, Sandy! And please tell your friends I don't think much of their little joke!" She got back into the car and slammed the door; we all looked horribly embarrassed as we helped Sandy to untie the pots, pans and chamber pots.

Three months later Sandy told me that Anne was expecting a baby. "Don't let on I've told you. She doesn't want people to know yet. But I had to tell someone, and I wanted it to be you." Pride filled him as I wrung his hand.

"Of course it means we won't be able to go on leave next month as we planned. They won't take pregnant women on board ship. As a matter of fact Anne's rather sick about it." Suddenly he looked shamefaced: "I mean, she's always wanted a child of course, but not quite yet. It's rather difficult." I felt he wanted to say more, but confidences did not come naturally to him; he turned away. Nor was he ever to confide in me about Anne.

The child was born prematurely, and nearly died. It was a sickly, febrile creature, a girl whom they called Imogen because this was the Shakespearian part that Anne had always wished to play. Since at first Anne would have nothing to do with it, it was put in charge of an Indian ayah, a wrinkled old woman with whom Sandy never ceased to discuss details of its care and feeding. Then, suddenly, Anne became jealously possessive: perhaps remorse had overtaken her, perhaps a belated maternal instinct had been aroused. She began to give to Imogen an unremitting attention without which the child would certainly not have lived. Anne nursed it through illness after illness, and with each victory over death her love was intensified.

At the age of three Imogen showed the first signs of epilepsy: I was present at the time and I shall not forget the horrifying shriek which was a prelude to the fit. It then transpired that there had been epilepsy in Sandy's family, though he himself did not suffer from it. The doctor suggested an institution, but Anne would not hear of it. "I know she'll grow out of it," she repeated stubbornly. Soon after she became interested in Christian Science, and there is no doubt that at the same time Imogen's health began to improve: but whether this was due to the Christian Science, to Anne's devotion or to natural causes I do not venture to decide.

Anne and Sandy now lived on the top floor of a block of flats to which I myself had moved. They had a staircase leading up on to the roof where Sandy had devised a garden: it was his great pride, and he would often make me go up there to see the marvels his gardener had produced under his guidance. Imogen was never allowed up alone, since Anne was obsessed with the dread of her having a fall during an unexpected seizure. Each year a kite festival was held in the town, and for a whole week the evening sky was dense with gaudy colours. The object was for each man to cut down as many other kites as he could with the string of his own, and as a kite drifted loose and began to flutter downwards crowds would rush round it, since the first man to touch it could claim it for his own.

Sandy bought Imogen some kites in the bazaar, but she was never really interested in them. Flaxen and pale, with pathetically thin legs and arms, and eyes sunk deep in a pinched and wrinkled face, she seemed to care only for her mother and the elaborate games of make-believe which she played with herself. However, with the polite condescension shown by children towards their parents, she half-heartedly joined Sandy in any amusements he provided for her. The kite festival thrilled him. Each evening, through that week, he would hurry up to the roof with Imogen as soon as his work was over. "You will take care of her, won't you?" Anne would each time say fretfully. "Don't let her stand near the edge."

We shall never know for certain how it was that Sandy took his eyes off the child. "But I only looked away for a moment," was his broken reply to Anne's accusations. I myself suspect, as I think Anne did, that in his excitement at cutting down someone's kite or having his own cut down, he entirely forgot Imogen. She had not had a fit for four or five months, and perhaps he had come to believe, as Anne so often declared, that she was 'over it.'

That evening I was working in my study on the ground floor when a sound made me run to the window. I flung it open and scrambled out. My one thought was to spare Sandy and Anne the sight of the smashed body. I pushed my way through the crowd of Indians who stood, chattering and exclaiming shrilly, before the door. I hurried to my bedroom, pulled a sheet off my bed, and covered her with it.

Late that same night I took my leave of Sandy and Anne, feeling sick and unutterably weary after hours spent in consoling them and seeing that all traces of the accident were removed. "Well, I'll say good night now, if you're sure there's nothing else I can do." "Good night, old man," Sandy answered. But Anne remained motionless as she had been for over half an hour; a cup of tea lay untouched on the table before her; she gazed out of the window on to the brown square of lawn flanked with concrete paths which made a 'well' to the building. "Good night, Anne," I repeated. After her first hysteria—I had had to drag her off the child's shattered body—it was strange that she should have all at once become so calm. Strange, but not, I suppose, unusual.

Since she still did not look at me or give me any answer, Sandy went across to her. I felt deeply touched; there was so much tenderness and love in his expression, he spoke so gently to her. "Anne, darling. . . . Please. . . ." As his large, clumsy hand came to rest on her shoulder an extraordinary thing happened. She leapt to her feet and blazed out: "Leave me! Don't touch me! Murderer! Murderer!" One hand pressed against her right breast as she yelled at him.

"Anne. . . . my dear. . . ." He had backed at the first shock of her onslaught, but now he moved forward to her.

She stared at him with a strange, terrible enmity; her teeth were bared. Then she spat. He did not wipe it off his face. Slowly, cumbrously he sank on to his knees and began to rock back and forth, sobbing.

A few weeks later she asked him for a divorce, but being a Catholic, he refused her. A change had come over her. 'Too much sacrifice makes a stone of the heart.' She had had to sacrifice the only thing she had ever really loved, and her capacity for feeling died at the same time. Her hardness amazed me. Sandy was stricken with remorse and grief, and she openly laughed at him for it. "Oh, he's hopeless," she said to me when I met her going out to a dance with a young subaltern only a few weeks after the tragedy. "I can't get him to do anything now. It's so stupid. What's the point in brooding over it all? And would you believe it, he wants to endow a scholarship at the convent—in memory of her." She gave an unreal, trickly laugh. "The masses he's had said! And the hours he spends in prayer! I'm beginning to think I've married a monk." The subaltern with her was by now pink with embarrassment.

I expected her to leave Sandy, but she did not do so. I suppose she feared to return to the financial insecurity from which she had escaped by marrying him. She was, moreover, a fundamentally conventional woman. She hated being talked about, and though in the course of the next few months her name was linked with one young man after another, she was never ostentatious in her infidelity. Sandy did all he could to regain her affection. He believed that only he himself had been to blame, and he accepted her indifference as a just punishment for the wrong that he had done her. He always spoke of her with a blend of tenderness and compassion. He loved her very much.

But only one thing could ever reconcile her to him; it was necessary that she should be rid of him. When, less than a year after the death of their child, Sandy himself was dead, it did not surprise me to hear her speak of him, between sobs, as "Poor darling Sandy" nor to see her, at his funeral, with tear-stained cheeks and fingers that never ceased to twist a sodden handkerchief. He had been very good to her, she told those who offered her their sympathy. She would never get over it.

It is strange how often theatrical things happen to theatrical people. Sandy had been found by her, when she came home late from a dance, with a knife wound in his throat: he had been murdered. Since his bearer had disappeared and, on Anne's own evidence, Sandy had that morning thrashed the man, the police had no doubts as to who had perpetrated the crime. But the assassin was never caught.

I, myself, expected Anne to marry after a decent interval. She had been seen about for several weeks before Sandy's death with the young police officer who was to find himself in charge of the case. He was an able and conscientious boy who had only just shortly come from England; he organized a cricket eleven among the police force, and his father was a clergyman. I had gathered, erroneously it seems, that he and Anne were in love with each other. I never saw them in each other's company after the tragedy, and before long the boy was transferred, at his own request, to another station. Anne herself left for England two or three weeks later. This was the last I saw or heard of her until our meeting on the pier.

XXXIII

I COULD not help feeling that as Paul listened to this story he secretly discounted much and tinged much with his own private notions. "What hell she's been through!" he exclaimed when I had finished. He must have thought me callous when I replied: "No actress could expect a juicier part, could she?"

XXXIV

"You look unusually spruce."

Paul blushed. "Do I?"

"Yes, you do."

"Well, I thought I'd better tidy up."

"I'm very glad to see it."

His hair had been coaxed flat with what I suspected to have been an application of my own special brilliantine. His face had a shiny, pink look, as if he had just scrubbed it with a nail-brush. Even his shoes had been polished. A handkerchief had been pushed into the breast pocket of his suit.

It was a large, not unattractive farmhouse of red brick, obviously built in the Victorian era: the garden, through which we walked up to the front door, was tended with utmost care and contained some rare and beautiful shrubs and plants. A number of dogs ran out and barked at us, until they were silenced by a broad: "Shut up, there!" from the other side of a high laurel hedge.

Tea was on the verandah. "I'm so glad you were able to come," Norah Patton said. I felt it was not the conventional welcome of a polite hostess, but an admission that she was lonely and liked to be visited. I had already sat down, but Paul, with the peculiar gaucherie which afflicted him on social occasions, still remained standing, flushed and fidgety. "Where will you sit?" she asked. "Next to Mrs. Wetherby?" Anne was alone on a canvas garden sofa, swinging herself back and forth without taking any notice of us. She was again dressed in black, her dark hair drawn straight back from her sad oval face.

"Yes—thank you," Paul stammered. He placed himself on the corner farthest away from Anne. Mrs. Patton glanced at me and something, perhaps his embarrassment, made her smile.

She was an excellent hostess. But in spite of her efforts to draw Paul and Anne into the conversation, she and I seemed to be carrying on a *tête-à-tête*. Anne had that curious, interior detachment which I had noticed about her at our previous meeting, and Paul was obviously too shy to say anything. I noticed how he kept glancing at Anne when he thought he was not being watched; she herself behaved as if he were not there.

Half-way through tea, a middle-aged, sturdy man in breeches and a tweed coat, his hair cut very short and greying at the temples, came out and joined us. This was Mr. Patton, whose voice we had already heard silencing the dogs. Instead of sitting down, he leant against a pillar a few yards away from us. He was not ill-looking in a rough, unintelligent way, but I could not understand what had brought so incongruous a pair together. He was obviously not at his ease in our company. He gulped his tea, wiped his mouth on the back of his hand, and then handed the cup back to his wife: "Same again." He turned to me. "This weather makes you thirsty, don't it?" Hair grew out of his ears and thick on the backs of his soiled hands. Mrs. Patton, whose manner had been cheerfully matter of fact to the rest of us, behaved towards him with a tenderness which seemed to get on his nerves. When for the second time she asked him: "Are you sure you've got all you want?" he replied crossly: "I'll say if I haven't." Meanwhile Anne creaked back and forth, swinging Paul with her.

Suddenly Patton asked: "Where's the girl?"

"I don't know. I suppose she's still milking."

"Hasn't anyone told her tea's ready?"

"I thought it best to let her come in her own time."

"You know you're supposed to tell her."

"Well, I'm sorry, darling, but she knows the time. She's only got to come round here."

With an exclamation, he strode to the end of the verandah and began to shout: "Lena! Lena!" Then he returned. As he did so, Mrs. Patton repeated with a pathetic contrition: "I'm sorry, darling." She held out a hand to him, but he took no notice.

Soon Lena appeared and was introduced to us. A land-girl, she had bright yellow hair, cut short and curled into bubbles, a prettily vacuous face, and an attractive figure: where her shirt opened, the vee of her neck was sunburned, and one could see the beginning of her small, childish breasts. "I'm sorry not to have called you," Mrs. Patton said.

"Oh, that's all right, Mrs. Patton." She spoke in a painfully refined voice, with a little giggle at the end. She looked round her, and her eyes rested on Paul. "Any room for a little one." She squeezed herself between Paul and Anne.

Simultaneously Patton said: "Bit of a squash there, Lena! Come and sit over here."

"All right. I'll move." Anne spoke with weary indifference.

The girl chattered to Paul about the cows; the rest of us said little. Joe Patton had moved and was now standing behind the seat, just above Lena. I guessed that he was attracted by her. It was the intense physical attraction which finds stimulus even in a proximity to the loved one.

I think it was then that I realized just how attractive Paul must seem to women. Everything Lena said was said for him exclusively; her eyes returned over and over again to him. But she was not the only one of the party to find him interesting. He was being watched, less obtrusively, by Anne.

At last Lena got up. "Well, I must return to my cows. Ta-ta, everybody." She turned to Paul: "Hope to see you again sometime." Patton followed her as she left us.

Anne returned to the garden seat. "Lena really oughtn't to go about looking quite so *décolletée*. It's hardly decent." She gave a short, humourless laugh: "Perhaps she doesn't mean it to be."

"Oh, my dear, she's only a child," Mrs. Patton put in.

Anne smiled but said nothing.

"How old is she?" Paul asked.

"Only just seventeen. She's a wonderful worker. Joe says he doesn't know how he'd manage without her. She works much longer hours than any of the men. Sometimes she doesn't go home until after ten o'clock." Again Anne smiled without saying anything. Then suddenly she leapt to her feet.

"Would you like to see over the farm?" she asked Paul.

I think he was as much surprised by the invitation as I myself. "Er—thank—you," he stammered. He blushed. "That is, if Mrs. Patton will excuse us."

"I like your nephew," the older woman declared as he and Anne moved off together.

"I like him, too."

"Anne seems to have quite taken to him. I'm so glad. She's still very unhappy, and it's difficult to interest her in other people. Nothing seems to interest her now. You knew her husband, didn't you? What a terrible tragedy the whole thing was! I'm not surprised the poor child feels that there's nothing left to live for."

I was beginning to feel uncomfortable; I had my own view of the 'tragedy' which I did not feel I could disclose to someone who was obviously so fond of Anne. "Is she going to return to the stage?"

"Oh, that's what I want. That's what I'm trying to persuade her. It'll give her something else to think about and take her out of herself. She's got talent—more than talent. Have you ever seen her act?" I nodded. "Then you know just how good she is. She still has things to learn, of course, and she's far from being a good learner.

But—I'll let you into a secret. You're an old friend of hers, so I don't see why you shouldn't know. I'm giving her regular classes. I used to be an actress once," she explained, with a pathetic blend of pride and humility. "Experience has an enormous value on the stage. It's what she lacks."

"A friend of mine was telling me about your triumphs in the old days."

"Oh, really?" She took me up eagerly. "So I'm not yet entirely forgotten. It's nice to hear that. It's such an ephemeral kind of fame: one leaves nothing behind but the reminiscences of a few tedious old men who tell the younger generation just how good one was. The younger generation are not impressed." She spoke light-heartedly, but there was an under-tow of bitterness to her words. All at once, her gaiety had left her and she looked old, ill and disappointed. "You know, I've never ceased to blame myself for being such a failure."

"A failure?"

"To give up when one has done only a fraction of what one ought to do—isn't that failure?"

"If it is, it's not the kind of failure for which one can blame oneself."

"I don't know. I think one can blame oneself for illness. It may be a medical heresy, but I think illness is nearly always self-induced. One's ill because, deep down in oneself, one wants to be ill."

"I think that's rather hard. I've been ill recently, but I'm certain I don't want to be ill."

"No? You're sure you don't want the sympathy and attention that illness buys?"

"I don't think so."

She laughed. "I was only joking." There was a pause in which she followed the intricate pattern of the lace table-cloth with the fingers of one hand: she was frowning to herself. "Perhaps," she resumed at last, "it's only a profound kind of selfishness for me to want Anne to be a great actress. I feel that, in her, I shall have a second chance. I want her to do all the things I failed to do. I'm terribly ambitious for her. That's rather a shameful admission, isn't it?"

"Shameful? Why?"

"It's rather horrible to live on the experiences of other people. One becomes nothing more than an ichneumon-fly. But what else is there for the aged and infirm?" In the silence that followed these words I remembered how May had said almost the same thing to me. She, too, had accepted the fact that the old must feed, like parasites, on the young. It was an idea which I immediately repudiated.

But was I myself guiltless?

XXXV

As Paul and I walked down the drive, my mind was still busy with my conversation with Mrs. Patton. I wanted to tell Paul about it. "Rather a remarkable woman," I said at last.

"Who? Anne?"

"No, not Anne." I had to repress the irritation that his words caused in me. "Mrs. Patton."

"Oh, yes."

"We had an interesting talk while you were gone."

"Did you?"

But I knew that he was really not listening to me, and said no more. He was thinking of other things. There was a long silence between us which he at last broke: "You know, I like Anne." He said it defiantly, as if he expected me to be angry with him.

Perhaps his instinct was right. At the admission my irritation intensified into an emotion that was not far from anger. But I said calmly: "Do you? Well, why not?"

"I don't understand her at all. But I think that's what I really like about her. She's strange and mysterious, and I keep on feeling that I want to find out more. Would you rather I didn't talk about her?"

"Of course not. Why on earth should I? You obviously want to talk about her. Go ahead."

"I'm glad you've said that." I looked at him, but he kept his face averted and would not meet my eyes. "I've always felt that I can tell you everything. I want always to feel it." He spoke with a candour which I, hampered by restraints and reticences, could never hope to emulate.

Incapable of saying anything, I slipped my arm through his.

I knew that he wanted to speak about Anne and that he would do so, in his own time, without my prompting him. "Weren't you surprised when she offered to show me round the farm?" he said at last.

"Yes, I was."

"I certainly was. I was so taken aback that when we went off together I couldn't think what on earth to say to her. 'How old are you?' she asked: I told her, only"—he reddened slightly—"I added on two years. I didn't want her to think me a complete baby. But she wasn't really interested—I don't know why she asked the question. We said nothing more until we reached the stables. She began to show me round, and then suddenly she asked me: 'Are you bored?' I said no, of course not. 'Well, I am. And I can't stand the smell of this manure.' I suggested we go back and join you and Mrs. Patton——"

"And what did she say to that suggestion?" I interrupted him.

"She said——" He broke off in confusion.

"Yes?"

"That she'd rather be bored in the stables than with you," he mumbled. "With both of you."

"And so?"

He was relieved that this information did not annoy me. "We walked round the garden. She asked me the names of a number of the flowers and I told her. Then, all at once, I realized that she was laughing at me. 'What's the matter?' I asked. 'Nothing. I just find you rather funny. That's all.' I felt myself blushing, and she explained: 'You were so pleased with yourself for knowing the names of all those flowers.' It was true, and her saying it and knowing it to be true made me feel a thousand times more embarrassed than ever. 'You know a lot about flowers, but they don't interest me one bit.' That sounds rude, but it wasn't, the way she said it. 'Then why did you ask me?' 'Because it amused me. Do you mind?' Funnily enough, I *didn't* mind. 'Tell me about yourself,' she said. 'Who are you, where do you come from, what do you do?' So I told her, and all at once she changed; she became sympathetic and friendly. I knew I could confide in her, I no longer felt embarrassed." After a while, he stopped. "That was all, really. But I'm certain you're wrong about her. She's not the sort of person you think she is."

I shrugged my shoulders. "When are you going to see her again?"

"I don't know. She—she said she'd ring me. Do you mind?"

"Of course not."

But I did mind. I knew that he would suffer and I wanted to protect him from her. Perhaps, too, I was afraid of losing him. I resented her influence over him and I wondered whether it would supplant my own. I tightened my grip on Paul's arm. It was as if this physical proximity could bind him to me.

XXXVI

THE next day three other guests arrived at the farmhouse; they were a distinguished pathologist, his wife and son. Dr. Stare was an insignificant, baldish man with a drooping moustache and an air of extreme lassitude; he asked me to play chess with him on the day of his arrival and beat me soundly. I found him dull and difficult to talk to. His wife, several years younger than he, was a large, complacent woman who ate heartily, laughed loudly and went for walks with their son while Dr. Stare remained indoors and read. This son was a medical student of nineteen, a tall, stooping youth with red hair and freckles, a hooked nose from which a dewdrop was usually suspended and myopic, fair-lashed eyes behind thick, steel-rimmed glasses. Though afflicted with a stutter, he was abnormally talkative and enjoyed holding forth on his own subject, medicine. His breath was bad, and he had the irritating habit of clicking his fingers when he had nothing else to do. His name was Charles.

As soon as I saw him, I recognized one of those unhappy people whose exteriors are so unattractive that the friendships they proffer to every chance comer are always being rejected. He was anxious to get on with everybody, and confident of success. But wherever he went, one noticed a chill or, at best, a polite toleration. He chaffed the maid, and though she giggled, it was obvious that she considered him a fool. He began to harangue our landlady on Socialism, and she excused herself. When he attempted to 'pal up' with Paul (that was the phrase which he himself used), he was received coldly. But each of these rebuffs, which would have deterred a nature less obtuse or sanguine, only had the effect of spurring him to an increased cordiality.

On the day after his arrival, he came out on to the verandah where Paul and I were reading with some bathing things under his arm. "J-just off for a dip," he informed us. He rubbed his hands together and beamed, showing his uneven, discoloured teeth. "Bit chilly, isn't it? N-no, I'm not f-funking it," he got out in a rush, as if to contradict an accusation which neither of us had made. He gave a laugh which emerged as a snort at the back of his nose. Then he leant over Paul: "What are you reading, old man?"

"Lawrence."

"Not *Lady Chatterley's Lover,* I hope."

"*Seven Pillars of Wisdom.*"

"Oh, T. E. Interesting man T. E. Lawrence. I mean, *psychologically* interesting." Paul went on reading. "Don't you think so?"

"Oh, quite." I thought Paul had been unnecessarily rude, but need not have worried: Charles chattered on, oblivious of any snub. He knew a man who had a theory about T. E. Lawrence; it was really a jolly interesting theory. He, himself, had never read *Seven Pillars.* . . . After twenty minutes I had run through both the *Spectator* and the *New Statesman* and Charles was still with us. Paul continued to turn the pages of his book. "Ah, well, I must get along or I'll be late for t-tiffin. Why don't you join me? Eh?"

"What? What's that?" Paul looked up from his book.

Charles slapped his thigh in merriment. "Don't look so startled. I said, 'Why don't you join me?' Come and get an appetite for lunch."

"No, thank you."

"Oh, come on, man. Come on!" He attempted to drag Paul out of his deck-chair.

"No, thank you."

Charles snatched the copy of *Seven Pillars.* He held it high above his head. "You won't get it back until you say you'll come."

"Oh, don't be such a bloody fool."

"S-say you'll come."

"Give me my book."

"S-say you'll come."

Paul leapt at him and they both crashed downwards on to the concrete. Paul was on top.

"Ouch!" There was a resounding smack as Charles's head struck the ground. It frightened both Paul and me. Paul scrambled to his feet and attempted to help Charles up.

"Are you all right?" he asked anxiously. *Seven Pillars* lay in a flower-bed.

"I—God!—yes, I'm all right. But you're a bit rough, aren't you?" He scrambled to his feet, rubbing the back of his head with the palm of his hand. He laughed: "It made enough noise, didn't it? Did you hear the crack? Like a gun going off."

"I'm sorry," Paul mumbled. "I shouldn't have lost my temper."

"That's all right, old man. Nothing to be sorry about. But you will come now, won't you?"

What could Paul do but say he would? "Attaboy!" Charles grinned delightedly as he thumped him between the shoulder-blades.

XXXVII

SINCE neither of them had returned when the gong sounded for lunch, I went in alone. "Have you seen Charles?" his mother asked anxiously.

"He and Paul went down to the beach about an hour ago."

"I do hope he's all right. He's such a poor swimmer. He had rheumatic fever when he was seven, you know, and they wouldn't let him bathe until he was nearly sixteen. He's never really got used to the water."

From time to time during the meal she got up and went to the window. "I wonder if you oughtn't to go down to the beach and see what's happened," she told Dr. Stare, but he shook his head and went on eating. "Nothing can have happened to the boy. It's not the first time he's been late for lunch." I could see that like most fathers he was irritated by his wife's excessive devotion to their son.

At last Charles arrived, but without Paul. He dropped his wet towel and trunks on to the dining-room floor and hurried over to join his parents. "I'm famished. Unless I eat something soon, I shall pass out." He snatched a piece of bread and began to gnaw at it.

"Where's Paul?" I asked.

"Oh, P-Paul!" He gave his snorting laugh. "He met some fair d-damsel while we were bathing. . . . Could I have some f-fodder?" he interjected to the waitress. "Yes, he swam out to the raft and she was there, I couldn't h-hope to join them. I'm such a putrid swimmer. I hadn't an earthly. When it was time to come b-back, I called to him but he just told me to go to h-hell." He again laughed, as he began to gulp down spoonful after spoonful of scalding soup. "Well, I w-waited several minutes—that's what made me so l-late—but he still didn't come, so I decided to pack up and leave him. Who is the lady friend anyway? I don't know that I entirely admire his t-taste."

It was not until three o'clock that Paul returned. He rushed breathlessly on to the verandah where I was reading: "I say, I *am* sorry! I tried to 'phone, but hadn't any pennies, and when I got some change there was such a queue outside the telephone booth. I'd no idea it was as late as this."

"Have you had some lunch?"

"Yes, we had lunch. . . . You seem rather fed-up. Were you getting worried?"

"No. Charles told me that nothing had happened to you."

"I'm afraid I've been rather casual."

I did not answer, but continued to read my book.

"You're angry with me, aren't you?"

"No, I'm not. But I think you behaved rather rudely to Charles." In fact, I didn't care how he had behaved to Charles, but I preferred to be indignant on someone else's account.

"Yes, I know." He looked shamefaced. "He's that sort of person. Of course, that's no excuse. Was he very hurt?"

"What do you think?" I was not going to tell him that Charles had treated the whole affair as a joke.

"I'd better go and say I'm sorry."

"He's out bird's-nesting."

All at once, we both laughed. "Poor Charles!" I exclaimed.

"Poor Charles!" Paul sat down on the floor beside my chair, clasping his hands round his knees. After his bathe, his hair had blown anywhere and there was a faint salt smell about his presence.

"What had Anne to say?" I asked casually.

There was a moment's pause. "I don't think I like her now," he replied at last.

"Oh?"

"She was nice at first, but then—then she changed. We met out at the raft—I expect Charles told you—and we fooled around for a bit. She kept on trying to duck me, but when I ducked her back she was absolutely furious. 'Oh, you're so rough and clumsy! You're just a schoolboy.' But that didn't last long and we were soon on good terms again. She suggested we have lunch together, and I said I'd love to, but I must ring you first. At that, she flared up just as she'd done before. She said she really couldn't wait for me and unless I left it we'd better say good-bye. That's why I didn't ring. Then she ticked me off because the waiter wouldn't serve us and she thought it was my fault. She kept on saying: 'Well, can't you *do* something about it?' As soon as we were served, there was a bit of peace—but not for long. It seemed I over-tipped the waiter. I was awfully nervous about it—it was that posh hotel by the pier—and I was anxious to do things properly. Anyway, she said it was quite as bad to over-tip as to under-tip. It 'gave one away', she said—whatever that meant. She was in a bad mood again, and as we sat out on the promenade, she kept asking me questions about myself—What was I going to do? What sort of things did I write? How old was I? I could see she despised me and thought me just a child. She said I oughtn't to be just lazing about as I am now—on your charity. She said I hadn't any guts because I'd stuck on the island instead of doing something on my own. She told me I was conceited and hadn't any manners—well, that's true enough, isn't it? That's what you say." He looked up at me and smiled. Then he frowned: "Worst of all, she began to make fun of my writing. She said the country was full of young men who thought they could write or compose or paint, when they'd be far more useful in an office or factory. 'What makes you think you have any talent at all? Have you ever earned a penny by your work?' There seemed to be a devil in her, and I felt utterly miserable. And the awful thing was that I came to think that perhaps she was right. Why should I imagine that people will ever want to look at the sort of rot that I produce? Isn't it all just a complete waste of time? Here I am, using your money and tinkering at the stupidest of stupid short stories when I might be doing something of real use! It's horrible when someone suddenly tells one the truth like that; it's as if the stopping had been picked out of a hollow tooth. I suppose she only did it to help me, and I ought to be grateful to her. What do you think?"

"I think you ought to take absolutely no notice of what she's told you. She's no right to discourage you like that."

"But mightn't she be right? Are you sure that I've anything to say that's worth saying? Are you sure that I can one day become a good writer?"

"One can never be sure. So many are called, and so few are chosen. But you've had the call, and you must follow it. It's a gamble and you may be one of the losers—one can't say. But it's always worth while to take the gamble." I put my hand on his shoulder; I wished to communicate to him the confidence that I had in his future; I was full of hope, and I did not wish him to be discouraged.

"I wanted to hear you say that." He put up his hand and took mine. "I want you to believe in me."

XXXVIII

In spite of my assurances, Anne had implanted a doubt. Was it not all a waste of time? He was obsessed with that question, and though he never again mentioned it to me, I knew that he was passing through a period when the hopes and ambitions of our first weeks together seemed all at once insubstantial. His was not a sanguine temperament; he could easily be elated and as easily cast down.

One afternoon he was seated at the drawing-room window,

reading a book, when all at once I heard him exclaim: "Oh, God!"
He leapt to his feet.

"What's the matter?"

"She's coming up the drive."

"Well, go upstairs quick, and I'll tell her you're out."

He made for the door, and then hesitated. He turned: "No. I
think I'd better see her."

"Don't be a fool. You know you don't want to see her."

"I think I'll stay."

He composed himself in the chair again and took up his book,
but I knew he was not reading. His hands trembled so much that
eventually he had to lower the book on to his knees.

When Anne was shown in, she gave me a curt good afternoon
and then smiled at Paul. She held his hand for several seconds
in her own, as she said: "Why haven't you been to see me? Why
haven't I heard from you? I waited until a whole week had passed,
and then I decided to ferret you out. What have you been doing
with yourself?"

"Oh, nothing much," Paul mumbled. His cheeks were flushed.
He would not look at her, but kept his eyes fixed on their clasped
hands.

"Then I have every right to feel hurt," she laughed. "Don't you
think so, Mr. Langworthy?" I made no answer and perhaps she did
not expect one for she immediately ran on: "Well, do you think
you could bear to take me out to tea?"

"This afternoon?"

"This afternoon?" she mimicked back. "You don't sound very
hospitable. I've been feeling so bored and lonely, and I was count-
ing on you."

"Of course, I'd like to take you out." At the words a panic apprehension overcame me. As he stood there, pink and trembling
with excitement, I knew that he was hopelessly infatuated with
her. Worse, there was nothing I could do about it.

"Good! Then let's go."

It was not until they reached the door that he remembered
me. He turned: "Is it all right? I mean—do you mind?"

"Of course not. I've a lot of letters to write. Will you be back
to dinner?"

He looked enquiringly at Anne, who said softly: "That's for you to decide."

He hesitated. "Yes—no——" He appealed to her. "You say."

She laughed. "You're not very good at making up your mind, are you? Women like a man to be decisive. You'd better learn that. Well, let's have dinner out as well, and see a flick."

"All right," he stammered. He gave me a last look, which at once besought me, excused himself and excused her.

"Have a good time," I said. I forced myself to smile, and was glad to see his face clear; he gave a sigh—of relief, it seemed. Then they were gone.

I tried to continue with my letter but could not. At last I got up, went to the window and peered down the drive, but they must long since have moved out of sight. The door opened and Charles came in.

During these days he was often our companion. He came unasked and though he irritated us we seldom had the heart to snub him. He was extraordinarily generous and every day he brought either me or Paul some small present—an orange, a bun, some sweets or an ice-cream. He would run errands for us and indefatigably wind up the portable gramophone. He so much wanted to be liked by us, but we could do no more than give him our grudging toleration.

"Just seen P-Paul as I came up from the beach—had that girl with him. They seem pretty thick, don't they? Either Paul didn't see me or didn't want to see me. I fancy the latter." He laughed cheerfully. "They were walking arm-in-arm. As I told you, she's not quite my c-cup of tea. Still . . ." He fumbled in his trouser pocket, and, like a child, brought out a small bag of glacier-mints. "G-go on. The whole bag's for you. I'll let you into a secret." He put a finger on his lips and whispered: "I g-got them off the r-ration."

XXXIX

PAUL was still not home at eleven o'clock that evening, and I decided to go up to bed. It was a still, heavy evening such as preludes a thunder-storm. I undressed and got into bed, but could not compose myself. I threw off the bed-clothes, rose and drank a glass of tepid water, and lay down again. Still I could not sleep. In the end I went to the open window and sat there, smoking cigarette after cigarette. I could hear people moving about in other rooms; in many of them lights were still burning.

Suddenly, I heard a rustle; a drop of rain fell, and then another. I put out a hand and let the cool drops trickle on my hot, sweating palm. The drops fell faster. There was a flash of lightning. The storm had come.

I was so lost in my relief that thoughts of Paul for a moment went out of my head. Then suddenly I heard feet pattering up the drive. "Thank God!" someone exclaimed, jumping on to the verandah below.

"Thank God!" a woman's voice echoed.

It was Paul and Anne. Leaning far out, without caring for the rain that streamed over me, I tried to listen to their conversation.

"How long are we going to stay here?" It was Anne, peevishly impatient.

"Until it's over. Then I'll see you home."

"But it may be hours. I wish you hadn't suggested walking. We could easily have got a taxi."

"At a price! Anyway, it was lucky we were so near the farm. Shall we go in?"

"No. Let's stay out here. It's rather exciting." Her irritation seemed to have passed.

"All right. But don't talk so loud."

"Why? Does someone sleep above here?"

"Yes."

"Who? Your fairy godmother?"

"Who do you mean?"

There was a soft laugh. "Your uncle, silly."

"Why do you call him that?"

"Why not? It's my nickname for him. Anyway, don't let's talk about him. He bores me."

"That's because you don't know him properly."

"Oh, I know him all right."

"Sh!"

"You're rather sweet."

"Don't be silly."

"I mean it. I mean it, I mean it, I mean it."

"I wish you wouldn't make fun of me."

"I'm not making fun of you." She whispered something which, strain as I might, I could not hear. A long silence followed. I was drenched, my teeth were chattering; a hopeless misery descended on me. I wanted to call to him, I thought even of going down; but in my heart I knew I could do nothing by interference. Anne I hated. At that moment I thought of her with a cold, murderous fury.

I heard nothing for so long that I thought they must have gone without my knowing it. But as I was about to turn away from the window, there was a sharp exclamation which might have come either from him or her. I heard Anne laugh. Then the whispering began again, but now, though I still could not make out what was being said, there was a note of passion in it; they were arguing, I thought; he was insisting, she refusing.

So it went on, until the rain suddenly, abruptly ceased. Anne spoke aloud: "Well, can I go back now?"

"I'll see you home."

"Will you?"

I watched the two figures move arm-in-arm down the dripping avenue of laurels. It would be at least twenty minutes before he returned, and when he did, it was unlikely that he would want to see me. But I felt that I could not go to sleep until I had spoken to him and reassured myself of I knew not what. I changed out of my wet pyjamas, put on my dressing-gown, lit a cigarette, took down a book and prepared to wait.

Half an hour later I heard slow, dragging footsteps approach up the drive. I looked out of the window to make sure that it was he, and then, with beating heart, sat down on the edge of my bed and took up my book. He must have seen my light burning, and perhaps he would come in of his own accord. Seconds passed. There was a clatter in the corridor.

"God, you're late, man!" It was Charles speaking. "It's past two. I got up to p-pay a penny, and wondered who on earth it was coming up the stairs. You're soaked!"

"Yes, I did get rather wet."

Charles whistled. "Well, you certainly have made a n-night of it. Enjoy yourself?"

"Yes, thank you."

"I bet you did—you old So-and-so!" He guffawed and then I heard him yawning. "I'd better turn in again. Happy d-dreams!"

"Good night."

Paul's footsteps receded towards his own room. Should I go to him? Better not. Yet an obscure, ludicrous anxiety filled me. What had happened? Was he all right? Fretted by indecision, I remained seated on my bed. He was coming back; I waited until his knock sounded and then with a strained casualness called: "Hullo! Come in!"

"I hope you don't mind my knocking you up like this, but I saw that your light was on." He was embarrassed; he was fiddling with his pyjama cord. But beyond his embarrassment, and obliterating it, was a happiness which he could not conceal. Anyone might think him a little tipsy.

"I couldn't sleep through the storm, so I began reading. I was afraid you might catch it on your way home."

He hesitated for the fraction of a second before he answered: "Oh, we managed to take shelter."

"Good." I gave no indication that I had heard them on the verandah. "Have a good evening?"

"Yes." He came impulsively towards me. "Oh, Uncle Mark——" He broke off.

"Yes?"

"Nothing."

I looked into his face, but he would not look back at me. "You're very happy, aren't you?"

He started. "How do you know?"

"It's written all over you."

All at once, his restraint was gone. He came and sat down on the bed beside me. "Yes, I am happy. I don't know why, but I am, I am."

"I can guess why."

"She's very nice," he said softly. "I want you both to like each other. If you really knew what she was like, and she knew what you were like, I know you'd be friends. Will you try, Uncle Mark?"

"Yes. I'll try to like her." At that moment I was willing to concede anything.

He pressed my hand: like a child he still found it easiest to express his emotions through some such small physical act of touch. At the gesture, I experienced release from all the anxieties that had been besetting me. I had feared to lose him, but I had been stupid.

I suppose he guessed this, for when he next spoke, it was to say with an almost naïve candour: "You don't mind my caring for her, do you?"

"I thought I did. But I don't now."

"I'm glad. After all, affection isn't like a cake which one can only cut into a certain amount of slices. There's no end to it."

I wondered if he was right. "I knew you'd fall in love sooner or later, and I'm glad it's happened. My only regret is—was" —hastily I corrected myself—"that it had to be Anne. But I'm prepared to admit that I may have been wrong about her."

"I'm sure you have." He spoke with a quiet, yet passionate conviction. "She has her moods—she wouldn't be human if she hadn't. She can be unkind and irritable. But I do believe—I do believe that she's a fundamentally honest and good person. After all, she's been through an awful lot and it's not surprising that it's made her superficially hard. I misjudged her, too. I thought as you thought. But now that I know her, I see how wrong I was."

There is something touching in the faith which lovers have in each other. I was certain that Paul would suffer for his belief in Anne's goodness, but could not say so. Warnings would have only angered him.

"Probably I've misjudged her. Anyway, I'm going to try again." I recognized the pitiful extent of my insincerity as I spoke the words. I smiled. "I have a great respect for your judgment. If you say she's all right, I feel she must be. Anyway, I'm glad you're happy. That's all that really matters."

"It was silly of you to worry—you were a little worried, weren't you?" He patted my arm affectionately. "Nothing can alter our friendship."

"I like to think that too."

XL

"NOTHING can alter our friendship." For a time there was a truth in the words. I now saw much less of him, he was often preoccupied, and yet when we were together we could resume our intimacy with no sense of strain. There was between us that perfect freedom which is the essential of all friendship; we could say anything, we could do anything, or we could just be silent: it did not matter. He confided in me every detail of his relationship with Anne, and asked me for advice. He was no less affectionate, no less sympathetic.

And yet, in spite of this, I could not help resenting the hours he spent with her, while I fidgeted away the time as best I could, reading, writing letters or going out with Charles. Charles was delighted to take Paul's place as my companion. He had conceived an affection for me, probably because I forced myself to talk to him when most people, including his father, told him to be off. He was good, and it seemed unjust that he should also be unpopular. In an effort to win my favour, he began to imitate Paul. He tried to write a story, in the back of an exercise book he had previously used for notes in the dissecting-room. He made lists of the books that he had seen Paul read and began himself to read them. He asked me if I thought it was too late for him to learn a musical instrument, and not discouraged by my assertion that it was, went down to the town three days a week to have lessons on the tuba from a retired bandsman.

I found him irritating, and yet I was often glad to have him with me. Charles, himself, had no illusions about our relationship: he knew that he was a stop-gap and with a humble gratitude he accepted that role.

Meanwhile, Paul's growing intimacy with Anne filled me with apprehension. I hoped always for estrangements, and yet for his sake I was sorry when they occurred. I think Anne enjoyed scenes, and created them for that reason. Paul hated them and yet in the end he, too, seemed to find in them a bitter substitute for the satisfactions she withheld from him.

Of their many quarrels one, in particular, now comes back to me.

He and Anne had gone to town for the day. He had followed her from shop to shop without complaining, though clothes bored him and the temperature was one of the hottest for that July. After two hours she had still bought nothing but a yard of ribbon, and he suggested that they should break off and get some lunch.

"Oh, but didn't I tell you? I can't have lunch with you. I'm supposed to be meeting Desmond Standing—you know, the portrait painter. I thought I made it quite clear." She saw the expression of chagrin on his face, and exclaimed: "Oh, for God's sake don't go into a sulk! Surely you can amuse yourself for an hour and a half. I'll be meeting you at two-thirty."

"I think I'll go home."

"Home! What do you mean? Back to the country?"

"It's so hot here. It's really no fun."

"I'm sorry you've had such a boring day."

"I didn't mean that."

"I don't know what else you meant."

"You know perfectly well——"

"Sometimes I find you more than a little tedious." All at once she changed. She slipped an arm through his, and gave her clear, tinkling laugh: "Don't let's quarrel just because there's a heat-wave. I'll tell you what. Let's go to Kew this afternoon. Would you like that? Yes?"

"All right."

She shook his arm gently. "But don't say it in such a cross voice."

"Kew would be lovely."

"Good."

Unfortunately they were not the only couple who had decided to go to Kew that afternoon. They wrangled about whether to take a train or bus, and when Anne got her way, as she usually did, bus after bus passed them without stopping. Paul could not resist pointing out that *if* they had taken the train—but Anne immediately snapped: "Oh, don't go into all that over again. Once one's decided a thing, it's hopeless to have regrets." In the end, they had to sway for twenty long minutes in a train which smelled of cheap scent, smoke and perspiration.

Surprisingly, however, Anne again recovered her good humour. "Well, it was worth it, wasn't it?" she said, as they jostled their way through the rose-gardens and found an open space beneath some trees. "Wasn't it? Come on, cheer up."

He pressed her hand. "Yes, it was."

But they had walked for no more than ten minutes when she declared that she was thirsty. Paul pointed out a drinking fountain only to be told crossly: "No, thanks! I don't want to catch some horrible disease."

"Well, I don't know where else you can get a drink of water."

"There's a tea-garden, isn't there?"

"Is there?"

"Well, of course there is."

At the counter she decided she would like something to eat with her cup of tea—"Just something to nibble." But the lettuce looked so crisp, there was real peach jam with the bread and butter, she could never resist doughnuts. . . . They came away with a large tray of food.

"Oh, these wasps!" One got caught in her hair. "Do something. Do something!" she cried.

"Sit still."

"It's all very well to say 'sit still'. Meanwhile, I shall get stung——" The wasp flew out. "Oh, you are clumsy!" In his hurry to help her, he had bent one of the ospreys round her toque.

"I'm sorry."

"It doesn't matter." But her sigh made it clear that it did. "I wasn't stung. That was the main thing."

As she put the spoon into the jam, two more wasps alighted on it; she dropped the spoon hurriedly. "Help me, will you? I'm such a coward over wasps." He put some jam on her plate. "That's rather a mingy spoonful, isn't it?" He gave her some more.

A wasp settled on her plate, and she pushed it away from her. Another buzzed round her, and she flapped her arms, exclaiming, "It's going to sting me," and eventually leapt to her feet, knocking her chair over. But it was Paul who was stung.

"Oh, you poor darling. Does it hurt terribly?"

"No more than a wasp sting usually does. It's only on my hand."

"They're such malevolent brutes. They just go for one for absolutely no reason at all."

"Well, if you will jump about at them. . . ." he said with a forced laugh.

"That's right. Blame me!"

"I'm not blaming you. Don't take everything so seriously."

"No one can say that I've no sense of humour."

"Come on. Let's sit down and eat."

She shook her head. "No, thank you. I'd rather go hungry than be stung."

"Don't be silly."

But she would not listen to him, and they had to leave the food for which he had already paid a large sum. "You're cross with me, aren't you?" she said, as they walked across one of the lawns.

"No."

"Yes, you are."

"Well, it does seem a pity to waste all that food," he broke out.

"I couldn't help it. Wasps terrify me. It's silly, I know, but I'm just made that way. I'm sorry." Once again she did all in her power to woo him from his sullenness. "Don't be angry, darling." ('Darling' was a word she seldom used to him.) "I'm just a baby—you don't have to tell me. Say I'm forgiven. Paul, say I'm forgiven."

Soon, he began to laugh: "If you knew how funny you looked—waving your arms and knocking over that chair!"

"Well, you looked pretty funny yourself when the wasp stung you!" She, too, was laughing.

"It didn't feel funny."

"Poor Paul. Has it swollen up badly?" She took his hand and caressed it. "I feel such a fool—it was all my fault."

"Of course it wasn't."

For a few minutes they were entirely reconciled. She suffered Paul to put his arm round her, though as a rule she refused any physical intimacy with him. She rested her head on his shoulder. A moment ago, he had been filled with irritation, and now there was nothing but tenderness and desire. They were passing one of the hot-houses.

"Oh, let's go and look at the orchids," Anne exclaimed.

"On a day like this?"

"I love orchids, and I love heat."

"And I dislike both."

"Come on," she cajoled. "To please me."

"Oh, very well." He gave in good-humouredly. "But, remember, if I faint, I shall blame you."

They spent many minutes looking at the orchids in an atmosphere that was heavy with their rank odour. Anne kept touching them, though there were notices forbidding visitors to do so. "I can't help it. They fascinate me." Paul's head began to throb; when he raised his hand to his forehead, drops of sweat trickled on to it. Anne remained strangely cool. More than once he urged her: "It's so hot. Let's go." The desire which all that day he had felt for her now translated itself into a mere animal lust; he attempted to conquer it, but could not. "That's as far as we can go here," she said. "We'll have to turn." Her face appeared to him as one of the pale, fragile orchids emerging through a dank swathe of steam. . . . He moved forward.

"Paul, for God's sake!" She pushed him away from her. "No, don't touch me."

He began to beseech her, but she reiterated: "No, no, no! I've told you—I don't like it." She gave a little laugh: "I'm not sure that you're nice to know."

He felt weak with shame, frustrated desire and the appalling heat. "Let's get out then. We've seen all there is to see."

"But I want to go through. There's more through there."

'Through there' he could see enormous fleshy leaves, a mat of creepers, and the back of an attendant who lolled, naked to the waist, against a tank of water-lilies. "There aren't any orchids through there."

"I want to see the bananas."

"But I can't stand this heat."

"I didn't ask you to come with me. You can wait outside."

"Please, Anne. Please!" He was almost tearful.

"Oh, don't make such a fool of yourself!" Angrily, she pushed her way through the door that separated them from that brighter, denser green, and he followed. A gust of hot air fanned upwards from the iron grid that ran along the floor. He felt he could not breathe.

At their entry, the attendant looked round and said in a slow voice: "Shut the door behind you." Paul fumbled and shut it. The man was watching them both with what, to Paul's exacerbated sensibilities, seemed to be nothing more than a smiling insolence. He looked as if he had once been a sailor; his arms and chest were tattooed with a pattern of anchors, mermaids and fish. He was large and muscular, with a broken nose, peculiarly bright, close-set blue eyes, a chin that was blue-black and a great mat of coarse hair on his chest. He was streaming with sweat.

Paul found him utterly repellent, and his one wish was to move away from him. But Anne now stopped: she was pointing down to the tank, and asking some question. The man answered her. She said something else, and they both laughed. They were standing close together, and it disgusted Paul to see how the transparent voile sleeve of her dress brushed against the man's gleaming fore-arm. He felt sick and ill. From time to time as the other two talked, he tried to attract Anne's attention. But she seemed purposely to avoid looking at him. For a moment he felt the impulse to drag her away by sheer physical force. In the green, hot light the attendant seemed curiously sinister.

Release came at last: the attendant was called away.

Anne and Paul continued to circle round the hothouse, she in front, he behind, until they had once more returned to the place where the attendant had been standing. "The attendant isn't back yet."

"I don't expect he stands here all afternoon." She waited for a while, staring down into the tank at her own reflection; he stared over her shoulder. Then she turned: "Oh, well, let's go." He noticed how as they walked out through the orchid-house, she not only peered down every turning, but kept glancing backwards.

As soon as they stepped over the threshold into the open, it was strange how, after the weakness and confusion of the last half-hour, he all at once felt clear-headed, sane and strong. Anne was looking in her bag.

"I must have dropped my handkerchief. What a nuisance! I'd better go back."

"It's in your pocket."

"Is it?" She looked down. "Oh, not that one. This is rather special. It's made of silk, and has my initials embroidered in one corner. I don't want to lose it."

"I'll go for you."

"No, I know how you hate it in there. You're looking quite faint. You sit on this seat for a moment and I'll be right back. Shan't be a moment."

She was gone, shutting the hot-house door decisively behind her, and he, doing as she had told him, sat down. But once seated, he was assailed by a thousand vague suspicions. He was convinced she had come out with no 'rather special' handkerchief—certainly, he had had no glimpse of it. Why, after she had kept him in the hot-house for over half an hour, should she all at once display so much solicitude towards him? Something in her behaviour when she had been talking to the attendant—Paul could not define it—had disturbed him. He remembered now how the man had looked at her while she was speaking, his eyes moving up and down her and a fixed smile revealing his large, over-white teeth.

Paul got up, and racked with uncertainty, hesitated at the door. Then he pushed it open, and entered once more into the damp, suffocating atmosphere. But he had barely walked a yard, when he came face to face with Anne. Far beyond her, through the door at the far end of the house, he imagined that he could see the attendant, lolling beside the tank as he had been when they had first seen him. But he could not be certain; he was never to be certain. Anne had already obliterated his view. Her face had become white; she stopped with only a few inches between them. "Well?"

Suddenly and inexplicably he felt afraid of her. "Did—did you find the handkerchief?" he stammered.

She stared at him for several seconds before making a reply. Then she asked: "What exactly are you trying to insinuate?"

"Insinuate?" he could only repeat after her.

"Why did you follow me?"

"I didn't follow you."

"I won't stand for it! I won't be spied on!" Suddenly she blazed out. "I'm not your property, whatever you think. You've no rights where I'm concerned, and the sooner you learn it the better. You're just a child, don't forget that. I won't be dictated to by you. See? See? See?" It was a scene of a crudity which overwhelmed him. She seemed to wish only to wound him, taunt him and make him realize how little he could expect from her. It was when she jeered at his youth that she inflicted the deepest hurt on him; to be regarded as a 'baby', not to be taken seriously by any woman, was for him, as for most adolescents, the supreme insult. He had thought that even if she could not love him in the way and to the extent that he loved her, at any rate in her own uncarnal fashion she did care for him. But that was an illusion which she had now destroyed. (Destroyed—but not for long. The illusion was to be recreated, before my eyes, within the next twenty-four hours.)

He could stand no more. He turned and hurried away from her, and she, realizing that for once she had gone too far, hurried after him. Her feelings were those of a cat which, having teased a mouse to death, is then sorry to lose its plaything.

"Paul! Don't go! I didn't mean it! Paul!" But he pushed her away from him and began to run. He ran on and on as if he were fleeing from some terrible danger.

He returned to the farm and told me the whole story. "I shall never see her again, I suppose. I don't know why she was so angry with me. Perhaps I did have suspicions—that was wrong of me, I know now—but I never said anything and surely there was no harm in going into the hot-house after her. What do you think? I can't understand it. It's so strange." He was very unhappy, and I was overjoyed.

Of that joy I was then, as now, ashamed. I had so often told myself that all that mattered was Paul's happiness and yet, deep within me, it seemed that I wished only to safeguard my own rights to him. I could not behave otherwise.

"You must try to forget about her," I urged. "Put her right out of your mind. I know it's hard, damnably hard, but it's the only thing to do. We'll arrange something for tomorrow—a drive or a few days away. That may help to take your mind off her."

When I tendered this advice, seemingly so sympathetic, what was I doing but reclaiming him for my own?

XLI

THE expedition we arranged for the next day was to Battle Abbey. Paul is the possessor of a wonderfully vivid historical sense, and ruins and old buildings fascinate him. It is a sense which I, myself, wholly lack; historical associations mean nothing to me. I have only æsthetic standards with which to judge a building, and for that reason I often shocked him by displaying no interest in places which, history apart, seemed to me hideous. When, for example, he and I visited the Tower of London, he was astonished at my telling him: "I can't stand this." To him, the Tower, with its many romantic evocations, was a strange, wonderful, disturbing spot.

In the same way, I expected him to lose himself in Battle Abbey. But he wandered over it listlessly, without enthusiasm. He had been cheerful enough at breakfast until the post brought him a letter from Betty and after that an impenetrable gloom had settled on him. It was a sad, hopeless letter and no doubt, vulnerable as his feelings then were, he had accused himself for her unhappiness. It seemed that her father had had a 'nervous breakdown' and had had to go into a home. She was now staying with Tilly and my mother, helping them with the house and garden. "I feel so alone—first you gone, then him. They won't even let me visit him—they say it would only upset him more. Oh, Paul, if you only knew how unhappy I am. There is nothing, *nothing* to live for. I often go the walks we used to go—I don't expect you to remember—and I think, think, think of you until I can bear it no longer. When will you come back? When will you write to me? When, when, when?" As a postscript she had written: "Do you remember Dr. Ferguson, the missionary doctor, who is on holiday from his leper-island—you forgot to come to his first lecture with me, it seems years and years ago? I think he wants to marry me, but he's so old and so serious and so dull. Yesterday he took me for a drive and did nothing but talk about his work. But I wasn't listening! There was only one thought in my mind—you, Paul . . ."

The despair and frustration of this letter must have weighed on Paul's conscience. He had accused Anne of being callous towards him, but in what way was he being less callous towards Betty? She, like himself, was tormented by a desire which could not be reciprocated, and in her plight he saw nothing but a mirror of his own. It was strange at one and the same time to be the victim and the torturer.

As we drove to Battle, he sat silent and glum beside me. I did all I could to draw him out and make him forget both Anne and Betty. But my questions were only answered with monosyllables; my jokes fell dismally flat. One small incident of that drive ought, however, to be mentioned. Paul was for the first time going to say something to me which was not an answer to some remark of my own. "Uncle Mark," he began. He broke off: "It seems somehow silly to call you Uncle."

"Does it? Well, what would you like to call me?" He did not answer. He looked acutely embarrassed; he gave me a brief, appealing, almost frightened glance and then turned his head away.

"You can call me Mark, if you like."

"All right," he replied, without enthusiasm.

"What were you going to say just now?"

"I don't remember. It doesn't matter."

At the time the incident puzzled me, but I thought no more about it. Having been round the Abbey, we had lunch at an inn. We were given an excellent meal of roast duck, *sauté* potatoes and green peas, but Paul ate only a few mouthfuls and then shoved his plate aside.

"What's the matter?"

"I don't feel hungry. I feel rather sick."

"Would you like to lie down?"

"No. I'll be all right."

"Let me order you a drink. Some brandy, perhaps."

"Oh, don't fuss over me!" he exclaimed, with a sudden irritation.

"I'm sorry." I went on with my lunch. When I had finished, we went into the lounge for coffee. I was going to ask him how he felt, but checked myself. As I settled myself in an easy chair, he walked over to the mantelpiece: "This clock has stopped."

"Has it?"

"What time is it?"

"Quarter to two."

"Quarter to two!" He threw himself into a chair, and drew both hands down his cheeks. "It seems such ages." He stared at the wall opposite him.

"I don't know what you'd like to do now, but I thought we might drive over to Brighton. You said you wanted to see the Pavilion, didn't you? We can stay the night there—if we find an hotel to take us. That'll make it less of a rush."

He remained motionless for several seconds before he answered; he might not have heard me. "I think we'd better go back to the farm," he said at last.

"Oh?"

"I've some things to do."

"Won't they wait until tomorrow?"

"I—I promised to have a bathe with Charles before supper."

"You can ring him up. He won't mind."

"No, I won't do that. I don't want to let him down."

I knew that it was the thought of Anne that drew him homewards, and for that reason I all at once wished to hurt him. "You're being unusually punctilious. You don't, as a rule, bother about Charles."

He neither answered me nor looked at me; he sprawled, wan and hopeless, with his eyes still gazing at the blank wall; the sight of him filled me with remorse for what I had just said.

XLII

PAUL and Charles were away bathing for less than half an hour. When they came in, Paul made straight for the stairs.

"Where are you off to, old horse?"

"To change."

"Oh, s-stay a minute; There's heaps of time." But Paul had already disappeared. Charles sat down opposite me: "W-well?"

"Well?" I reiterated. I was too preoccupied with Paul's affairs to wish at that moment to speak to Charles. The physical repulsion which I had at first experienced in his presence and later overcome, now renewed itself. He was wearing a grimed pair of khaki shorts, a belt which fastened with a silver snake, a grey flannel shirt, open at the neck, such as one usually sees on schoolboys, and gym-shoes. A finger explored his nose.

"If you haven't got a handkerchief, do go and fetch one," I snapped.

"S-sorry," he said with perfect good humour. "It's an awful habit. I've done it all my life." He pulled a filthy, sodden handker-chief out of his shorts, emptying a shower of hay seeds on to the carpet at the same time, looked for a dry corner and then blew. "What's b-biting Paul?" he asked, still muffled by the rag.

"Nothing, so far as I know."

"Perhaps he's l-liverish. He didn't exactly p-put himself out to be friendly to me."

"Well, he sacrificed a trip to Brighton in order to come back and bathe with you."

I had wished to snub him, but my words had precisely the opposite effect. "Did he? Did he really? Oh, I say—— Do you mean——?" He gazed at me in delighted incredulity. "But why?"

"Why? Because he'd promised you that he would. That's why."

"Oh, but it was nothing as d-definite as that. Of course I'm jolly glad—it was d-damned decent of him. But I just said that if he was b-back in time and if he wanted to . . . That's all."

"I see." But I think I had known all along.

Immediately after dinner Paul announced that he was going for a stroll. "Would you like me to come with you?" I asked.

"No, thank you. I think I'd rather be alone."

"As you wish."

A few minutes later Charles joined me out on the verandah. "All alone? Where's P-Paul?"

"Gone for a walk."

"With the lady-friend?"

"I don't think so."

"How about a game of bézique?"

"No, thank you."

"You're frightened of l-losing to me as you did l-last time! Chess, then?"

"No, thank you."

He sighed, and creaked into a wicker chair. "I swopped these stamps in the l-little shop in the High Street. Care to p-peep at them?"

"Look, Charles, I very much want to get on with my book. Do you mind?"

"Of course not. Why didn't you say so before? I'll buzz off. See you later!"

I sat alone, but I could not read. One, two, three hours passed. It was growing dark, and I shivered slightly. I was just going indoors when I heard a firm, confident step on the gravel of the drive.

"I hoped I'd find you here." Paul, flushed, excited and joyful, threw himself into the wicker chair. "I've seen her. It's all right. It's all made up."

"Good. I'm very glad. Tell me about it."

"Do you really want to hear? It won't bore you?"

"Of course I want to hear."

"Very well, then . . ."

He had wandered disconsolately out towards the Pattons' farm, with no thought of going in and asking for her. He leant against their gate and stared up the drive, his hands in his pockets. He was certain that somewhere, up there in the house he could not see, Anne was seated, talking or sewing or listening to the wireless, without a thought of him. He gave himself over to a serene melancholy; it was almost pleasurable.

"Paul!" The voice that startled him came, not from the house, but from the main road. "What are you doing here?"

"I—I——" He could only stammer incoherently.

"I wanted you to come round. It was so stupid of us to quarrel as we did yesterday. I'm afraid I said a lot of things I didn't mean. Will you forget about them?"

"I've forgotten about them already," he lied.

"It must have been the heat. It always makes one quarrelsome . . . Come up and have a drink."

"Oh, no—I mean——"

"Come on!" She took his arm and propelled him gently forward. "You don't have to meet Ma Patton—or Farmer Giles." She alluded to them with a patronizing facetiousness. "We can sit out on the lawn."

Paul waited for her as she went into the house and returned with a tray of drinks. She sat down on the bench beside him, in an arbour which was fenced round by syringa bushes; a heavy, pervasive smell from the withering flowers lay all about them. They talked as they drank, and then putting down their glasses, they were silent. Anne slipped an arm into his, and said in a soft, vaguely mocking voice: "You may kiss me, if you like."

"May I?"

"A token of reconciliation."

His lips brushed her cheek, and then, with an uprush of desire, he pressed his mouth against hers; his hands sought her out. She drew away from him, a little breathless, laughing a little. When he pleaded with her, she shook her head: "No more."

"That's the first time I've ever kissed you on the lips."

"Perhaps it'll be the last time."

"Why?"

"Because—because . . ." All at once she became grave. "Do you really want to know?"

"Yes."

"Once I was terribly in love with someone—he was killed. You've probably heard that already?" He nodded. "He was everything to me, and I gave him everything. When I lost him, all that ceased to interest me. I don't think it will ever interest me again." The corners of her mouth sagged; suddenly she looked much older than her twenty-eight years.

"I understand," he said simply. "I love you very much."

"You're rather a dear." For a moment her fingers rested lightly on his cheek.

Someone was calling from the house. "Anne! A-Anne!" It was Mrs. Patton.

"Oh, damn her!" Anne exclaimed.

"What does she want?"

"She wants me to go and recite Shakespeare to her," Anne said scathingly. "I'm supposed to have a lesson. I'm already twenty minutes late for it. That's your fault."

"Oughtn't you to go?"

"I'd much rather stay out here."

"Well, shouldn't you tell her?"

"No—I don't think so." She laughed. "I can't be bothered. She'll soon get tired of calling for me."

"I think that's a little unkind," he deprecated.

"Yes, I suppose it is." She sighed. "You don't understand. You don't know how I feel. I *have* to assert my freedom. She's always trying to take it away from me. I must be free, I must—at any price. You don't understand that. You prefer not to be free. You like to be owned by someone else. But I—I hate it." She shuddered. "That's what I hate about old people. They're like spiders, wrapping you round and round and round in their webs. I know what you say—'Well, why not? The web's warm, the spider's kind.' . . . Ugh!" She pulled a face.

This was as much as Paul then recounted to me of their conversation; but, later, in one of the many excursions we were to make into the past, he added a few more sentences. His reasons for concealing them at the time of this narrative will be apparent. It seems that she then turned to him and asked: "Don't you ever feel you'd like to be free? Don't you?"

"What do you mean?"

"Don't you ever regret the months of bondage?"

"Bondage? To whom? I don't understand you."

"You've sold your soul and you don't realize it," she mocked. He was still mystified, and she sang out softly: "The fairy godmother! The fairy godmother!" He was appalled as he realized for the first time just how much she hated me.

"It's not like that. You don't understand. There's no slavery about it."

" 'In whose service is perfect freedom?'" she jeered. He did not answer, and all at once she softened: "Don't let's talk about those two old fogies. They're dead, we're alive. . . . You can kiss me again," she whispered. This time she did not wait, but with a passion that frightened him, glued her lips to his.

After that evening, she would, from time to time, allow him

to caress her. But she would grant nothing more, and she laughed when he spoke of marriage.

XLIII

PAUL made a number of attempts to reconcile us to each other; but whatever the occasion, Anne continued to behave towards me with a cool insolence: she had decided that I was an enemy and nothing would make her change her mind.

On one occasion Paul arranged that we should all go down to the beach together. He and Anne were going for a walk, and I was to meet them at the Pattons' farm at a certain hour. When I arrived, myself a few minutes late, I was told they had not yet returned. "Never mind," Mrs. Patton called from the drawing-room. "Come in and talk to me. I'm a little hurt that you so seldom visit me." She was making lace of an extraordinary fineness and beauty; I went across and admired it. "It's a way of passing the time," she sighed. In the past she had been a disconcertingly hearty woman, but now a profound discouragement seemed to have settled on her. "I get so bored with it. It's awful when one knows there are only a limited number of things one *can* do. That's why I reproached you for not coming to see me oftener."

"I didn't wish to abuse your hospitality."

"That's not the truth!" She said it as if it were a joke, but I knew she meant it. "You prefer the company of the young people. I don't blame you." She threw down her work: "Well, you're here now—that's the main thing. For a few minutes I have you to myself." Momentarily, her old gaiety returned; she began to gossip away to me. But then, all at once, she broke out: "Oh, I've been so bored, bored, bored. You've no idea. And I really blame your nephew for it."

"My nephew?"

"Before I did at least have Anne. But now——"

She shrugged her shoulders. "She spends as little time as possible with me. She misses her lessons when it suits her. She's changed—she's not the same person." She shook a finger at me.

"Yes, it's all due to that handsome nephew of yours. I know I shouldn't be jealous. I ought really to be glad. I *am* glad. I only want her to be happy—that's all that matters, after all. But it would be a pity if she lost her interest in the stage—a great pity. I've already told you of my ambitions for her. I hope I won't be disappointed."

I found a pathos in this aging cripple whose only joy was to live vicariously on the success of another woman; it was a pathos intensified by something which Paul had told me only the previous evening. It seemed that Joe Patton was having an affair with the land-girl whom we had met on our first visit; and Mrs. Patton knew of it.

Suddenly she said: "I expect that you're in rather the same sort of position."

"How do you mean?"

"I don't suppose you see much of your nephew now, do you?"

"Oh, quite a lot," I answered casually. "It doesn't really worry me."

"You're lucky then. I wish I could feel like that." There was, perhaps, a trace of irony in her words. "To let go—that's something I've never been able to do. But it's so foolish *not* to let go. One can be so unhappy. Don't you think so?"

At that moment Paul and Anne joined us. They excused themselves for their lateness in a manner which annoyed me. "Anne insisted on taking a short-cut which wasn't a short-cut at all," Paul explained.

"I like that! It saved us at least five minutes. It was you who first lost the way——"

"Me!"

They wrangled amiably, laughing and pretending to be indignant with each other; that they had kept me waiting was obviously a matter of indifference to them.

Anne had been turning a bracelet round and round on her wrist and now, in the middle of this absurd argument, she suddenly burst out to Mrs. Patton: "Look at the bracelet Paul's given me. Isn't it a beauty?"

"My dear, it's lovely. It really is lovely."

I tried to catch Paul's eye, but he would not look at me; his cheeks flushed, he stared down at the carpet. I now knew why that same morning he had asked me for a month's allowance in advance: I felt hurt that, instead of telling me the real reason, he had merely said he had a thing or two to buy.

Anne turned to me. "Don't you think it's a beauty?"

"It's very nice."

"I'm afraid poor Paul must have been horribly extravagant. At first I refused it, but he insisted. I'm still not entirely happy about it. I feel as if I'd committed a robbery."

"Let's go," Paul intervened.

I was in an ill-humour as we set off, but Anne, for reasons of her own, decided to be pleasant to me. Paul left us to walk on ahead of him down the narrow shingle path; I knew that he was pleased that at last we were treating each other as friends. It was clever of Anne to talk of India, her dead husband and the past we had shared together, for on these subjects I was most vulnerable, but all the time I asked myself: "What's the catch?"

Then she moved on to Mrs. Patton. "I'm glad you had a few minutes for a talk to her. Poor darling, I'm afraid she gets very lonely. I try to be with her as much as I can, but you know how it is. As a matter of fact, I'm thinking of buying her a dog. Don't you think it a good idea? I've heard of someone who breeds borzois. Terribly expensive, of course, but it would be rather lovely. I think if she had a dog it might make such a difference." She looked over her shoulder at Paul, who was still following behind us: "Paul agrees with me."

"You're sure she really wants a dog?" I asked.

"Oh, yes. She had one and it was run over, and she said she'd never have another. But people always say that. I know that once she sees it, she'll fall in love with it. Paul and I want to go and choose it tomorrow. The place is only about twenty miles from here. As a matter of fact, we—that is, Paul—well, we wondered if we could borrow your car. . . . You see, it would make it all so much easier," she hastened to explain. "If we saw a dog we liked, we could bring it straight back. It might be difficult on a train. Do you think we might have the car? Do you?"

"But Paul can't drive."

"Oh, I can drive. I'm very careful, I promise you."

"Oh." There was a pause: I did not want to lend the car, and yet could not see how to avoid doing so. "Oh, very well. But I must have it in the afternoon. Can you do your trip before lunch?" I had promised to visit the daughter of one of my friends at a sanatorium near Brighton; I was to have tea with her.

"That'll be quite all right. Thank you so much. It really is most frightfully good of you."

"I told you Uncle Mark would say yes." The path had widened as we came down to the beach and Paul slipped his arm into mine: it was a gesture of affection which met with a look of fleeting distaste from Anne.

Her object gained, her next remark to me was one of almost childish insolence: "I expect it's too rough for you to bathe today."

"I don't think so."

"I had an idea you were a weak swimmer—I can't think why. Perhaps Paul said something about it."

"I said nothing of the sort."

"Didn't you?" She gave a clear, tinkling laugh. "Then I'm just being stupid."

Once we were in the water, it seemed to anger her that Paul should race, not with her, but with me. When he tried to duck me, she called out: "You are a child, Paul!" She said it with a laugh, but it was not a pleasantry.

After our bathe, we lay out in the sun for several minutes. Paul wanted to go in again, but Anne and I refused: I, myself, was tired and she seemed to be still piqued. "You old fogies! Well, I'll leave you both to it." He had been exhilarated by Anne's initial politeness to me and did not realize that there had been a change; he was delighted to leave us both together, confident that our relations would be yet further improved.

We lay back and watched Paul as he ran down to the sea and hurled himself in. He squirmed over on his back and waved to us. I waved back; Anne did not move. The sight of him, young, beautiful and utterly happy, brought a strange, foreboding chill to my heart.

"He's very charming," Anne said. She had a pebble in her hand which she kept tossing up into the air. I did not answer. "It's funny he's so unambitious."

"He has ambitions."

"Literary ambitions, you mean? Yes, there are those. But at the moment his life seems so aimless—no plans, nothing. He's curiously indecisive. Don't you feel that?"

"Most young people nowadays are like that, I think. There's so little that's settled in the world. One can hardly blame them."

"But I've never met anyone quite like Paul. He seems to be quite content to go on living this perpetual holiday. The thought that he must make his own way in the world doesn't seem to have occurred to him."

"He has his own ideas about what he wants to do. I shouldn't worry about him."

"Oh, heavens, I'm not worrying! I'm just—interested. I like him, he's a nice kid, and I don't want to feel he's going to become a complete drone. That's what your kindness and—and generosity may make of him."

"I don't think so. Why shouldn't he do nothing for a while? Anyway, he's never idle. At the moment, he's preparing—as every writer must prepare."

"Writer!" she exclaimed. "Well, of course, you and he both believe in his artistic mission. That makes all the difference. It excuses so much and explains so much. . . . But sometimes—sometimes I wonder. . . ." She hesitated, deliberately, I thought, so as to give emphasis to what followed. "Do you think it's really a good thing to fill him with all this talk of the unique gifts that he possesses? After all, is he really so out of the ordinary?"

"I don't think I've gone in for that sort of exaggeration. He needs confidence, though. I have tried to encourage him."

"Of course, he admires you enormously, doesn't he?"

"We're good friends."

"Oh, but he worships you—just worships you. He relies on you for everything."

"If he did, I should be as worried about him as you yourself appear to be. But Paul has a will of his own, and he uses it. I'm surprised you haven't learnt that for yourself."

At that moment Paul himself appeared: shaking himself like a dog, he flung himself down on the sand between us. He grinned and pushed the hair away from his eyes. "What have you two been talking about?" he asked.

"You," Anne said.

"Me? What have you found to say about me?"

"Lots of things." She got up and made for the bathing-tent. "It's getting cold. I'm going to change."

"What have you been saying about me?" Paul asked again.

"Nothing. She's only trying to pull your leg."

He grinned. "I'm glad you and Anne are getting on so well. I knew you'd like each other in the end."

XLIV

THE next day Anne and Paul failed to return the car until after four o'clock. By that time I had worked myself into a fury. I had had to ring up the sanatorium and tell them that I shouldn't be able to visit the girl that day. The matron's distressed: "Oh, yes. Yes, I see. Oh, dear. . . . I'm afraid she'll be very disappointed" exacerbated my feelings yet further.

When at last I heard them drive up, I went out on to the terrace; I said nothing, but stood, watching them, my hands on my hips. Paul leapt out: he was pale and agitated. "I'm terribly sorry. Everything went wrong." In an undertone he murmured: "Anne and I have had a row." I still did not speak. "Are you very annoyed with us? Are you?" He looked up at me pleadingly. "Why don't you say something?"

"I'm afraid I've been struck momentarily dumb by your surpassing casualness. I don't mind for myself," I went on, my rage boiling over into a hot spate of words, "but you knew I was going to visit this girl at the sanatorium. It probably never entered your head that she might be disappointed."

"But it did, it did!"

"Then why the hell didn't you get back when you said you would?"

"You haven't heard me explain——"

"Oh, I'm sure you have some excellent explanation. You always do. Well, what is it? Well?" But he was silent; misery and weary resentment covered his face. "Well?" I repeated harshly. I knew that each of my words hurt him, and I was glad that it was so. "A moment ago you were bubbling over with excuses. What's happened?"

I had forgotten Anne entirely, and it was with a start that I heard her say: "There's no need to bully Paul. It was my fault." She spoke with a cool insolence, her gloved hand still resting on the wheel of my car. For the first time I saw the borzoi puppy in the back seat.

"That I can quite believe."

"It wasn't her fault, it was mine," Paul shouted.

"Paul, Paul! Don't get so excited. You know I'm to blame—why not admit it? I've no sense of direction and no sense of time. I'm sorry. I can't say more. Can I?" Her tone accused me of being unreasonable. "Do you mind if I just drive the puppy home—I gather you've definitely abandoned your visit to the sanatorium? He's not very strong on his legs, poor thing, and I'm afraid that steep path would do for him. He is rather a beauty, don't you think?"

Her calmness left me without an answer. "Coming, Paul?" But he pushed past me and ran into the house. "Oh, why does he go off the deep end so easily?" she asked. "Why don't you come? Mrs. Patton will love to see you. Then you can drive the car back, and save me a journey."

"I'll drive my car there, too, if you don't mind."

"As you wish!" She laughed.

We set off in silence; I had every intention of showing that I was still in a rage with her, and it was with a deliberate noisiness that I changed the gears. "Oh, oh, oh!" she exclaimed. "I think even I could do better than that."

"No doubt." I scowled at the road ahead, as we swung recklessly round a hair-pin bend. At that moment the dog leant forward and took my left ear in its teeth. It did not bite me, it only wished to play, but in my present mood it so infuriated me that I gave it a malevolent slap across the face. It immediately set up a high-pitched, hysterical crying.

Immediately I felt ashamed of myself; I expected that Anne

would make some scathing comment. But when I glanced at her, she was only smiling; it was an indulgent, pitying smile, and it made me feel far more uncomfortable than any words.

Mrs. Patton was delighted with the dog. It was nervous and I think her loud, bell-like voice terrified it; it slithered down on to its stomach, and looked up at her with large apprehensive eyes. But she only exclaimed: "He's feeling rather coy just at present." She put out her arms. "Give him to me." I picked up the dog and gave him to her.

"He's quite a weight already." Mrs. Patton rubbed her nose against his muzzle. "Chickery-chick! Chickery-chick!" she began to croon.

The dog struggled for a while and then vomited into her lap.

But Mrs. Patton only laughed; she did not mind.

XLV

WHEN I returned I found Paul in his room. He was reading by the open window, the evening sunlight touching his unnaturally flushed cheeks and forehead. "Hullo." I tried to behave as if nothing had happened.

"Hullo," he mumbled. He did not look up.

"I'm sorry." No answer. "I shouldn't have lost my temper." There was still no answer. I was surprised. Paul had often sulked when we had first known each other, but since then he had outgrown the habit. "Can't we forgive and forget? I said things I didn't mean to say. I wasn't just. I know now that it wasn't your fault——"

"It was my fault!" he exclaimed with angry vehemence. I shrugged my shoulders. "You want Anne to take the blame because you hate her. But it was my fault, not hers."

"Anyway, I don't really mind—now. I've said it—I don't mind. Why don't you cheer up and forget about it all?"

Then he broke out: "Because I feel ashamed. Because I've treated you badly. And your not minding only makes it worse. I hate myself."

"You are silly, Paul." I spoke kindly, gently.

It was strange how even so small an admission of sympathy could draw me to him and allay my vexation.

XLVI

He was now frequently asking me for the loan of money. His allowance had been paid to him for four months in advance, but he still came to me. It was a generous allowance, and though I gave in to him, I felt peeved that he could not manage on it. There is nothing more humiliating than to have to ask for money, and it was not surprising that he should be ungracious and irritable when he did so. But however much I told myself that it was far better that he should ask in this way rather than with a cringing obsequiousness, his attitude rankled in my mind. When he borrowed, with hardly a thank you, a sum which he would probably never repay to spend on a woman whom I disliked, it seemed to me that I was a fool to hand him what he asked. Yet I felt sorry for him. Anne, I learnt, had other men-friends and naturally Paul wished to treat her as lavishly as they did. He was always afraid that she regarded him as a child instead of the man-of-the-world which he would like to be. Shame filled him when he had to make a fresh demand of me, and I knew what harm that shame could do to our friendship. Where there is a sense of obligation, affection withers. I was worried, and I decided to increase his allowance.

"We'll wipe out all old scores, and begin afresh. I'm afraid I've been rather stingy with you. When I was your age, money was worth so much more."

"But it's a large allowance already. I can't take more." He looked miserable.

"It's not a large allowance. Anyway, the money's no use to me. I earn far more than I know what to do with. I'm glad that you should have it."

"I wish I could repay you in some way."

"You do that all right."

He sighed heavily and shook his head. "You've done so much for me."

"Not nearly as much as I should have done. Think of all the

years that I neglected you—ten shillings at Christmas, ten shillings at your birthday, and that was all! I've a lot to make up."

"Well, so have I for that matter."

I did not quite understand what he meant, but I patted his shoulder: "Never mind about asking me for money. Once you really start to mind, it'll make a difference to our friendship—or once I start to mind. But I won't do that, I can assure you."

"I'll try not to mind."

In the event, it was not money but something at once more subtle and more surprising that altered our relations with each other. He and I had been up to the Pattons for tea. It was an over-cast day, and the atmosphere at the house when we arrived seemed heavy with unspoken reproaches and anxieties. Mr. Patton and Lena had gone to a Reading cattle-show and had stayed away the previous night; the borzoi had distemper; it was obvious that Anne and Mrs. Patton had been quarrelling. The older woman's eyes were red and her cheeks blotched with tears. The dog lay in a basket at her feet, shivering and grunting.

Anne soon led Paul off, and Mrs. Patton and I were left alone. "I've hardly slept a wink these last two nights. It's not that I can do much, but I just lie awake and worry. Poor little thing!" At first I thought she was speaking of Anne, but then I realized that she meant the dog. Fingering the pearls which hung about her massive neck, she went on in a dragging, tragic voice: "It would be too cruel if I were to lose him. I don't know what I should do. I suppose he must have had this wretched germ when Anne first bought him. You remember how he was sick that day? There's so little one can do. They haven't made any of the serum during the war, you know. One's utterly powerless." She could speak of nothing else. Even when she mentioned her husband, it was in connection with the dog: "I do wish Joe were back. He's wonderful with animals. He has an instinct. People with their roots in the soil seem to understand in a way in which we can't." Her hands still played incessantly with the pearls; the flesh of her sagging neck was red and crumpled. "Anne hasn't been much of a help. She doesn't care. She just thinks the dog's a nuisance." Before, when she had spoken of Anne, it had been with indulgence: now there was an implacable hardness in her voice.

On and on she went, monotonously tearful, while the dog continued to grunt and wheeze. It was sultry and most of the windows were shut. All that day I had felt off colour, and now I was certain I was going to have one of my attacks. My loins and back ached, I began to shiver. I wished that Paul would return, so that we could go home.

At last he came back, and a few minutes later, without telling anyone how I was feeling, I said that we must go; we had been there barely an hour, and it was obvious that Mrs. Patton accepted this news as yet another blow from adverse fortune.

"Why did you want to rush away like that?" Paul asked, as we made our way down the drive.

"Oh, I don't know." Recently I had tended as far as possible to conceal from him my occasional bouts of illness.

We walked on, Paul oblivious that there was anything wrong with me, until I suddenly had to interrupt the easy flow of his conversation: "Do you mind if we sit down for a moment?"

"Of course. Are you feeling all right?"

"Yes, quite all right. I just felt giddy for a moment. It must be this sultry weather, it makes one liverish."

We sat down on a low stone wall, and soon my head cleared. "How are you feeling?" Paul asked, with the anxiety which he always showed when I was unwell.

"Much better already. Shall we continue?"

"Oh, let's stay here for a bit. It's so wonderfully peaceful."

"All right." There was a silence such as often arose between us, unvexed by the uncomfortable need for speech. It was I who in the end asked: "What were you and Anne up to?"

"Oh, we just wandered round the garden, and talked." He glanced up at me: "About you."

"What did you find to say about me?"

"Anne thinks I rely too much on you. She doesn't understand. There was a lot else. We've been over it all so often before. She thinks you're possessive of me—and a 'bad influence'." He gave a laugh; his candour seemed all at once to bring him near to me. "I wish I could tell her," he said. "I can't, of course—I understand that. But I wish I could."

These last words mystified me; they filled me with a nebulous dread. "Tell her what? What do you mean?"

"About—us," he said simply.

"Us? What about us?"

All at once he became horribly, painfully embarrassed; the blood mounted to his cheeks and forehead and he began to wrench up handful after handful of grass from about his feet. "You know," he said. "Our—our secret."

"My dear Paul, I don't know what you're talking about."

"I mean that I'm your—that you're my . . ." Panic overwhelmed him. The colour drained from his face as rapidly as it had mounted there. "It doesn't matter," he said hoarsely.

But I had realized; suddenly I had realized. We looked at each other, and for a moment our embarrassment left us both speechless. "Do you mean——? Did you think——"

"Then—then aren't you?"

"Your father? Of course not!"

He buried his face in his hands. I turned away. We could not bear to look at each other.

"Whatever made you think I was?" He did not answer; his hands still covered his face. "Paul!" I repeated the question.

"I don't know." He spoke in an abrupt, frightened voice. "I always assumed—— I always imagined—— Ever since you told me all about my mother. And—and we were so fond of each other. I felt certain. So many things you said—your kindness to me . . ." The abrupt, jolting sentences were almost sobs.

"I'm sorry. I never guessed . . . Paul, don't be so upset." I attempted to put an arm round him, but he drew away.

"I must think. I must try and get it all straight. I feel all muddled. I can't explain."

"After all, to all intents and purposes you are my son. That's how I think of you. What does the physical part matter. Spiritually, you are my son."

He shook his head. "Don't say anything now. I must think. It's made everything different." He was so distraught that I thought he was going to break down.

We walked back in silence, and gradually he became calm. "You're shivering," he said, as we neared the farm.

"Am I?"

"I feel rather sick myself."

"Oh, I think it's just another of my attacks. But I'm upset about this, too. I'd no idea——"

"Please, don't let's talk about it. I've been such a fool."

"Very well."

We dragged up the path which led to our verandah.

"You'd better go to bed."

"Yes, perhaps I'd better."

At that moment I felt so faint that I had to grip the back of a wicker chair for support. Paul advanced as if to offer his help, but did not touch me. I dragged myself into the hall and began to mount the stairs, with him following. On other such occasions he had made me lean on him, and I was surprised that he did not now do so. But I felt too ill to worry about it.

"Shall I get you some of your pills?"

"Please."

I fell on to the bed and watched him as he crossed the room. First he took the pills from their bottle, and then he went to the wash-hand stand to fetch a glass of water. As he held the carafe above the tumbler, a tremor suddenly passed through his hand. Water splashed on to the floor.

"Here you are."

I opened my mouth for him to place the pills in it, as he usually did, but he set them down on the coverlet.

"Water?"

"Thanks."

He placed the glass on the bedside table, still without looking at me. I rinsed down the pills. "Thanks," I repeated.

"Is there anything else?"

"I feel very hot; perhaps you'd better just pull the eiderdown over me."

With abrupt, clumsy movements he jerked the eiderdown over my trembling body. Then, for the first time, his eyes met mine and I was horrified by what seemed to me a vague, barely perceptible distaste.

"If you want anything, tap on the wall. I shall be in my own room."

"I don't think I shall want anything."

"I'll go then."

Obviously he wanted to leave the room as soon as he could. I lay, shivering and sick in the light of evening; I wanted to sleep, but could not. As usual during these attacks, all my senses became unbearably acute. I was oppressed by the scent of the roses beneath my window, my clothes seemed stiff and rough, and from all about me I could hear sounds—feet in the passage-way, birds, voices, the distant rattle of a car. I went over my conversation with Paul many times, and could find no rest.

XLVII

IT was dark, the house was silent, and still I lay gazing up at the luminous patch which was all that I could now see of the sky beyond my window. I dozed, but woke almost immediately. I dozed again, and woke with the memory of falling downwards through miles and miles of space. My fever had passed, but my clothes were drenched with an icy sweat. I got up and began to take them off; a rancid smell came from them.

I started: Paul was moving about in his own room. I looked at my watch, saw that it was past one o'clock in the morning, and wondered what he was up to. No sooner had I climbed back into the bed than I heard his door click open, followed by a soft, hesitant knock at my own.

"Come in."

For a moment he stood blinking, his eyes unaccustomed to the light. In his striped pyjamas and a camel-hair dressing-gown that he had long since out-grown, he looked no more than thirteen or fourteen. His hair was tousled and he was wearing no slippers.

"Hullo."

"I heard you moving about, so I came to ask you if you could give me something to make me sleep. I've lain awake for hours and hours." He did not advance into the room, but remained standing by the door.

"You'll find some aspirins on the wash-hand stand."

"I thought perhaps—perhaps you could let me have one of your sleeping-tablets."

"I don't think that's a very good idea."

"But just this once."

"I'd rather you didn't."

"Please! . . . I know I shall never get to sleep unless I take one."

"Those tablets are not supposed to be taken without a doctor's prescription. If you have one tonight, you may find you can't get to sleep without one tomorrow night."

He shrugged his shoulders, and without saying anything, opened the door.

"Paul!"

"Yes?"

"Take one if you want to."

Still without a word, he crossed to the wash-hand stand and took a tablet. Then, with a murmured good night, he was gone.

XLVIII

From that day on I felt that he was changed. Outwardly, our relationship was much as it had always been, but beneath the surface I sensed inhibitions of which neither of us could ever bring ourselves to speak. A spontaneity was missing; however hard he tried, he had ceased to be at his ease with me. We were constantly in each other's company, he still confided in me, but we were really miles apart. I noticed how he avoided any physical contact; if our hands accidentally brushed each other while we were out walking, he would move away; if at night he came to my room to talk to me, he would never now sit on my bed. I told myself that he was growing up, and these restraints were inevitable; they meant no diminution in his affection for me. But I could not believe it.

Suddenly, he even seemed to look different. His shoulders had broadened, his body was no longer that of a boy, but of a man. His face, too, had acquired a new strength and heaviness; the delicacy of feature had gone; he had begun to shave every morning.

Since meeting Anne, he had gradually shed his ill-manners and gaucherie; at first I had been pleased, but later I regretted the ingenuousness and freshness which had been lost at the same time. Outwardly, and perhaps inwardly, he was beginning to conform to a pattern.

He had once been impatient of social functions, but now he and Anne perpetually went up to town to dances, parties and first-nights. He was using money freely, and I again had to increase his allowance. He often spent a night in town; I had let my flat to some old friends on the condition that it would be free for me at the weekends, and though I, myself, did not make use of this arrangement, Paul often did. Anne, it appeared, had friends in town with whom she could always stay, and it was convenient for him to have his own *pied-à-terre*.

I was hurt by the change in his attitude to me, though for a time I did not disclose my feelings. When I did, it happened that he was himself in a state of acute nervous tension. (Of course, I did not at the time know this; it was not until he told me, many weeks later, that I realized how unlucky I had been.) I shall relate the events here, not as I learnt them, but in the order in which they actually took place.

XLIX

ON one of the many excursions that Paul and Anne made to town together, she broke it to him that she was again going to visit Desmond Standing, the portrait-painter.

"He wants me to sit for him," she explained casually. "You can come along if it doesn't bore you."

Recently, she had often talked about Standing and Paul had become jealous of him. Now he showed that he was piqued.

"Oh, don't be such a bore!" Anne exclaimed. "Come, if you want to come. Otherwise we'll say good-bye. It's too hot for a scene." Paul checked himself and said nothing. "Well?"

"I'll come."

Desmond Standing lived in a small, elegant house off Sloane Street; Paul decided that he disliked him at the first touch of his limp hand and that impression remained, in spite of the charm and distinction of his manner. About forty years of age, he had prematurely grey hair coaxed in smooth, glossy wings away from a broad, unlined forehead, a soft, over-precise voice and a foppish taste in clothes. He was a successful man and he looked it.

Soon he was talking about himself with the gentle, faintly ironic deprecation that egotists take to be modesty. Previously, he had told the maid to bring them in some tea. "I feel quite exhausted! It's so nice to talk to intelligent people after the old blunderbuss I've had here all morning."

"Oh, who was that?" Anne asked.

He mentioned an eminent general.

"But it's rather exciting to be painting him, isn't it?"

"It's an awful bore. Still"—he sighed—"six hundred guineas is six hundred guineas. I wish I could do without money, but I can't. I'd be no good at starving in a garret and turning out neglected masterpieces. But sometimes—*sometimes*—I get a twinge of conscience. It's rather awful to have sold one's birthright for a mess of pottage."

He continued to speak regretfully of the talents that he had prostituted, but Paul could feel no sympathy for him. If Standing had sold his soul to the devil, it was obvious that he was well satisfied with the bargain. In any case, had there ever been a soul to sell? It is not unusual for financially successful artists to imagine that if they had wished, they could have achieved a success of a more durable and austere kind.

With a frankness that was intended to win their sympathy, Standing alluded to the details of his past career. Skilfully he established himself as a character in his own fiction: he was the young man who, for the sake of a wife he no longer loves and children he never wanted, goes down to the market-place and sells himself to the highest bidder.

"The awful thing is that having taken the first step there's no going back. One forges one's own fetters. Food, clothes, taxis and holidays in expensive hotels—I can no longer do without them." He turned to Paul. "I suppose you despise me for my weakness? Anne tells me that you want to be a writer. Well, look at me and learn your lesson. You can't serve both God and Mammon, and of the two, choose God. I mean that." He spoke with an earnestness which made Paul want to giggle.

"Show Paul some of your pictures," Anne suggested later.

Standing groaned. "Oh, God, no! If you knew how I loathe them!" But he went out to his studio and brought back two small canvases. "I don't mind your seeing these. I painted them when I was only nineteen. They're immature, but they may give you some indication of what I could have become." He sighed. "I wish I could paint like that now." The canvases, plainly derived from Picasso's cubist period, seemed to Paul dim and dated.

Standing gazed at them lovingly. "Heigh-ho!" he murmured.

Later he began to talk of the painting he was going to do of Anne. "It's to be quite different—no chi-chi tricks, no slickness. . . ." He ran on, describing this picture which was to redeem all the trash he had painted in the years of success, until, suddenly, there were a series of thuds, thumps and screams from overhead. "Oh, blast those children." He leapt up and flung open the door, shouting: "For God's sake stop that row! I can't hear myself think. Amy—Amy——!"

"Yes, dear?" His wife answered from another room. "What's the matter?"

"What's the matter! Do see what the children are doing. They'll have the ceiling down." He spoke with a tartness which would have offended any servant. Through the open door Paul had a glimpse of his serene, well-bred features contorted into rage. But as soon as he returned, the rage vanished: "Sorry for that interruption," he said jovially. "They tend to get rather out of hand."

Paul wondered when Anne would leave. He tried to catch her eye, but at the same moment she took off her hat and began to slip out of her light summer coat; Standing immediately leapt up to help her. "Thank you." She smiled up at him, and he smiled back; all at once Paul felt out of place.

"Doing anything this evening?" Standing asked her.

"Nothing special. Why?"

"I've had an invitation to a party from——" He brought out the Christian name of a famous artist. "Amy won't come, I know— in any case, she'd be hopelessly out of it."

Anne accepted eagerly; she asked questions—Who would be there? Could she go in the dress she was now wearing?—which Standing answered with a faint show of patronage. He was still standing beside her, and at one point in their conversation he slipped in a casual "darling." They had forgotten all about Paul.

"Well, I'd better be going along."

"Oh, must you?"

"Will you be spending the night in town, Anne?"

"Will I?" She looked up at Standing as if expecting him to answer for her. "Yes, I suppose I will."

"I think you'd better," Standing said. "The party won't break up until the early hours. We can give you a bed here."

"Oh, thank you."

"Good-bye, Anne."

"Are you off?" she said absently.

"Yes."

"I'll see you out." Standing opened the door for him.

"I can find my own way." He pushed past and ran out into the street, hearing in the distance Standing's cheerful: "Good-bye, old boy." At that moment Paul hated him—for his house, his clothes, his assurance, his wealth, his distinguished friends and, above all, the interest Anne had in him. Paul could laugh at him, he could see through him and tell himself that he was a conceited nobody. But in his heart he feared him more than any other man.

L

IT was when he returned from this visit, hot, dispirited and in a state of nervous excitation, that I tackled Paul. I had come downstairs for dinner and was surprised to find him seated on the drawing-room sofa.

"Hullo! You back already! I didn't expect you."

He glanced up from his book and said in a flat, sullen voice: "Didn't you? I thought I told you I'd be back earlier."

"Well, I'm very glad to see you. What's become of Anne?"

"Oh, she was going out with some friends anyway."

I placed myself on the sofa next to him, and could not fail to note how he withdrew himself into the farthest corner. Suddenly, on an impulse, I asked: "Why do you do that?"

"Do what?"

"Move away from me."

He flushed as he answered: "I hadn't noticed it. I suppose I wanted to give you more room." He got up and went to the window.

"You've done it again."

"Done what? I don't understand you."

"You don't like being near me."

"Oh, don't be silly. It's hot, that's all."

I gazed at him; he stood with his back to the window, the heel of one shoe kicking against the wainscot. There was a peevish, discontented expression on his face. "You've changed," I said quietly. "It's not the same between us."

He did not answer, and I repeated: "You've changed, Paul."

"I wasn't aware of that."

"What's happened? What's come between us? I don't understand." I got up and went to him. "Have I done anything—said anything?"

"Oh, don't be silly!"

"Has Anne said anything?"

"What do you mean? Of course not!"

"Has she made any mischief?"

"I don't know what you're driving at." He shrugged his shoulders angrily.

"Why not be honest? It's better in the long run."

"I don't know what you want me to be honest about." He spoke with a sudden coldness. "As far as I'm concerned there's been no change. You've only imagined it."

I shook my head. "You know that's not true."

"Oh, you're impossible!" he broke out. "Why can't you let things happen ordinarily, naturally—without this perpetual fidget, fidget, fidget! It makes everything so impossible."

"Personal relationships are the only things that matter to me."

"You and your personal relationships!" he exclaimed contemptuously. "You care so much about them that you fuss them out of existence. You're like a child with a watch, tinkering until it breaks the main-spring. You weary me with your endless analysing."

"A friendship isn't worthwhile unless it can survive the truth. I'm not interested in the sort of friendship that is built on illusion and pretence. Our friendship was once real; it's ceased to be that."

"Only in your mind! As far as I'm concerned it's as real as it ever was."

"Perhaps it never was very real where you were concerned." I regretted the words as soon as they were spoken. I had hurt him, I knew.

"You may be right," he said in a voice that was all at once quiet. "Perhaps it was all an illusion. Perhaps . . ." He hesitated, and at the same moment the dinner-gong boomed out from the hall. He turned and went out without saying anything more. I was left, standing indecisively at the open window.

Feet hurried down the stairs. Doors slammed. I heard the tinkle of crockery and Charles's voice exclaiming: "Chicken! Good show!" above the murmur of conversation. Perhaps Paul had been right. After all, what he had told me, I had been told many times in the past by May. "You're like a bear, hugging its victim to death," she had once said, and on another occasion, when I had accused her: "You don't care for me as you used to care for me," she had flashed out in exasperation: "I wish you'd realize that each time you tell me I don't love you, you make me love you less." A cynic in all other matters, it seemed that I was a hopeless idealist where my affections were concerned; my standards were too high, my demands too great. Yet anything less than perfection failed to interest me. I was doomed to go through life asking of people what it was not in them to give.

A maid put her head round the door: "Are you coming in to dinner, sir?"

I started, and then said: "Yes, I'm coming."

"I thought as you mightn't 'ave 'eard the gong."

"Thank you." I went through to join Paul.

LI

FROM then on it was as if we had raised a wall between ourselves; I had the sense of some invisible yet solid object against which I bruised myself whenever I made to approach him. True, there were still chinks and crannies through which I could peep, and if I strained to stand on tiptoe I might sometimes have a glimpse over the top; but it was an effort, and soon even this communication was to be denied me.

Two or three days later Charles brought me a letter from the friend to whom I had lent my flat. I imagined that it was the usual weekly rent-cheque and slipped it into my pocket without opening it. It was not until several hours after that I read the news that it contained.

The man who had written it was one of those individuals who all through their lives are forced by their principles to do disagreeable things; one admires them, one pities them and secretly one thinks them damned fools. Hebden had been prime minister of an Indian State, earning an income four times the size of what the British Raj paid to me; but, disapproving of the matrimonial irregularities of the young Rajah, he had quarrelled with him and then retired. It was the kind of sacrifice that I suspect Hebden rather enjoyed making, and it harmed no one but himself. But, unfortunately, if the opportunity arose, he showed himself no less eager to immolate others on the altar of his high principles. On this occasion it was Paul and I who suffered.

Hebden 'thought I ought to know'—how often such people use that phrase!—about Paul's weekend visits to the flat. "Loath as I am to interfere in the private affairs of others, I feel I am doing no more than my duty in telling you that for some weeks past your nephew has been coming here accompanied by a woman. I have this information from General Rankin—he has taken the Cottons' old flat—and, of course, his evidence is beyond question. In any case, Molly and I had ourselves suspected something of the sort. . . ." Stunned, I read the well-meaning, officious phrases many times; I pushed the letter into my pocket only to take it out again;

I turned it to the light as if to decipher it more clearly. I could not believe it. Never once had Paul even hinted to me that Anne slept at the flat; she had some friends, it was always made clear, with whom she stayed during their visits up to town. Yet, here, on the incontrovertible evidence of three middle-aged busybodies, it had been proved that Paul had been deceiving me for several weeks past. It was the deception that cut me to the heart; in comparison the rest seemed unimportant. Fool that I was, I had imagined there to be no secrets between us, and all the time he had probably been laughing at me for my credulousness. What had he imagined? That I should be shocked by such an intimacy? That I should forbid him to go on with it? Had he so little confidence in my affection for him? Did he imagine me to be so devoid of understanding?

My first impulse was to go to him and pour out my reproach-es, but he and Anne had gone up to town and would not be back until the evening. Meanwhile there were three or four hours to while away until their return. I could not sit still, I could settle to nothing. Perhaps it had all been an error; perhaps they had mis-taken someone else for Paul, or made up the whole story; perhaps . . . I felt I must have some confirmation, I must discuss the whole thing. But with whom . . . ? I remembered Mrs. Patton.

"I had to come and see you." I was hatless, flushed and out of breath. "I've just had something. . . . Look!" I thrust the letter at her. She gave me a bewildered, alarmed glance; my behaviour must have seemed utterly eccentric to her. "Read it!" She hesitated, and then took the letter from me.

I waited impatiently for her to finish, and then burst out: "Well?"

I was astonished by the face she raised to me; the colour had drained from her cheeks, her lower lip was trembling. "I can't be-lieve it. I refuse to believe it. Anne wouldn't do such a thing. It can't be true." I had expected her to be surprised, shocked even; but such horror and grief filled me with astonishment. Then, in a moment, I realized. . . .

"But she never told me. She always said she was staying with these friends of hers. Why should she want to deceive me? There've never been secrets between us—never, never. Oh, no, it can't be true. There must be some mistake."

"I'm afraid there can be no doubt about it. I don't want to believe it any more than you do. But there it is—beyond any possible argument."

She opened the letter again, her eyes moving along the lines with fevered haste. "Who wrote this letter? Who is this person? Who is he?"

"An old friend."

"An old fool!"

"He was only doing what he thought right."

She folded it slowly, reluctantly, as if it were something fragile and beyond price. "I wish you had never shown it to me. I wish I had never known anything about it all."

"I feel that, too. It's rather cowardly."

"Cowardly? Why?"

"One shouldn't be afraid of losing an illusion."

"But nearly all happiness is built on illusion."

"Nearly all—but not all. And the happiness that is built on truth . . ."

"Yes?"

But I shook my head. I was no longer certain. Like most middle-aged people I had long since collected my beliefs like so much bric-à-brac to be carried round with me wherever I travelled; I had got used to the pieces and had long since ceased to question their value. But now, for the first time for many years, I was seeing them as they were.

"When they get back, are you—are you going to speak to Paul about it?"

"Naturally."

"I suppose that's wise."

"I don't know whether it's wise or not. I only know that I can't possibly keep silent."

"I don't think I shall say anything to Anne. You're right—I'm a coward." Again she opened the letter; for her, as for me, it had a peculiar, deadly fascination. "Of course, I knew they were in love with each other," she said in a quiet, mournful voice. "When people are in love, they become remote—even people one has known all one's life. All at once, they're strangers and there's no way of getting into touch with them. . . . I felt that with Anne. For a time, we knew everything about each other and then, suddenly, we knew nothing. I think she realized what had happened, and because she hates to hurt anyone, she felt guilty and wanted to make up for it to me. She was extra attentive; she gave me the dog; she did all she could to please me. But it wasn't the real thing. When that peculiar sympathy dies, no amount of artifice can bring it back to life."

"But it may revive of its own accord."

"Perhaps. One hopes." She passed a hand across her eyes. "I must go and give the dog its medicine. Perhaps you could push me through to the garden-room? I don't want to worry the maid."

"Of course." I set off behind her. "How is the dog?"

"I should like to believe he's better, but. . . ." she shrugged her shoulders helplessly, the tears she fought back making it impossible for her to go on. "We can only wait for it to run its course." At that moment there was a horrible, almost human yelping from the far end of the corridor. "What's that? Quick—go and see! Leave me here, and go and see."

The animal writhed convulsively. Froth, tinged with blood, worked at the corners of ceaselessly chattering jaws. Its feet, scrabbling backwards and forwards on the waxed parquet floor, made a noise which so set my nerves on edge that I felt I must at any cost stop it. I raised the animal in my arms, and as I felt it against me, my gaze looking down into its own blank eyes, my disgust changed to a strange serene tenderness. Slowly, it quietened and I set it down again; only then did I become aware that Mrs. Patton had been shouting to me.

"What's happened? Is he all right? Tell me what's happened?"

"He's all right now. He had a fit."

At that moment Joe Patton appeared through the door that led out on to the garden. "What was all the noise?" he asked. Then he saw the dog and he went across to it; he knelt down and shook his head slowly. I went and fetched Mrs. Patton.

"I was afraid this would happen." He was still kneeling by the dog; his hob-nailed boots had made long scratches on the parquet floor. "There's no hope now."

"No hope!" Mrs. Patton exclaimed. "Of course there's hope. What do you mean?"

"I mean that he'll go on having these fits until one takes him off," he retorted with matter-of-fact brutality.

"How can you say such a thing! Dogs often have fits."

"Not this kind of fit. You'd better let me put him away for you."

"Leave him alone!" she screamed. "Don't touch him! You're callous, you're utterly callous. You don't care what happens to him. You don't know what it is to care for an animal."

He flushed angrily. "Go on then! Let him suffer for a week, or two weeks, or three weeks. But don't tell me I didn't warn you." He stamped out and shut the door.

"He doesn't understand," she said piteously. "He doesn't care." Her voice sank to a tragic whisper: "Nothing can bridge that gap—nothing."

The dog raised its head shakily and then lay back again; it closed its eyes. "Give him to me," Mrs. Patton said.

"He's covered in froth."

"It doesn't matter." I hesitated and she repeated: "It doesn't matter."

I could do nothing but lift up the pathetic, sodden bundle and lay it in her lap. She began to caress it with slow, long, lingering gestures; a tear escaped from each eye and trickled down her face. "He must get well, he must get well," she reiterated, almost under her breath. I think she had forgotten all about Anne.

LII

WHEN I left the house, I met Charles standing indecisively half-way up the drive.

"What are you doing here?" I asked in astonishment.

He blushed. "Oh, waiting for someone."

"Someone? Who?"

"Oh, someone."

"Anne?"

"G-good God, no! Paul has the copyright in her—not that I'm interested. N-no, you wouldn't know this girl. She works on the farm."

"You don't mean Lena?"

"That's right! Have you met her?" Eagerly he began to question me. "D-don't you think she's wizard? I wait for her here almost every evening now. She goes up to the house from the cow-sheds at f-five o'clock. What time is it now?"

"Five o'clock."

He plunged his hands into his baggy flannels and waltzed across the drive. "She'll be here any moment then." There was a crunch of gravel, and he swung round, his face flaming. "Hullo, Lena." His embarrassment was that of a comedian on a music-hall stage; one stork-like leg rubbed against the other; grinning, he laced and unlaced his fingers.

"Oh, hullo. It's you, is it?" She spoke in a bored drawl. Then she saw me. "Evening, Mr. Langworthy. Close, isn't it? A spot of rain tomorrow, I shouldn't wonder." She was going to walk on towards the house, but Charles called her:

"One moment, L-Lena."

"Yes. What is it?" She turned impatiently, her hands on her hips. I had not seen her for several weeks, and I was surprised how in that short time her physique had changed. There had been a childishness about her which she had now wholly lost. Her features seemed coarser, she was using a great deal of make-up, and she had become much more plump; her breasts, once small and pointed under the constriction of her thin Aertex shirt were now voluptuously full. There could be no doubt of what had happened since I had last set eyes on her.

"Are you d-doing anything this—this—this—evening." It was with great difficulty that he got out the last word.

She rolled one of her platinum curls round her finger.

"Well, I don't know, reely—— That's the truth. Mr. Patton may want me on the farm, and there's a friend of mine down at the bus garage who's promised to take me to the Palais if he's not on duty."

"But if he is on d-duty?"

"I'll be free, I suppose."

"Then you could c-come out with me?"

"But I'm not certain——" she objected.

"I don't mind c-coming up here on the off-chance," he said eagerly.

"Oh, very well. But I don't promise anything."

"I'll be up at seven."

" 'Bye, Mr. Langworthy." I guessed from her intonation and the glance she gave me that she was one of those women who, paradoxically, are interested only in the men whom they themselves cannot interest.

Charles talked excitedly about her until we reached home. "She's absolutely first-rate, isn't she? Everyone in the place is c-crazy about her. Of course, I haven't an earthly. I know she laughs at me—I can't really blame her." He sighed heavily. "Oh, it's hell to care for someone who you know will never care back. You don't know what it's like."

"Why not?"

"You're the type that women f-fall for."

"Only women I don't want."

"I should be g-glad of even that. I wonder if anyone will ever care for me enough to m-marry me. I want to m-marry. I want to have at least six children. I should like to m-marry someone like Lena—b-beautiful, intelligent without being in the least b-bookish; k-kind, amusing . . . But it's all only a dream. There's something about me—I don't click."

At any other time I might have condoled with him, but now his words filled me with nothing but an ungovernable irritation. As soon as we reached the house I left him and went upstairs. It was a tranquil summer evening and I sat at the window waiting for Paul to come in. I held the letter in my hand and from time to time I read it yet again.

At last there was a knock.

"The maid said you wanted to see me as soon as I got back."

"Yes. Come in. Shut the door. I've just received a letter that I think you ought to see."

Mystified, he took it from me and began to read. I watched him, but he gave no sign of emotion. It could not have taken him more than a minute to glance through the letter, but to me the time seemed interminably, cruelly long. Panic seized me. I wished that I had destroyed the letter, and concealed all knowledge of it. But it was too late; there was nothing I could do now.

I shut my eyes so as not to have to look at him. My despair was absolute.

"Well?" The coolly insolent monosyllable was like a blow; I had a sense of giddiness and of things colliding together before my eyes. "Well?" he repeated.

"Is it true?"

"It's true that she sometimes sleeps in the flat."

"In fact, for the past six or seven weeks she's been your mistress?"

He flushed deeply. "I decline to answer that question. It's nothing to do with you."

"Nothing to do with me? When you use my flat? Is that nothing to do with me?" I felt myself tumbling headlong to destruction, but could not stop myself. It was too late. I was possessed with the desire to hurt him, no matter what the cost to my own self. "For all this time you've been deceiving me—for weeks and weeks and weeks! I must have seemed a damned fool. It's not hard to deceive people when they have implicit trust in you. It's not hard, but it's just a little shameful. Why on earth couldn't you have told me? Didn't you feel I had the right to know? Didn't you feel you owed it to me?"

"That's right. Harp on my obligations to you." There was nothing but contempt in his voice—no anger, no contrition, not even the hurt which it had been my one desire to inflict on him. "You think you've bought me, don't you? You think I'm just here to do your will? I wish I'd never taken a penny of your money!"

"You know that's not true. I want nothing from you—there are no debts between us. But, don't you understand, I'm afraid for you. I'm terribly afraid for you, Paul. You're going to mess up your whole life, and I can't stand by and let that happen. I care too much."

"I'm not a child. I know what I'm doing. I don't want advice, yours least of all."

"But she'll destroy you. She's changed you already, and she'll go on changing you, until there's nothing of you left. She's dangerous. One of my best friends married her and I know, I know only too well. There's nothing she'd stop at, nothing, nothing!"

"I refuse to listen to this absurd nonsense about Anne. I suppose you realize that if I chose to repeat some of the things you've said about her, she could take you into court. I advise you to be careful."

"What do you know about her?" A hysterical giggle which I could not check broke from me. "You're in love with her. You've always been in love with her. When one loves a person, how much do you think one sees? You don't know the real Anne."

"I know her better than you do, at all events. If love blinds, what about hate? Hate has poisoned you and filled your mind with lies. Do you deny that you hate her?"

"No. I don't deny it. But—I have good reasons."

"What reasons?" Suddenly, terrifyingly, the icy crust of his rage splintered. "What reasons?" Incoherently, he choked and sought for words. "Obscene, disgusting reasons! Don't imagine I haven't guessed! Don't imagine I haven't realized! Anne was right about you, she was right all along. I was a fool not to listen to her long ago. I should have seen through you. I should have known the kind of person that you were. I never realized—how could I have realized?"

"I don't know what you're talking about. What are you trying to say? What lies has she told you about me?"

"Oh, don't try to appear so innocent. It worked once, but it doesn't work now. I'm not the child I once was, and don't you think it." He stood over me, his fists clenched, his body trembling; there was a pause in which his mouth remained open as if he were about to retch. Then, like a hot, bitter vomit the words poured from him. He seemed possessed. The force and vulgarity of his accusations stunned and appalled me. All these weeks beneath the tranquil surface of our friendship there had been fears, shames and the most insulting of suspicions. Perhaps it was just because of this period of repression that they now broke from him with so crude an impetus.

At last he had finished. Sweat and tears of rage mingled as they trickled down his face. As if after a fit, shudders ran through his body. He waited, obviously expecting me to make some reply. But a terrible lethargy had descended on me, without either the hope or the desire to refute his charges. I lay back in the chair, turning my head sidewards to look out the window; the cushion felt strangely cold on my burning skin.

Suddenly, he was sobbing; he put one hand and then the other up to his mouth, and ran from the room. I remained where I was. It was growing late and the garden was almost dark.

LIII

"MAY I come in?"

"What do you want?"

"Shall I put on the light?"

"Put it on if you like."

He must have decided not to; as he crossed the room to me his face was no more than a pale blur in the surrounding blackness. I was glad. I did not want him to see me.

"I came to say I was sorry. I lost my temper."

"That's all right. It was my fault as much as yours. I shouldn't have interfered—you had every right to be angry with me."

"I—I didn't mean all that about—about——" He could not go on.

"That's all right," I repeated.

"I didn't. I swear I didn't. You must believe me."

"I don't know what I believe just at the moment."

"I wish I'd never said it. I only said it because I was hurt and wanted to hurt you back."

"Perhaps."

"How can I convince you——?" He knelt down at my feet and took my hand. "I meant none of those things. I'm so ashamed. Please, please believe me——"

I loosed my fingers from his. "I don't want to talk about it now."

There was a pause; then his head, which had been bowed, was raised; he was looking at me. "Would you like me to go back to the island?"

"Back to the island! Of course not. Why should I?"

"I don't suppose you want me with you now."

"Yes, I still want you."

"Then you forgive me?" he asked eagerly.

"I still want you."

"Then you're willing to forget all this, and—and begin again? Can we? Can we?"

"I don't know. But I want you here. I don't want you to go away."

"It'll be different from now on. I know I've—I've behaved badly towards you. I know I've been casual and ungrateful "

"Please. Please, Paul. I think you'd better leave me now. Go to bed. Go to sleep."

My mood of apathy and weariness must have puzzled him; he seemed at a loss how to deal with it. "Are you all right?"

"Quite all right."

He rose slowly to his feet and stood hesitating before me. "I've hurt you terribly."

"Good night."

He turned away. "Good night."

LIV

I WAS left to the heart-searching and self-accusation which were to obsess me for several weeks. He had hurled his wild charges at me, and in spite of all subsequent protestations, he must at the time have believed them to be true: a person as unmalicious as Paul does not invent such things. Over and over again I repeated to myself: "No, it's a lie. It's a lie." But was I certain? Could I be certain? I told myself that there had been no tinge of perversion in my love for him, but the doubt persisted and obsessed me. I examined all our past intercourse; I went over scene after scene, conversation after conversation.

Our affections grow, like blooms, out of a profound darkness; of their roots we can see nothing, and if we grope, who knows what obscene shapes our fingers may not touch? But sterner than any judge I was determined to explore that darkness. I gave myself no rest until my conscience was satisfied. . . . And before that, many weeks were to pass.

LV

"WE can behave as if it had all never happened." Those were Paul's words, and I was often to repeat them to myself, finding in them the bitterest of irony. Had he really imagined that after such a scene we could take up the threads again and efface all memory of what had been said? It was impossible—for him as for me. Always that recollection lay between us. . . . So the last brick was placed in the wall, the last cranny was stuffed up. Our isolation from each other became complete.

LVI

AFTER this crisis I could only guess at what was happening between him and Anne. I had not taken the key of the flat away from him and I supposed that when they went up to town together, they still slept there. He had asked me: "Would you like me to stop using the flat?" but I had answered: "Of course not." I added with careful emphasis: "Use it exactly as you used to use it."

"You're sure you don't mind?"

"I don't mind."

I never doubted then that Anne had been his mistress, and it was with astonishment that I was to learn the contrary from him many weeks later. It seemed that though she allowed him the most intimate of caresses and even initiated him into pleasures of which he had previously had no knowledge, yet for all his protestations she would never give herself to him in the absolute sense of that phrase. It amused her to witness the shame of his ungratified desires, and to intensify their violence. For days she would withhold herself from him; then she would seem to be about to yield all only to break off at the last moment with a laugh, a yawn or a cross word. Moreover, she was torturing him by means of her friendship with Standing. She went for almost daily sittings to the house in Knightsbridge, and would often cancel an engagement with Paul in order to remain there. She never wearied of hinting that she and Standing were in love with each other. "It's sad that he's tied to that old cow of a wife and the three brats. We understand each other so well. Poor lamb! He feels that his whole career might have been different, if he'd met me earlier."

Paul felt that she now only used the flat because she found it convenient to do so; she did not really wish to be with him; she was becoming more and more impatient of his advances. "Oh, don't maul me about so. You'll spoil my dress!" She would get off the sofa, her mouth pouting. "You know, you're becoming something of a bore. It's partly my fault, of course—I shouldn't have encouraged you to begin with—but do try not to be quite such a nuisance."

Paul realized that he was already losing what little he had ever had of her; nor did he know how to regain her interest. Desperately, he lavished his attention on her, little realizing that in this way he spurred her to even grosser cruelties. His devotion and submissiveness maddened her; she longed for him to fight back, and because he would not, could not, she became the more implacable.

Inevitably, a crisis was reached. It was Charles who brought me news of it, for Paul had never again mentioned Anne to me after our scene together. It was strange and not a little ironic that he should in the end have to confide in Charles whom he had once so much despised. I can imagine that he felt he must tell someone of his misery, and who else was there, now that he and I were isolated from each other? I repeat the story as I then heard it.

LVII

WHEN Anne told Paul that she was going away for a few days to stay with friends, he was naturally disappointed at being separated from her but nursed no suspicions. Shortly before, she had asked if she might have her own key cut to the flat. "It'll be so much more convenient," she explained. "Often you and I are out at the same time, and then I have to get the porter to let me in. Do you mind?"

"*I* don't mind. But I think I'll have to ask Uncle Mark first."

"I knew you'd say that!" she exclaimed angrily. "Of course he'll refuse. You know how he dislikes me."

In the event—need I mention?—Paul never asked me, and Anne got her key.

On the Sunday of the weekend Anne was spending with her friends, Paul developed toothache. The local dentist was away on a weekend holiday, and neither of the two men in the neighbouring town would see him until the Monday morning. "You can't wait till then. I'll ring up my London man. We're old friends, and he'll see you as a favour to me."

"Don't bother. I can wait. Honestly, I can."

"No, you can't. In any case, I'd much rather you saw a good dentist instead of the old dodderer here."

I wanted to accompany Paul, but I had already arranged to play bridge that evening and he assured me that he would be all right. "I'll spend the night in the flat, and come back first thing tomorrow morning."

"I don't know if I ought to let you go alone."

"Don't be silly. I've grown out of the hand-holding stage!"

After the dentist had given Paul a local anæsthetic and taken out the tooth, he put him into a taxi; it was past ten o'clock. His gum was still frozen; and as he was driven from Harley Street to South Kensington, he congratulated himself, prematurely, on having got rid of the trouble with so little pain.

. . . Turning the key in the door of the flat, he was surprised to see that there was a light on in the hall. He could hear voices and the sound of a bath being run. He stood for several seconds in the doorway, unable at first to make out what was being said. He only knew that it was Anne and someone else. Standing! Who else could it be?

"Do give an eye to the bath. It'll overflow."

Standing passed at the far end of the passage without seeing Paul; he was wearing a dressing-gown, tied carelessly, so that as he walked most of his naked body was exposed. The sound of the rushing water ceased. Coming back, he turned his head, blinked at Paul in horrified incredulity, and then exclaimed: "Good God! What are you doing here?"

"I might ask the same question."

"Anne and I are just putting up for a night." He attempted to pass it off casually. "She said you wouldn't mind. Come in, old man. Have a drink."

"What's that?" Anne's voice shouted from the bedroom. "What are you saying?"

"It's Paul."

"What? I can't hear you."

"Paul's here."

"Who's here?"

She, too, was in a dressing-gown. "Paul! What brings you here?" But unlike Standing she was only faintly surprised. She looked at him and then laughed: "What's happened to you?"

"What do you mean?"

"Your face—it looks so funny! It's all swollen."

"I've just had a tooth out."

"Oh, poor Paul! Did it hurt a lot?"

He did not answer. He did not know what to say or do. Suddenly, he felt his mouth fill with a salt discharge from the already thawing cavity; a twinge of pain ran up his right cheek to the temple, making him wince. He pulled out his handkerchief, and holding it to his mouth, spat into it. Standing repeated: "Come and have a drink, won't you?"

Paul gazed at him and wondered what attracted Anne: in his clothes he looked well enough, but there was nothing impressive in the white, skinny body now revealed by his open dressing-gown—each rib distinct, the shoulder-blades like lopped wings, and the one exposed nipple surrounded by four or five long hairs. Their eyes met, and Standing looked away; Paul felt nothing but a detached contempt. Once again he raised the handkerchief to his mouth and spat into it. Then he said quietly: "I think I'd better go. . . . I was going to spend the night here," he added in explanation.

For a second or two he stood before them, but neither Anne nor Standing said anything. He knew that they were impatient for him to make a move, but he found it impossible to do so. He lingered until Anne said: "Well, good-bye." Then with a sudden, abrupt movement, he took a step and slammed the door behind him.

He hailed a taxi, and sat back in it; he could feel the blood throbbing about the raw hole where the tooth had been; the muscles of his neck and head ached at every jolt. Curiously, all his thoughts centred on his physical condition; he did not think of the scene in the flat, and the self-pity he felt was not for any betrayal but merely for the pain he now suffered. At Victoria he got out and made his way to the train.

He was alone, and mile upon mile of rain-sodden country passed by him in the faint, grey light of evening. He huddled into one corner of the carriage and sank his chin on to his breast. Spasm after spasm of pain shot across his face; a dull agony pulsed in every wrenched sinew. He groaned, sank farther into the dusty cushions and closed his eyes.

Suddenly, he saw Anne, clearly, as she had been when she had said good-bye to him. He remembered the rise of her breasts under her silk dressing-gown, her throat, her hair, her smile. A voluptuous longing swept over him, filling him with recollections of the intimacies he had once known. So intense was it that he could almost persuade himself that she was there with him in the shabby, empty carriage. He wished to put her image away from him, but even when he opened his eyes and looked out on to the dark fields, it would not leave him. He had never known such an intensity of desire; his loins ached, his body shook with it.

The salt, bitter discharge seeped once more into his mouth; he gulped it down, but more came and again more. It nauseated him, and in the end he got up and pulled down the window. He leant far out and spat repeatedly, the crimson threads whirling away from him into the dark and rain.

Then he collapsed on to the cushions and began to weep.

LVIII

When he returned, I guessed that something was wrong. "I thought you were going to spend the night in town."

"I decided not to."

"You look bad. You'd better go straight to bed. I'll get you a hot drink and some aspirin."

"No, please. I'll be all right. I think it's just this local anæsthetic."

"No harm in taking an aspirin."

When he was in bed I brought the aspirin up to him with a glass of hot milk. There was also a letter.

"From Betty. A West African stamp."

He took it from me and began to read. But after only a few seconds he threw it down on the floor beside him. "She's a fool!" he exclaimed with an almost childish petulance.

"What does she say?"

"She's married that man, that missionary doctor."

"Well, isn't that a good thing?"

"A good thing!" Suddenly he was in a passion. "What do you mean? She's gone out to that leper-colony with him. It's madness. If she doesn't catch leprosy, it'll be some other disease. In a few years she'll be dead."

No less suddenly his rage flickered out; an expression of despair and chagrin settled on his features. He gazed up at me and I gazed down at him. A word, a sigh, a gesture—but a thousand restraints seemed to come between us. We could not say any of the things that we wished to say. In the end I murmured good night and went out.

LIX

THE next morning Paul told everything to Charles and Charles told me. "Poor P-Paul! He seems pretty c-cut up, doesn't he? I always thought that w-woman an out-and-out bitch." He assumed that I already knew everything. "I wish there was s-something one could do to cheer him up."

"Is—is it all over then?"

"Well, I should think so, don't you?"

"I don't know. You see, Paul hasn't told me yet."

"What!" He was astonished, but I could also see that he was pleased. Paul had chosen him, rather than me, as confidant; he would not have been human if his vanity had not been flattered. "I thought you *must* know everything about it."

"No, I don't."

"I expect he's just waiting for a good opportunity to tell you," he said with clumsy kindness.

"I doubt it."

"You haven't quarrelled, have you?" I detected a note of eagerness in his voice.

"No. But there are gulfs between the old and the young. The young seem to confide in the young."

"Yes, but you and Paul were always such friends! Age made no difference." It is extraordinary how brutal the well-meaning can contrive to be.

I shrugged my shoulders. I was eager to question him, but I felt that to do so would be to humble myself utterly. In any case, it was not necessary. Charles had no thoughts that he might be betraying Paul; he wished only to parade his superior knowledge. The whole story tumbled from him. "I don't see why I shouldn't tell you. After all, he must want you to know, and probably just can't bring himself to say it. You know how it is."

Poor Paul! So it was all over. Compassion for him mingled with a joy which I tried to put away from me and which made me feel utterly ashamed. I wanted to go to him. I wanted to comfort him. But how could I? Surely he would resent it? Surely he would imagine I was interfering?

From this indecision I was saved by Charles. Before supper that evening he came up to my room. "I've just seen P-Paul. I've told him you know everything."

"Oh."

"He d-didn't seem to mind. In fact, I think he was r-relieved. He just said, 'Thank you.' Quite quietly and casually."

"Just that."

"Yes, just that."

I did not say anything until after dinner, and Paul himself remained silent; he ate hardly anything and seemed to avoid my eyes. Before the sweet, he excused himself: "I'm feeling rather faint. I think I'll go out into the garden."

"Are you sure you're all right?"

"Yes, quite all right."

"I'll join you out there, then, for coffee."

I found him sitting at the far end of the lawn, his hands deep in his pockets. There was a chill wind blowing and I repressed an involuntary shudder as I sat down beside him. "I've told the girl to bring our coffee out here." He remained silent.

I glanced at him, and then with a thudding heart, began: "Paul—I was awfully sorry to hear from Charles about—about Anne." There was no reply; he might never have heard me. "He oughtn't to have told me, I suppose. I hope you don't mind. Do you?"

"It doesn't matter," he said in a flat, expressionless voice.

"I wish there was something I could do to help you."

He turned slowly; so far his face had been averted from me. "I want to go away."

"Away?"

"On my own."

"But where to?"

"I don't know. I feel I must get away."

"Well, of course, of course. When do you want to go?"

"Tomorrow."

"You can have any money you want. Is there anything else?"

"I don't think so."

"Sure?" He did not answer; his dark-ringed, tragic eyes were fixed on the distant house. I had to say something or do something to comfort him. "Are you terribly unhappy, Paul?" Silence. "Paul." On an impulse I took his hand between my own, but he drew it away immediately and rose to his feet.

"I don't think I want any coffee. I must go and do my packing."

"I'll get Mrs. Hackhurst to cash me a cheque. Will twenty pounds do to go on with?"

"Thank you."

I watched him as he moved with slow, dragging footsteps across the lawn and went indoors.

LX

THE next day he left, taking with him no more than a suitcase. I was anxious, and that night I had considered refusing to let him set off alone. But in the end it seemed best to let him do what he wanted. "If there are any letters for me, you can send them to the flat. I'll call in there from time to time."

"You'll be in London then?"

"I don't know."

"I hope you'll be all right, Paul."

He shrugged his shoulders impatiently.

"Let me hear from you," I pursued. He did not answer and we said good-bye.

Days passed. No letter came, there was no news of him. I wrote, but without answer. I thought of going up to London to find him, but restrained myself. I knew that he would never forgive me if I did so. The day he left I had been to see Mrs. Patton and she had given me some advice I had not forgotten.

"Yes, I know," she said as soon as I was shown in. "It's all over between them. Anne's been here to collect her belongings. She told me."

"Has she gone?"

"Yes, she's gone. For good, I suppose." She sighed deeply. "I knew it had to happen, but none the less it came as rather a shock. I had such plans for her. It was my own fault, of course. I needn't have lost her if I'd shown an ounce of sense. Now it's too late."

I sank into a chair. "What's she going to do?"

She shrugged her shoulders. "God knows! She can't marry this man, that's certain. His wife won't give him up. They've taken a cottage in Cornwall and I suppose she'll live with him until she wearies of it. Yes, she rather fancies the role of the woman who defies convention for the man she loves. It's new, it's exciting, and she'll play it for all it's worth." There was a rasping malice in her words; but all at once she stopped, appalled. "No, I mustn't speak like that about her. Poor Anne! She's been through too much. It's sad, you know. She rushes through one experience after another in the hope that something—anything—may at last make her feel. She can't feel, she's lost the capacity, and that terrifies her. That stunning blow of losing first her child and then her husband finished her. But in her frantic efforts to wake out of her trance she does so much harm. . . . Paul must be terribly upset."

"He was very much in love with her."

"I know."

"He went away this morning."

"Went away! Where to?"

I shrugged my shoulders. "He wouldn't tell me. I didn't want him to go, I'm desperately worried, but what else could I do? I couldn't keep him here against his will."

"No, you were quite right. The secret of friendship is to know how to let go. It's a lesson I've learnt these last few days. Open the door of the cage and the bird doesn't want to fly away. If only I'd been wiser—if only I hadn't clung to Anne—she might still be here. I did everything to bind her to me, and it was fatal. Utterly, utterly fatal. I'm very unhappy."

There was a touch of self-pity in the last words which repelled me. I felt sorry for her, but I could not comfort her. "It's easy to suffer for the foolishness of others, but when one has to suffer for one's own foolishness . . ." she went on, "that hurts. I sacrificed everything to my friendship for Anne—my time, my thoughts, my interests. Even"—her voice sank—"even my husband's love. Yes, I sacrificed that, too." She looked up at me and then down at the ground. "Lena lives here now."

We talked a little longer until the maid came in to say that Charles had called; he had brought a present for Lena, and would wait out in the hall for me until I was ready to leave.

"I hope you didn't m-mind my sending in that message, but I thought we might w-walk back together," he explained when I met him. "It's Lena's birthday and I came up with a b-brooch I'd bought for her." He sighed. "I don't know why, she didn't seem to like it." He laughed ruefully: "It was expensive enough."

At that moment we were both startled by a shot. "What was that?" Charles asked.

"Oh, probably just Patton shooting a rabbit."

"But the noise came from the yard."

Someone was calling: "Mr. Langworthy! Mr. Langworthy!" The anguished voice came from the drawing-room where I had just left Mrs. Patton. I flung open the door.

"He's done it! He's done it! I know he has! He said he would!" Shrieking hysterically, she attempted to get out of her wheelchair and stand up. Her face was contorted with agony. Charles and I rushed to her, but we were too late. She swayed, strained to move forward, and then crashed on to the floor.

We raised her with difficulty. "What was she saying? You'd better go and see," Charles said in agitation. "That shot . . ."

"The dog."

"Oh . . . I thought . . . I thought perhaps . . ." Relief passed across his face. "Is that all?"

Mrs. Patton's enormous body was shaken with grief; she had twisted a finger as she fell and now massaged it, rocking back and forth. Patton came in.

"Get out!" she screamed at him as soon as she saw him in the room. "Get out! Murderer! Murderer! Murderer!" We had to hold her in the chair as she struggled to get up and attack him. He went out.

We calmed her as best we could and then, nearly half an hour later, made our way down the drive.

A voice called. "Hey—Langworthy!" It was Patton.

"Yes."

"About that dog . . ." He was flushed, and he would not look up at us. "I didn't want you to think . . ." he mumbled. "I had to do it. No good letting it live on for two or three days more when it was suffering like that. But she couldn't see that. I told her there was no chance. She wouldn't listen. So—so . . . Well, I don't like to see an animal suffer like that on my farm," he got out with a sudden defiance.

"I expect you did right. She was very fond of the dog, but if, as you say . . ."

"There wasn't a chance—not a chance!"

"I'm only sorry for her sake."

He shook his head and frowned. "I've never known her to be so fond of an animal."

He was not unkind, I rather liked him; but he was insensitive, and I wondered if he might not have set an insurmountable barrier between himself and his wife. He had understood the needs of the dying animal, but he had not understood hers.

She would probably never forgive him.

LXI

WITHOUT Paul, the days dragged slowly. I was once more suffering from insomnia, and as I lay awake through the interminable hours that stretched between midnight and dawn, I would go over the wreckage of our friendship, reproaching myself for a thousand imagined faults and failures.

Charles was often with me. Insensitive though he was, I think he guessed what I was suffering and wished to help me as best he could. At first, his obtuse kindness irritated me and I could not bear to be with him; I was rude to him and must often have hurt his feelings. But in the end I found a certain solace in his presence; I came to rely on him and felt peevish and restless when he was not with me.

He was, himself, in low spirits. He was still in love with Lena and she regarded him as no more than a joke. "Hostility or indifference I c-could stand—but to have her laugh at me——! I suppose you know that she's l-living in the house now. She says it's more convenient than being with her parents in the v-village, but everyone declares she's Patton's m-mistress. What do you think? Do you think it's true?"

I did, but I hadn't the heart to say so. "Oh, hardly! You know how people talk."

He sighed and shrugged his shoulders. He was not convinced.

Each morning he asked me: "Any news from Paul?" He, too, was anxious, not solely on my account, but also because he had admired Paul and felt an affection for him. One day, as we returned from a walk together, he suddenly took my arm: "I know what you're thinking."

"What?"

"You're wondering if there's a l-letter waiting for you when we get in. Right?" I nodded. "You mustn't worry so much," he said.

"I can't help it."

There was a moment's silence and then he blurted out: "I'll tell you something. I-I'm sorry P-Paul's gone, I wish he'd c-come back, and yet—yet part of me's glad that he's not here—glad that I have you to myself. I know I'm only a s-substitute, but I don't care. If Paul were here, I'd begin to irritate you; you'd become bored with me."

"Nonsense."

"You d-don't have to pretend it's not true. I know. All my life it's been like that, and I think I've learned not to mind now. I shall always be second best, and I might as well accept the fact."

"Oh, don't be so silly!"

But he only gave a wry smile.

LXII

SINCE the scene over the dog, I had not been able to bring myself to visit Mrs. Patton. I often planned to go, only in the end to shirk it and find some excuse. One evening, after supper, Charles suggested that I should walk up with him. "I want to see Lena. She p-promised to meet me at the cinema the day before yesterday, but never turned up. Since then I've heard n-nothing, and when I ring up, they always say she's out. I think I'd better see for myself."

"I don't know that I really feel equal to the walk this evening."

He laughed. "Now no excuses! You know you're always s-saying you must go up there. You c-can't put it off for ever."

"It's not a case of putting it off," I said crossly.

"Oh, come off it." He gripped my arm and shook me in a way which I found particularly exasperating. With a gesture of impatience I thrust away his hand.

"You will come, won't you?"

"Not this evening."

"But why not?"

In the end, from sheer weariness I gave in and we set off. I was in a bad temper, but Charles took no notice. He chattered away to me, sputtering over every second word in such a way I could only understand a third of what he said. When I had first met him, shyness had made him pick his phrases with some care, but now that he was at his ease with me, he discharged words like a machine-gun, the saliva spraying in volumes from his clumsily agitated tongue and lips.

I answered him in no more than monosyllables, until suddenly and unaccountably, he fell silent. Although we were walking at no more than a stroll, he had all at once begun to snort and grunt as he breathed; his face was white. "What's the matter?" I was going to ask, when he turned and halted: "I don't think I'll come and see Lena after all."

"Why on earth not?"

"Oh, what's the use! It's all so futile. I'll sit here and wait for you."

"Well, I only came because you persuaded me."

"I know," he said miserably. "I'm sorry. I just haven't the courage any more. Nothing will ever come of it."

His dejection was so extreme that I could not help pitying him. I touched his shoulder: "Cheer up. Don't wait for me. I'll go on as I've come so far, but you go back."

"I've nothing to do, so I might as well stay here. Don't feel you've got to hurry." He threw himself under a tree, looked up at me and smiled: "See you l-later."

When I was shown into the drawing-room, Mrs. Patton was seated in her wheelchair before the window. "What became of your friend?" she asked. "Why didn't he come all the way with you?"

I looked at her in incredulity, and she smilingly raised a pair of field-glasses. "I saw you through these. They've been lying hidden away in a drawer for years and years. I got them out four days ago, and it's as if they'd given me a new life. Yes, I mean it. You know how I was when you last saw me—there seemed nothing left, I felt hopeless and miserable. But now I've a perpetual source of interest. I can sit for hours and hours, here or on the terrace, and watch, watch, watch. You've no idea. All of a sudden I've made a host of new acquaintances—people I never knew existed before this. There are the two families in the cottages down the hill, the maiden ladies from your farm who always walk up here every day, the postman, the grocer's boy, the farm labourers . . . But that's only from this window. From the terrace, I can see the pier, the beach, the high street and the London road. Even in this short time I've learnt so much. Did you know, for example, that the lovers all go to the stretch of beach east of the pier? Don't ask me why they should, but every evening I see them there. The place is thick with them! And yet the beach at this end has hardly a soul on it."

She spoke hurriedly, excitedly, her flabby white hands never ceasing to play with the field-glasses. It repelled and yet touched me to think of her, spying on the life in which she could now have no part; I imagined her, seated for hours on end with the glasses to her eyes, while those whom she watched remained oblivious of her scrutiny. A slight shudder went through me. Just as she had once lived vicariously through Anne, so she now lived vicariously through a host of strangers. Could one blame her? Yet the idea filled me with disgust.

"You don't look well," she said.

"Don't I?"

"What news of Paul?"

"None."

"None! No wonder you're worried. I haven't heard from Anne, either. But—surprisingly—I don't seem to care. It's funny how life creates its own compensations. When I heard I should never walk again, it seemed so appalling, I didn't know how to face the future. But gradually I found new interests—books, needlework, music. I learned how to get pleasure from just looking at things. Sight, touch, smell—they took on an importance they'd never had before. . . . And so, now, after losing Anne, I've found yet another substitute. . . ."

As she spoke, I could not decide whether she was a very weak or a very courageous woman. But I envied her—how I envied her!

"I suppose your friend was coming up to see Lena, and then changed his mind?"

I nodded.

"Is he in love with her?"

Her curiosity irritated me. "I don't really know," I answered coldly.

"I think he must be." She raised the binoculars to her eyes: "He's still sitting there, waiting for you. He looks very dejected. Poor boy!" She put down the glasses. "I suppose you know what's being said about Lena and—my husband?" I flushed and was at a loss to make an answer. "Of course you know!" She was laughing at my embarrassment. "Yes, he's living with her. And that, too, doesn't seem to matter now. Why should it? He's been faithful to me for twenty years—that's almost unbelievable, isn't it? You can guess how strong his appetites are—and how little I can do to satisfy them. Oh, I owe him more than I can ever repay, and I don't grudge him this. He's always wanted a child, perhaps she'll give him one. At heart, he's a peasant and he's always regretted that I could never do that for him. I don't think I shall mind even a child. He's happy, and I'm glad that he's happy."

Weakness or courage? I still could not decide, as I walked down the hill to rejoin Charles.

"We're being watched," I said as he rose to meet me. I felt as if I were divulging some shameful secret.

LXIII

"Mr. Paul has arrived." As we came in, the maid put her head round the green-baize door which led to the servants' quarters.

"Paul!" When, during those sleepless nights I had imagined this happening there had been relief, joy and love in my heart. But now I felt nothing but panic. I looked at Charles as if expecting him to help me.

"Where is he?" he asked the girl.

"He went up to Mr. Langworthy's room. He asked me to tell you when you came in."

Again I looked at Charles. "I'd better go up," I said at last.

"Shall I come with you?"

"Yes—no. No." I began to mount slowly. Charles waited beneath me in the hall. On the landing I halted and stood for several seconds, one hand pressed to my heart. What should I say? How should I greet him? How behave? I was trembling and I felt vaguely sick.

All at once I strode to the door and turned the handle. "Paul!" I stared in horror. "Paul!" I shut the door behind me, crossed to the bed where he lay with his face downwards, and shook him by the shoulder. Again I shook, again and yet again, with frantic movements. Then I stood still. I gazed. Seconds must have passed. My bottle of sleeping tablets lay on the floor, empty. I knelt beside him and clutched the arm which dangled over the side of the bed. I pulled him over, and looked at his unshaven face, the cheeks abnormally flushed, the mouth open.

"Charles! Come up here! Come up immediately!" I ran out on to the landing and shouted down the stairwell.

Charles bent over Paul, raised an eyelid, and put an ear to his chest; I stooped for the empty cardboard box and held it out to him.

"I'll get Father. Wait here."

Shuddering uncontrollably, I stood beside the bed until, after what seemed many minutes, I heard the slow, firm tread of Dr. Stare. Charles put an arm round me. "You'd better go out. Wait in my room."

"But is he——? Will he——?"

"He's not yet d-dead. There's just a chance."

"Here, Charles! Get a glass of water. Quick."

"Wait in my room," Charles repeated.

I sat down on his bed, and held my head in my hands. In spite of my grief and terror, I was aware of many things: of the late birds twittering beyond the window, of the smell, sour and frowsty, which seemed always to follow Charles, of the gleam of my white face in the shadowy mirror opposite, and of the steady tick, tick, tick which came from the alarm-clock on the bedside table. I leapt up and strode to the window. Suddenly, unexpectedly, my stomach heaved and I vomited down into the darkness. I clutched the window-sill, feeling weak and dizzy.

Then I was standing in the doorway of my own room. Neither of the other two noticed me; they were too busy. I could hear their strained breathing, and the strange, terrible grunts, snorts and hiccups that came from Paul.

Two hours later, Charles gripped my arm. "He'll be all right," he whispered. "We've pulled him through." He was tired but exultant. "I didn't think it possible. Did you, Dad?"

My gaze went across to the rumpled bed. Paul's eyes were open and they were looking up into mine.

"Why didn't you let me die?" he asked.

LXIV

THREE days had passed.

"You know, you and Charles really needn't be afraid of leaving me to myself." All that morning he had sat apathetically on the verandah, doing nothing. We tried to talk to him, but he only answered us in curt, bored monosyllables. His face was white and curiously thin since I had last seen him; a nerve twitched uncontrollably on the left side of his mouth.

"Don't be silly."

"It's you that's being silly. You don't realize that it's not a thing one does twice."

I took a chair beside him. "I'm worried about you, Paul."

"Oh, please!"

"You said something I can't get out of my mind. It was the first thing you said after—after they brought you round."

"I meant it."

"But why, why? What's happened? Whatever made you want to do such a thing?"

"Charles has been asking me that all this morning. Now it's you." He spoke with a contemptuous indifference which wounded me more than his actual words could ever do. "Do you really want to know?"

"Of course."

"If I tell you, it'll only be so that you and Charles need no longer be tormented by curiosity. I don't want your sympathy. You understand that? . . . Call Charles."

I did not move.

"Call Charles," he repeated.

I shook my head. "I don't want to hear—not like that."

"But surely Charles is entitled to an explanation"—he seemed to be laughing at me—"after all I owe him. Think—what a scandal there would have been if Charles hadn't hushed the whole thing up for me. His father would have talked his head off otherwise." He plucked a rose from the trellis behind him, and began to tear off the petals with swift, agitated movements. More and more I felt that he was not himself.

"Why are you looking at me like that?" he suddenly asked.

"Like what?"

"Oh, with that sad, saintly forgiveness in your eyes!"

"I have nothing to forgive. But I'm worried about you. I want to help you and I don't know what to do. I seem only to get on your nerves."

He made a tentative gesture—for a moment I thought he was going to grasp my hand—and then slumped once more into his chair. He smiled, not amiably, but with a bitter derisiveness. I felt that my solicitude, my care, my very presence filled him with contempt. I could not understand it.

LXV

A WEEK later Charles and his parents left for home. "Write to me, don't let's lose touch," he repeated with a pathetic insistence, and I assured him that I would. But I think that he and I both knew that the promise would be broken. He was kind, he meant well and I was under many obligations to him, but in my heart there was no desire to maintain our intimacy. I am ashamed to write this now, but it happens to be the truth.

Letters came from him, two and three a week, some of which I forced myself to answer. But the intervals between my replies became each time longer and the replies themselves shorter. In the end the fat envelopes, many of them unopened, accumulated in my writing-desk were forgotten, and at last ceased to come. I have no notion what has become of Charles, but when I think of him, I always experience a vague pang of conscience.

Already, before Charles's departure, the village had begun to empty itself. Summer had merged into autumn, the leaves were yellowing, and I found it too cold to bathe. There seemed no reason for continuing to stay in the country except that, as far as I could gather, Paul was disinclined to move. From day to day I put off making any plans, hoping for some change in him, but none came. He remained morose, dull and lethargic, and any efforts I made to rouse him seemed only to get on his nerves. He would sit for hours on end staring out of a window with so little show of interest that I wondered if he saw anything at all. He ate little. Sometimes he would take up a book, but after turning over a few pages he would put it down again. When I suggested a walk or an excursion, he came with me but said nothing and behaved as if he were in a dream.

I was worried, and found it impossible to concentrate on anything else. I had had a letter offering me the job which May had for so long coveted for me, but I felt a complete indifference. If I accepted, I should have to return to India in four weeks' time, and to leave Paul seemed unthinkable. I wrote to refuse, but was told that I should be given a fortnight to reconsider my decision. There seemed to be no likelihood of my doing that. The thought of returning to a position of great responsibility appalled me; I felt I no longer had either the strength or the inclination to take up the threads of a career again. I was obsessed with one thing to the exclusion of all else.

LXVI

FROM my bedroom window I could see him at the far end of the garden, doing nothing. Huddled at one end of the seat, with his hands in his lap, he looked thin, ill and hopeless. As I stood there, the wind kept blowing dead leaves past me into the room so that they made a dry, scraping noise against the wainscot. There was a spring-like transparency in the light and a spring-like chill in the air; far off, I could hear the sea, and the sound intensified the melancholy that had filled my heart.

Suddenly, Paul took up a book and began to read, but a moment later his eyes moved from it and he gazed out into the distance. Impossible to tell what he was thinking—if anything at all. He continued to stare for what seemed many minutes, oblivious of the way in which the wind kept blowing his hair into his eyes. Then he raised the book and looked down again.

With a sigh, I left the window and went to join him. When I was away from him I felt restless, and yet when I was with him, there was nothing I could do. Either way, concentration was impossible.

He glanced up as he heard my footsteps. "How are you feeling?" he asked. I had had a slight attack of fever.

"Oh, not too bad. You oughtn't to be sitting out here without a coat. You'll get a chill."

"I'm all right." His voice was curiously hoarse and indistinct.

"Let me fetch your coat for you."

"I don't want it, thank you." He seemed to dislike to have me do anything for him.

"What are you reading?"

"Nothing."

He was going to close the book, but I slipped a finger between the open pages. "Housman!" I exclaimed. When I had first met Paul I had attempted to argue him out of what seemed to me an excessive admiration for this writer. "Which poem were you on? This one?"

He nodded.

I began to read aloud:

"*Into my heart an air that kills*
    From yon far country blows;
What are those blue remembered hills,
    What spires, what farms are those?

That is the land of lost content——"

Suddenly I heard a gasp; he had turned his face away from me. I looked and saw that he was crying.

"Paul!"

"Don't, don't!" He pushed me away from him.

"Paul, what's the matter?"

He made an incoherent noise which I could not understand. Then, in an attempt to silence his sobs, he pressed one hand, fist clenched, against his mouth.

"I'd no idea. . . ." Clumsily trying to make amends, I slipped an arm round his shoulder. "Paul, don't cry! Don't cry!"

For a moment he resisted me and tried to push me away. Then, strangely, wonderfully, he pressed his face against my coat, his hair brushed my lips. He seemed to surrender everything—his grief, the past, the future, his very being. "I'm so unhappy. It's been horrible. You don't know." Like a child he clung to me, one hand crushed between his chest and mine.

I do not know what I said to him, but slowly he calmed, slowly he began to tell me the story of those days in London. As he spoke, brokenly, often incoherently, the tears did not cease to trickle down his cheeks. What he related then I shall relate here, but in my own words. I should weary the reader if I attempted to reproduce the hesitations and repetitions of his own narrative.

LXVII

HE left us with no real notion of what he would do when he reached London. Vaguely, he planned to look round for a room, to write, to meet people and above all, to forget Anne. He left his belongings at the flat and decided to sleep there that same night; the next day he would start looking for accommodation. All at once, he felt alone and dispirited; when he had said good-bye, it had seemed a fine, exhilarating thing to set out on his own, but now he had to put away from him the desire to give in and return to the country.

He wandered out, had a meal in a cafeteria, and began to stroll through Hyde Park. The sight of the lovers under the trees brought a strange pang to his heart. He did not wish to think of Anne, he did everything in his power to obliterate her image, yet again and again his mind filled with recollections of her. He remembered how he had once walked here with her and his hand had been round her waist. He could remember even her perfume.

Gradually, his memories of her obliterated all else and created their own reality. He seemed to touch her flesh, to stroke her hair; her body seemed to press against his.

Aimlessly, he drifted into the crowd that had gathered about one of the speakers; but he did not listen, his thoughts were all with Anne. He allowed himself to be pushed by those who were struggling to get in front of him and swayed as the mob swayed. Then, all at once, he realized that he was being stared at. He glanced up and hurriedly glanced away again. But the eyes would not leave him. They belonged to a man of about thirty years of age who wore dusty green corduroys, a check shirt with no tie and a tweed jacket. He had a straggly beard and was entirely bald in front; behind, his red hair had been allowed to grow so long and thick that it looked as if it were a bun. He had turned half round, with his back to the speaker, and was looking at Paul with a faint, almost contemptuous amusement.

In the end this scrutiny made Paul feel so uncomfortable that he extricated himself and walked rapidly away. He placed himself on a seat, forgot the stranger, and once more gave himself up to his thoughts of Anne. The melancholy with which they filled him all at once became strangely pleasurable.

"Excuse me. Have you a light?"

Even before he looked up, Paul knew who it was. Reluctantly, he drew out a box of matches.

"Thanks." The man sat down beside him, lit his own cigarette and then asked: "What about you?" He proffered a crushed packet of cigarettes: "Only Woodbines. I don't suppose you smoke them." There was an insolence in the drawled way he spoke the words.

"I don't smoke anyway."

The man pulled at his cigarette, tilted his head back, and blew out the smoke in half a dozen fat rings. Paul noticed now that there were red hairs on his cheek-bones, in his nostrils and in his small, delicate ears. His nails were bitten, his fingers were grubby and stained with nicotine.

He looked round at Paul. He had long eyelashes and green eyes with a slight cast in them. "I saw you listening to that pharisaical old bastard over there. I wondered what you were thinking."

"Oh."

"What were you thinking?" Paul coloured; he did not know what to say. But before he could stammer anything, the man had cut in: "You were a little bit shocked, weren't you? You hadn't realized just how much you were hated."

"Me?"

"Your class. The first time, it is a shock. I know, I went through it myself—though you mightn't think so now. Of course, one knows that the people want this, that and the other thing, one may even be a socialist oneself; but when one comes up against that crude malevolence for the first time it's like a blow in the face. It *was* the first time, wasn't it? I could see from your expression."

All at once Paul was interested. Though in a sense it was under false pretences that he had got this man to speak to him, he did not now regret it.

" 'It's so unjust!' one thinks at first. And then a terrible sense of guilt comes over one. Either that, or defiance." Again his eyes rested on Paul; he gave his slow, contemptuous smile. "In your case I should say guilt. Right?"

"Well—yes. Perhaps."

"Don't feel so ashamed at admitting it!" he laughed. "Though there's a certain irony in that old humbug—" he indicated the distant speaker—"causing you a pang of conscience."

"Why?"

"Because he's not one of the exploited. He's on the other side—your side. If there's a show-down you won't find him near the barricades." Paul's bewilderment delighted him. "Oh, I know he calls himself a communist and he's very eloquent about it all. But it means nothing; it's no deeper than the skin which he'll save at any cost. I can tell you a thing or two about that man. I know him. I was once in his party." His eyes narrowed. "Remember the Spanish Civil War? You were probably only a kid then. Well, that man used to stand up where he's standing now and declare that the British Government should send out every man, plane and gun it could. I was one of those who heard him. I went." He drew up his trouser-leg and showed a long, glistening scar. "I got this—and quite a bit besides. Oh, I'm not regretting having gone, I'd do the same again. I believe that what he said then was true, and what he says now is true. But if ever I have to go to Spain again, I should like to be certain that he's beside me." He took another cigarette and lit it from the one he had just finished. "It was the same when the war came. What was he doing? During the week he worked in an aircraft factory, and on Sundays he came out here and said the Government ought to damn well start a second front. I was on the landing-beaches. My best friend was blown up just in front of me." He jerked a derisive thumb in the direction of the speaker. "Oh, he's a clever man, he is! You won't catch him getting himself into that sort of mess. He's clever, he's bloody clever. . . ."

Paul had never met anyone like this; admiration and shame for his own lack of political experience filled him to the exclusion of any thoughts of Anne.

"Have you been out of the army long?" he asked.

"Six months in a glass-house," the man said laconically. "Then they slung me out. Insubordination."

"Insubordination? What happened?"

"Oh, I told a damned fool of an officer just what I thought of him." He laughed. "I don't regret it. I regret very little. . . . Now that you've heard all this, I suppose you're beginning to feel sorry you ever got to know me."

"Of course not," Paul repudiated indignantly. "Why ever should I?"

"What would your people say?" the man mocked. "I don't expect they'd take to me, would they?" He scratched under his arm: "I'm dirty, I smell, and I need a shave. I have what's called a 'bad' record and my political views are deplorable."

"Don't be silly!" On an impulse he added: "I'm glad I've met you. The only thing is . . . you make me feel so. . . ."

"Yes?"

"So mean—and selfish—and cowardly."

"There's no need to feel that. How old are you? Eighteen? Nineteen?"

"Eighteen."

"Only eighteen? You've lots of time yet." He looked at Paul through narrowed eyes and then declared slowly: "You're all right. I can see that. You're all right. You're one of us. You won't go far wrong."

This verdict brought an exultant rush of blood to Paul's face.

"But I've so much to learn. I know nothing. I—I don't know what to do—how to begin."

"Not so fast," the man laughed. He rose: "Let's have a drink. I'm feeling thirsty." He plunged a hand into his trouser-pocket and then pulled a face: "I spoke too soon. Not a penny left."

"Oh, that's all right. I've plenty of money. Come on!"

The man drank heavily, and it was always spirits: but Paul did not care. He was glad to pay for him, and it was with a strange, constricting tenderness that he watched him gulp down glass after glass of neat whisky. All the time he talked volubly, his words filling Paul with visions of a new, sterner, nobler life of service and initiation. At closing time they wandered back into the Park again, took off their coats because of the sultriness of the evening, and knees clasped, continued their long conversation. . . .

At last the man yawned: "I must go and get a doss." Far off a clock struck one; clocks, strangely loud, reiterated the sound from all about them. He rose unsteadily to his feet.

"Come back to my flat if you like."

"No, I won't do that. But thanks all the same. I've told you—I wouldn't fit."

"There's no one there."

The man only shook his head: he swayed a little, his face a grey blur before Paul.

"But I may see you again?" Paul said.

"If you like."

"Can I have your address?"

The man laughed. "I haven't one! You give me yours."

Paul drew an envelope out of his pocket and held it up to the light of the moon so that he could see to write. "There you are!" He handed it to the man. Shyly, he said: "It's been wonderful meeting you. I can't explain. You'd only laugh. But you will let me hear from you—soon, soon?"

The man patted the trouser-pocket into which he had stuffed the envelope. "I'll be here tomorrow evening same time, if you like."

"Good!"

That night Paul dreamed, not of Anne as he had done for so long, but of his new friend; hope, strength and confidence were

with him even in sleep. He woke, wonderfully invigorated and
alert. But when he went to put on his suit, he found his wallet
missing. Nor could the police help him; they even seemed to think
him rather a fool.

LXVIII

FORTUNATELY, since the man had not taken the few shillings of
change that Paul had been carrying with him, he was not yet entirely destitute. But that meagre sum would be exhausted in the
next day or so, and then he would have to think, make plans, do
something.

"Why on earth didn't you get in touch with me?" I asked.

"Why? Because I couldn't possibly make any further demands
on your generosity. You'd done so much already. Anyway"—he
smiled—"don't you remember how you begged me not to carry
the whole twenty pounds around with me in my wallet? I didn't
want to hear you say 'I told you so'."

The whole of that next day he wandered about London—sitting in Parks, taking aimless bus rides, drifting through picture galleries, eating at milk bars, loitering at street corners. More than
once someone would try to fall in with him, but he gave no en-
couragement. A hag selling bunches of white heather pursued
him through Trafalgar Square, incapable of believing him when
he told her he was broke.

When evening came, he wandered into the Café Royal.

"What can I fetch you, sir?"

The vastness and the imagined splendour of his surroundings
flustered him. He had no notion what to say. "Oh—er—some,
some rum."

"Some rum, sir?" Was there a note of surprise in that upward
inflection? "Very good, sir. And anything to go with it?"

"Some—some——" He looked frantically from table to table.

"Some ginger perhaps, sir?"

"Yes, that'll do."

"Very good, sir."

The girl at the table next to his was looking in his direction.

He wondered if she was laughing at him, but the expression in her eyes was one of dreamy, almost stupefied content. She lay, rather than sat, in the arms of a young man who wore a cheap blue suit and appeared from time to time to nibble at her left ear. She was plain, plump and dowdy, but as her eyes met Paul's, she gave him a slow, vaguely provocative smile. Women were queer: there she was, held by another man, and yet, even at that moment, she could think of making herself attractive to a total stranger.

Paul looked away; he felt uncomfortable at holding her gaze so long while the young man, wholly oblivious, drew her even nearer to him and began to press her bust rhythmically upwards. He looked away, and then, hurriedly, he looked down. Too late.

Wandle, whom he had not seen since that far-off weekend we had spent with May, had half risen from his chair and was waving to him. He waved sheepishly back. Wandle beckoned and Paul had to go over to his table.

"How nice to see you! You're looking remarkably bonny. That tan suits you. Sit down." He pulled a chair back. "Let me introduce you. This is Paul," he told the three young men who were with him. "Don't let's worry about surnames." He pointed to each of the young men in turn. "Michael, from the stingiest of all publishing firms, Tony from the B.B.C., and Kim. . . . I can't remember where you come from, Kim."

"Oxford" was the sulky reply.

"Of course. Well, there you all are!"

The three young men looked Paul up and down, and smiled with a vague, uninterested condescension.

"Now tell me all about yourself. Where have you been? What have you been doing? Why have you never sent me anything as you promised?" Before Paul could answer, Wandle rushed on: "So much water has flown under the bridge since we met at that dim, dreadful house-party. You heard about the accident?"

"The accident?"

"My dear, don't say you never heard about my accident. It happened on the journey back from that very house-party!" The three young men, obviously bored, had begun to whisper and giggle together. "I was in hospital for nearly a week. Frightful. I can't bear illness. The very sight of enemas, bed-pans and bottles gives me a nasty sinking feeling. .... You remember Tom?"

"Tom?"

"You *must* remember Tom. Tom Badson. My secretary." Paul nodded. "Of course you remember him. Well, it's all very mysterious, I simply can't even pretend to understand it, but I'm absolutely convinced that he did the whole thing on purpose. There was no proof, of course, and in any case he was killed, poor boy, so there was no point in going into it. He was a strange character. I suppose he had some grudge against me, God knows what. He'd been sulking all that weekend, you may remember. It was an awful moment when I saw him swing the wheel round and the embankment came to meet us—awful! The sad part is that he was such a wonderful secretary. At the same time I didn't really appreciate him, but now I know. The types I've had since—refugees, Girton girls, bearded old maids and hairless young men who've never even touched a typewriter. I give them an average of a week each." Suddenly an idea came to him; his monocle fell downwards. "You—what about you? You're doing nothing, are you? It's quite an easy job. With your intelligence you could do it standing on your head."

"But I've never—I mean, I know absolutely nothing about being a secretary. I've no experience."

"My dear child, that's a minor consideration. You'll pick it up in next to no time. The important thing is that you're 'sympathetic'; that's what really matters. Any fool can learn to hammer on a typewriter."

"Well, I can type a bit." Suddenly, Paul began to feel excited. After all, even if Wandle was personally odious, he was a writer of distinction and much could be learned from him.

"You can! Well, what on earth are you worrying about. Is it all fixed then?" His hand, the palm curiously hot and clammy, descended on to Paul's.

"If you really think I'll be all right."

"I'm absolutely sure of it." His delight struck Paul as being childishly excessive. "We must celebrate this. Boy! Hey, boy!" He clicked his fingers at an elderly and palsied waiter.

One of the young men—Tony, was it?—turned to Paul. "Did I

hear that you were going to be Wandle's new secretary?" Paul nodded, and the young man turned to the other two: "Meet Wandle's
new secretary." They all looked at him with what seemed to be a
new interest.

When, two hours later, they at last left the Café Royal, they
were all a little drunk. "Take my arm," Wandle said to Paul. "I
can't see in the dark. Night-blindness." He belched and leaned
heavily against him. "Find a taxi."

The others were beginning to say good night. "My dears,
you're not *all* going to desert me?"

"Paul's still with you."

"Oh, very well. Then nighty-night, everyone. Take care of
Kim, Tony. You know what happens to young men who won't stop
fidgeting with their hair." They all giggled weakly, and then, with
repeated good nights, went their separate ways.

Paul found himself seeing Wandle home in a taxi.

LXIX

THE next morning when Paul arrived for work, Wandle was break-
fasting in bed. He lived in a large, luxurious service flat at the top of
a building in Piccadilly, full of books, modern pictures, and signed
photographs in silver frames. He called Paul in to him: "Let's discuss business." He patted the bed, and Paul sat down. In between
mouthfuls of toast and gulps of coffee, Wandle indicated Paul's
salary (it was not large), his duties (they were as much domestic
as secretarial), and the hours he would be expected to keep ("it all
depends on the work in hand"). After the excitement of the night
before, these details all seemed rather flat and disappointing.

Perhaps Wandle guessed this, for when he had finished he
asked with a certain sharpness: "All right?"

Paul nodded.

"Good." Wandle covered a piece of toast with butter and hon-
ey and held it out to Paul.

"No, thank you. I've only just had my own breakfast."

"There's one other thing." Wandle bit into the piece of toast himself. "I really think it would be more convenient for both of us if you could come and live here."

"In this flat, you mean?"

"There's a very nice bedroom through the door there. Tom used to have it. I believe some of his things are still there, but we can have them cleared out. Take a look."

Paul opened the door, and at once experienced a sense of foreboding and oppression. A large photograph of Wandle looked down at him from the mantelpiece: next to it were three small snapshots—a bald man working in the garden of a semi-detached house, a middle-aged woman with a hat pulled down over her eyes, and a blurred, faded cat sunning itself on one corner of a window-sill. "Like it?" Wandle called from the bedroom.

"Yes, thank you."

A slight shiver ran through Paul as he closed the door behind him.

"That's settled then." Wandle threw back the bed clothes. "I must get dressed. Due at a committee meeting at eleven-thirty." He swung his legs out of bed and smiled: "Do you think you could possibly fetch my slippers? They're just under the chair."

LXX

ONE of the first of Paul's jobs each day was to go through the pile of unsolicited manuscripts that arrived by the morning post. Those which he thought would interest Wandle were put on one side; the rest were kept for a fortnight, unread, and were then returned. At first Paul's and Wandle's tastes had not coincided and there had been some peevishness and exasperation. For example:

"I thought this rather good."

"Mavis Cook," Wandle read out with extreme distaste. "Norbury. Whoever heard of anyone called Mavis Cook of Norbury writing a short story! . . . What's this?" He pulled a manuscript out of the heap of Paul's rejections.

"That? Oh, it's a bit of 'reportage'. Dull, and not very well written. About the lower-deck."

Wandle began to read. "*I* don't think it's dull," he said coldly. "And I don't know what you find wrong with the style. Simple, clear, economical—what more do you want? I know you have a taste for fine writing, but you shouldn't let that blind you to other, perhaps even more important virtues." He read on.

"Are you going to accept it?" Paul asked meekly, after a minute or two had passed.

"I don't know. I'm not sure that it's *quite* good enough. But obviously the lad ought to be encouraged. He's young, I imagine, and will improve. Give me a rejection slip."

Paul watched him as he wrote: 'Sorry. I like this, but can find no room for it. Let me see some more of your work.' Wandle signed the card with his initials and then asked: "What else?"

"I don't know what you feel about this one." Paul handed him the work of an elderly and distinguished poet.

"Oh, dear! Oh, dear, oh, dear!" Wandle was agitated. "This is very awkward. It won't do, it won't do at all. No one wants to read him now. What on earth am I to say?"

"Couldn't you say what you've said to A/B whatever it is? 'Sorry. I like this, but can find no——'"

"Oh, don't be so fatuous. He's an old friend of mine. We belong to the same club. In any case, I can't afford to rub him up the wrong way." He sighed. "It'll have to go in, I'm afraid. I suppose we should feel honoured that he sent it to us."

This sort of conversation taught Paul much; soon he could predict Wandle's reaction to any work with complete accuracy. He had made good. "I'm very pleased with you. You seem to have got the hang of the thing in next to no time. I always knew you were the person I was looking for." On the occasion when he spoke this encomium, Wandle went to his bedroom and returned carrying a tie: "A little present for a good boy. It doesn't suit me, but it's the very thing for you. Silk," he added. "It cost thirty bob."

Paul liked the tie no more than Wandle did; he would never wear it. But as a token of success in his new job, he took it, thanked Wandle, and wrapped it away in a drawer.

LXXI

ONE afternoon when Wandle had gone out and Paul was working alone in the flat, there was a ring at the door. It was Monica
Dean, the girl we had met with her brother John at May's house-
party. For a moment she did not seem to recognize Paul, then she
exclaimed: "Christ! Fancy seeing you again!" She gripped both his
arms with a heartiness to which he found it difficult to respond.

"I'm Wandle's new secretary."

"What!" she screamed. "How could you? You must have been
in a bad way." Laughing, she tossed her bag on to the desk and
heaved herself up beside it. Her skirt was short and it was rucked
so far up that he could see her suspenders. "Well, what news since
we last saw each other." Pulling off her hat, she began to run a
comb through her thick black hair.

"Oh, nothing much."

"What about the uncle?"

"He's in the country."

"And you're on your own?"

"Yes."

"Living here?"

"Yes."

"What does Wandle pay you? He'd skin a flint for a farthing."

She continued to question him in a way which he resented:
her voice was too loud, she brought with her not only her perfume, but a vague, unpleasant female smell, and as she kicked her
legs her high-heels made small nicks on the polished mahogany of
the desk. And yet, in spite of all this, he was glad to see her there
and did not wish her to leave. There was much that was vulgar
about her—the great bang in which she wore her hair above her
forehead, for example—and yet it was this very vulgarity which
appealed to him. His senses were peculiarly stirred by having her
near to him; even her coarse, uninhibited laugh and her loud,
slangy voice filled him with a vague pleasure.

"Look how I'm wasting your time!" she exclaimed after twenty minutes. "What'll Auntie Wandle say? And I haven't even mentioned what I came about."

"Oh. What was that?"

"It's this number Wandle's planning—you know, about John." Suddenly she became serious, even grave. She got off the desk and sat down in a chair. "He wants me to do an article for it—you know, family background, all that sort of thing. Well, I've tried, but I just can't write about him somehow. I suppose it's all too near."

Paul was bewildered. "What number is this? It's the first I've heard about it."

"The memorial number. Hasn't he told you?" Then seeing the puzzled expression that was still on Paul's face, she explained: "John's dead. You can't have heard." All at once her voice became small and flat.

"Dead! I'd no idea. . . ."

"Three weeks ago yesterday."

"I'm terribly sorry."

"He'd have been a great poet if he'd lived." For a moment, he thought that she was going to break down, but instead she gave herself a small, almost imperceptible shake and continued in her normal voice: "Wandle had plans for the memorial number almost before he was in his grave. He used to be rather malicious about John's work, but you should seen his grief! He told everyone just how heart-broken he was. To hear him, you'd think he and John had been life-long friends." She spoke with a malice and hardness that shocked Paul. "When I'm with Wandle now, I get a strange feeling. Suddenly, I begin to think that John lived and wrote and died for only one reason—to give Wandle the pleasure of grieving for him. You know, the number's to begin with a poem of Wandle's—a ghastly free-verse 'In Memoriam'. He hasn't written poetry for years now, so you can imagine how thrilled he was when this one came to him." She stopped: "Oh, but why talk about Wandle? Tell him I called, will you? I'll come again, or give him a tinkle, or something. . . . I wonder how long you'll keep your job."

"I quite like it."

"At the moment."

He felt he must see her again, and he was just going to ask for her address or telephone number, when she said: "You must come and see us." She pulled a used envelope out of her bag. "That's the address." In one corner she scribbled her telephone number in a large, childish script.

"Thanks. I won't forget," he said eagerly.

"Good." She took his hand in her own, and then suddenly, unexpectedly she raised her lips to his and kissed him. "Good-bye." She laughed and was gone.

LXXII

Two nights later Paul was woken by a loud rap at his door. Someone was by his bed. He had never felt at his ease in this room in which Tom Badson had once lived and he gave a startled cry as his hand fumbled for the light.

"It's only me." It was Wandle.

"Oh. You gave me rather a fright."

"Were you asleep then?"

"Of course I was."

"I'm sorry. But I couldn't stand it any more; I had to see someone—talk to someone. Otherwise I should have gone mad." His cheeks sagged, his face was grey; he was breathing heavily.

"What's the matter?"

"It's this damned asthma of mine." His voice became tearful with self-pity. "Nothing helps. I just lie awake for hours and hours and hours. I don't expect you've ever suffered from insomnia. Strange, unreasonable fears come to one; one's mind goes round and round everlastingly like a dog chasing its own tail. And the loneliness! One feels that everyone has slipped away to some place where one can't follow." He sat down on the bed beside Paul, and hung his head between his knees. He began to cough, exclaiming with each gasp: "Damn! Damn! Damn!"

"Isn't there something you could take?" Paul asked anxiously.

"Oh, my room's full of bottles. But nothing's any good. I've had it for years and years and I suppose I shall go on having it until I die. . . . Until I die," he repeated. "It's funny, but when I have these attacks I can't stop thinking about death. It's an awful feeling. Every instant, every tick of the clock brings one nearer to it, and there's nothing one can do about it—absolutely nothing. One's as powerless as a rat in a cage." He ran his fingers through his hair, making it stick up in absurd tufts: "Oh, I must put it out of my mind. I must, must, must! Talk to me, say something, suggest something."

All at once Paul felt sorry for him. People described Wandle as 'impressive', but there was no hint of this quality in him now. He had become a frightened and lonely old woman.

"Let's make some tea." Paul swung himself out of bed. "Why don't you play me some of your records? You always say that you will, but you never do."

At once Wandle brightened. "What a wonderful idea! But I hate doing this. I hate dragging you out of bed."

"It doesn't matter."

"You are kind to me."

They went into the sitting-room and turned on the electric fire. While Paul made the tea, Wandle began excitedly to go through his records, heaving down album after album and littering the floor with disks. His taste was almost entirely operatic. He chose from Puccini, Strauss and Wagner music whose sumptuousness moved Paul and yet made him feel uncomfortable; he was too much of a Puritan to give himself to it as it demanded. Wandle lay back in his chair, with closed eyes; all at once he seemed happy and at peace.

The last record he put on was 'One Fine Day' from 'Madame Butterfly'. Familiarity made the music seem trite and sentimental to Paul, but when he glanced across, he was surprised to see that tears were trickling down Wandle's cheeks. "Oh, how unfailingly that music gets one!" Wandle exclaimed as the record ended. He smiled through his tears. "I feel so much better now. I feel I could sleep. And for that I have to thank you." He crossed the room and sat down at Paul's feet.

"I am lucky to have you for my secretary. And friend," he added, fixing his long-lashed, mournful eyes on Paul's face. He was not wearing his monocle, and its absence was as conspicuous as the gap left by an extracted front tooth.

This compliment embarrassed Paul, and he shifted uneasily in his chair. But Wandle continued to stare at him, until after several seconds he suddenly exclaimed: "You know, you really look very fetching in those blue pyjamas." Paul coloured. "You mustn't be embarrassed. I mean it." Again the sombre, yearning eyes were turned up to Paul. "You're very beautiful."

"Oh, don't be so silly." He made as if to rise, but an obscure fascination kept him where he was.

Wandle had taken his hand. "Would it surprise you to learn that I care for you a great deal? Care for you as I've never cared for anyone else. . . ."

Five minutes later, Paul had locked himself into his room. It was obvious that a new secretary would have to be found in the morning.

LXXIII

WHEN Paul looked at the envelope that Monica had given him, he was surprised to see that it was addressed, not to 'Miss Dean' but to 'Mrs. Sloan'. He assumed that she had given it to him in error. At any rate, he had her telephone number and so could get in touch with her.

She seemed delighted to hear from him and asked him to tea that same day.

"Can you tell me the address?"

"I thought I'd given it to you."

"Yes, you did, but there must have been some mistake. The envelope says Mrs. Sloan. . . ."

"I am Mrs. Sloan."

"Are you married then?" he asked in astonishment.

"Yes." All at once her voice became indistinct. "I'll tell you about it when we meet." Hurriedly, she rang off.

At four o'clock he arrived at the semi-detached house in Crouch End, puzzled at finding her in such surroundings. With a desire for physical proximity which seemed to be characteristic of her, she greeted him by taking both his hands in her own and then threw a comradely arm round his shoulder. Her appearance was slovenly. She wore slippers, trodden down at the heels, a skirt with the zip-fastener undone, and a woollen jumper of no particular shape or colour. Whisps of her coarse black hair had escaped from the combs that held it up and straggled down her neck. Yet, once again, in spite of all this, her presence stirred Paul so that he wanted only to be near her and watch the slow, lazy movements of her limbs under the soiled, untidy clothes which covered but could not conceal them.

"I fell asleep after lunch and only woke up a few minutes before you arrived," she explained.

She showed him into a room littered with books, papers and belongings of an even more personal kind. A handkerchief lay on the floor and she stooped to pick it up. The sofa was piled with rumpled cushions and Paul guessed that it was there that she had been lying. He felt an absurd desire to sit in the same place.

"I'll put on the kettle." She went out, and without her, he at once began to feel restless. He got up, wandered about the room and at last went to the bow windows that overlooked the small back-garden. A man sat out at the far end of the lawn, reading a book. Both his thinness and his stature were remarkable; he had a bulging forehead, high cheek-bones, and eyes that looked enormous behind their thick glasses. Sitting slouched in such a way that his head seemed to grow out of his narrow chest, he was too absorbed to notice that Paul was watching him. From time to time a nervous tic convulsed his whole face.

"My husband."

Paul started at her voice; she had come in without a sound.

"I'd no idea you were married."

"It was only a few days after that house-party. He writes. You may have heard of him—Morgan Sloan."

"Yes, I believe I once read a short story of his. I rather liked it. A sort of—of fairy story."

"A fairy story!" She laughed. "Yes, I'm afraid he'll always be regarded as a writer for children. It's rather sad."

"I'm sorry. Have I said the wrong thing?"

"Of course not! . . . He was John's best friend, you know. John said that no children should be allowed to read his work. He said that grown-ups didn't like it, not because it was childish, but because it was too adult for them."

"That's interesting." But he was not really thinking about literature. "And do you agree with that?"

She shrugged her shoulders. "I know nothing about writing, only what John taught me. I'm a complete Philistine." She threw herself full-length on to the sofa. "In any case, I've read only three or four of Morgan's stories." She looked up, and smiled: "Does that surprise you? Frankly, they bore me." She added: "I'm not in love with him you know."

"But I thought—you said——"

His incredulity seemed to amuse her. "Oh, he knew that when I married him. He said it made no difference. I was unhappy at the time—I'd just heard that John had no chance of recovery—and he was very kind and gentle to me. He's one of the kindest people I know. John always wanted me to marry him, and it seemed the best thing." She tore at a fingernail. "There were other, more sordid reasons, too. I thought I was going to have a baby. Not his. Even that he didn't mind. But it all turned out to be a mistake—the doctor told me it was impossible for me to have a child without an operation." She leapt up: "Damn! I'd forgotten all about that kettle."

Paul liked Morgan Sloan. He appeared to be almost blind, and through tea innumerable little mishaps befell him; he knocked a table over, he filled his cup too full, his cigarette burnt a hole in one of the chair-covers. He spoke in a grave, courteous voice, showed a sincere interest in Paul, and made him feel that he was liked and appreciated.

"How are you getting on with George Wandle?"

"I've left."

"You have!" Monica, who had lost herself in a kind of animal stupor while they were talking, suddenly woke up. "I am glad. Aren't you, Morgan?"

"I think it's probably a good thing."

"I'm damned sure it is. What are you going to do now?"

"I don't know yet. I've saved most of my pay while I've been with him, but that won't last long. I'm not even certain where I'm going to live."

"Why don't you live with us?"

Monica would listen to none of his objections. Why not? What could be better? If he liked he could pay them a few shillings a week, but it was quite unnecessary. She turned eagerly to Morgan and he, too, added his persuasion.

Paul wanted nothing better than to be near Monica, and yet he was afraid—of himself, of her. He hesitated, and at the same moment he felt her knee press against his own. How did she dare with Morgan sitting opposite to them? Then he realized; the evening sunlight glinted on the cruelly thick lenses.

"Say 'yes'," Monica urged.

"Do say 'yes'," Morgan reiterated.

LXXIV

HE was horrified, he wished to leave and yet somehow he could not. Disgust filled him. He told himself that this was what he had all the time been secretly desiring and yet, now that it had happened, it sickened him. It was far worse than he had ever imagined: taking advantage of Morgan's short sight, Monica would attempt to caress him even when her husband was present. Under the breakfast-table her hand would seek his knee; meeting him in the corridor as she came from a bath she would press herself against him; one morning she even came to his bedroom. He felt that his very presence in the house was a betrayal of Morgan's hospitality. Moreover, he was committing a worse betrayal: the betrayal of his love for Anne.

Compared to that love, what he felt for Monica was something base, trivial and ephemeral. So he told himself, only to discover that an infatuation of the senses can be as potent as any other kind of infatuation. He despised Monica, there were moments when he even hated her, and yet she obsessed him to the exclusion of all else. Time and again during the four days he lived at the house in Crouch End he had to repudiate her suggestion that they should sleep together. Yet, in his heart, he knew that this was what he desired and would in the end do.

His persistent refusals made her ill-tempered, even hysterical. She was for ever nagging at Morgan, as if she blamed him for Paul's reluctance to satisfy her desires. Perhaps she was not far wrong. Morgan's gentle trust was what really kept Paul from her.

"But why not?" she asked one evening, in exasperation. "Why ever not?"

"I've told you."

"You're too absurd! You're just a baby!" She picked up a cushion and then flung it back on to the sofa. "What's the matter with me? What don't you like about me? Do you think I've got some disease?"

"You know it's not that."

"Then what the hell is it?" He did not answer, and she exclaimed contemptuously: "I know: it's Morgan. Oh, don't be such a damned prig. Anyway, how many times have I told you that when we married it was only on the condition that I should be free, absolutely free?"

"Even so, I couldn't do it. I couldn't betray him like that. I should be ashamed for the rest of my life."

"You're such a little gentleman," she said with ruthless sarcasm. "You and Morgan between you—you make me sick. I wish you were dead, both of you. I wish—wish——"

The door-handle turned and Morgan peered in. She swung round in a fury: "What do you want?"

"Sorry. I just came for a book."

"You were listening outside! You were spying on me! I've told you, I won't stand for it. I won't be spied on."

"My dear Monica——"

"Don't dear me!"

"Monica——"

He put out a hand to touch her, but she slapped him across the face. His glasses clattered down on to the floor. His eyes, curiously small and weak now, attempted to focus on the face they could not see. There was no reproach, no hurt, no anger in them; only tenderness and love.

"Get out!" she screamed. "Don't stare at me like that! Get out of here!"

"Very well. But let me find my glasses first."

She gave them a kick out into the hall. "They're in the hall now."

He groped his way out, and then went down on his hands and knees; before she slammed the door behind him, Paul had a glimpse of him, long, thin, ink-stained fingers scrabbling outwards over bare linoleum, eyes peering. Strangely, Paul felt no pity now. He wanted to hurt Morgan as she had hurt him; he wanted to tread on him, kick him and hit him in the face.

By the unspoken sympathy that exists between lovers Monica must have guessed. She came to him and laid her head on his breast.

"You make me so unhappy."

"Do I?"

She looked up. "I'll come tonight."

"Tonight." He could still hear Morgan lumbering about in the passage but he did not care.

LXXV

"In the past I had often imagined what it would be like at that moment: there would be rapture, tenderness, exaltation and in the end a sad peace when we lay, utterly satisfied, in each other's arms. No. The reality was quite different. I was sobbing with rage, humiliation and disgust, and she herself seemed to be possessed by a demon. At last I thrust her from me, but she pleaded: 'I needn't go yet. Morgan doesn't matter. Let me stay. A little longer, just a little longer!'

" 'Go, go, go!' She tried to cling to me, but I put both arms round her waist and half carried, half pushed her from the room. Frantically I turned the key in the door and then stood leaning against it—breathless, sobbing, appalled. Slowly, I went back to the bed, tidied the bed-clothes and lay down. My sobs had ceased. My face against the pillow, I was utterly still but for a shudder that from time to time ran through my whole body.

"My soul seemed to fall, precipice by precipice, gulf by gulf into a darkness of shame and outrage. I thought of Anne, of Morgan, of you and then, strangely, of Betty. Why of Betty? I don't know; I suppose because she was associated with a kind of love that I knew I should never again experience. It was not only a conventional, physical innocence that I had lost—that, after all, was inevitable and unimportant—but I felt that I had betrayed something at once less obvious and more precious.

"Betrayal. . . . That was the word which again and again passed through my mind, each time searing it with the same deadly anguish. You, Betty, Morgan, Anne—again and again I thought of you. Yes, I thought of Anne, but my feelings for her had all at once altered in a subtle way. I loved her still and felt that I had betrayed that love, and yet I was at last seeing through her for the first time. I had at last got to know her. . . . You see, it was only then that I realized that she and Monica were, at heart, the same. They did not want me for myself, but for what I could do to them. And that was their attitude to everyone else—though Anne concealed it with a subtlety Monica lacked. To them, everyone was an experience, and that was all.

". . . It's strange, I can speak like this about Anne, I know her utterly, through and through, and yet—" he shrugged his shoulders—"I still love her. I love her not less, but more. But with a love that has altered—more serene, more profound, more durable.

". . . It was growing light. I watched the melancholy, suburban dawn and then got up and dressed, packed my things and went down to breakfast. Monica pretended to be surprised when I said that I must leave; I offered some excuses, but cared too little to make them sound convincing. When Morgan went out to re-fill the teapot, she suddenly gripped my wrist, her sharp, crimson nails digging into it. 'Stay, stay, stay!' she whispered. 'Don't go. Don't!' I shook my head, and at the same moment, Morgan came back. We went on eating as if nothing had happened.

"Morgan walked down to the station with me. 'I'm sorry you have to go like this. You must come and stay with us again.'

" 'Thank you.'

" 'I mean that. We shall miss you.'

" 'You've—you've been very kind,' I stammered.

"His hand rested on my arm. 'You mustn't mind my asking you this, but have you—do you need any money? Please don't be offended, only I thought that *if* you did——"

" 'I think I have enough. Of course I'm not offended.'

"We arrived at the station, and he turned to say good-bye. His hand seemed to grope for mine, but then held it firmly. 'Good-bye. Best of luck.'

"From the remoteness created by his height and his thick glasses, he looked down at me. I knew that he liked me. I knew that he knew."

LXXVI

"THAT's all. Except for what happened here."

It was almost dark. From the tree under which we were seated a leaf fluttered down on to my lap. I crunched it in one hand.

"And now?" I asked.

He shrugged his shoulders.

". . . You know, I can't help feeling that all this has been partly my fault. I took you away from the island, I promised you so much. And the awful thing is that from the very start I had forebodings. All the time a voice was saying: 'Don't, don't, don't.'"

"Oh, but you mustn't be so silly. You're not to blame. It had to happen, the awakening had to come. And the fact that it came with such a jolt was not your fault—was no one's fault. Life begins in a dream from which one must sooner or later rouse oneself. It's horribly painful when one first wakes and sees things as they are—without the comfort of illusion—and one's immediate impulse is to shut it all out; to close one's eyes and sink back into the old, comforting dream. But that's fatal. That's what I feel I must at any cost avoid doing. 'Life begins where the search for truth begins.' And if life, then art also. I think my only hope as a writer is to keep my eyes open—however much it hurts; to refuse to fall asleep again. Many, many times during these last few days I've resisted the impulse to shield myself behind some new illusion—if not the old illusion of everything being for the best in the best possible of all worlds, then, the natural converse of that—the illusion of life's utter hopelessness and worthlessness. . . . Any illusion would comfort me now, but having once woken I want to stay awake." He turned to me, but it was too dark to see his face. "Don't you agree with me? I'm right, aren't I?"

"I'm sure you're right."

He sighed. "I wanted to hear you say that. It's only that belief that has kept me going these last two or three days. Otherwise—I should have tried again to kill myself. . . . Through all my unhappiness and shame and longing for Anne, I've gone on saying to myself: 'You're awake. Your eyes are at last open. You've achieved something.'" He broke off. "Perhaps I'm only deceiving myself."

"I'm quite certain you're not."

". . . I like to feel that when I write again—perhaps not for three or four years—it'll be different. The dream is over, the reality begins. . . . And funnily enough it's just this that I first want to write about—I mean, about the transition from sleep to waking; about the disenchantment that comes—I suppose?—in all our lives, but is so often delayed or disregarded; about truth and illusion, and the superiority of truth; about the importance of reality to any writer. . . . Above all about my own personal crisis——"

"And mine too," I put in quietly. "I haven't been just a spectator."

"Yes, I know. I realize that now."

There was a long silence which I at last broke:

"Well, I'm glad you've told me."

"I'm glad too. I wanted to before, only——"

"Only?"

"Somehow I couldn't."

"Why on earth not?"

"You seemed so far away. It was as if a rampart had been built between us. Every word, every action, every feeling was somehow chilled."

"I don't understand that. Didn't I seem sympathetic enough? Didn't I——?"

"Oh, of course you were sympathetic enough. You were wonderful. That was half the trouble." He saw my perplexity. "It's curious and paradoxical, but if you had been angry and reproachful with me I think I should have found it easier. You might have reduced the terrible feeling of guilt that I always had when I was with you. I discovered something rather strange. It's easy enough to forget the injuries that are done to you, but the injuries that you do to others—they can't be forgotten. The thought of what I've done to you . . . I never imagined our friendship would survive it."

"Oh, but you've been tormenting yourself needlessly. You've never done me any injuries."

"I have! I have!" he exclaimed. "And now I'm so ashamed. I want to make amends."

"If you've injured me, then good heavens, I've injured you."

He shook his head. "I misjudged you horribly. I was selfish, stupid, ungrateful. . . . I was afraid and ashamed to love. As if love were ever wrong! The wrong can only come in the expression that we find for it. You know, it was through Wandle—yes, through Wandle—that I realized that. From the bad we recognize the good, from the base, the noble—I suppose that's how it was. . . . Suddenly that night I saw that your feelings towards me were different from his feelings. I knew then that probably in my whole life no one would care for me with the same unselfishness and devotion."

"I don't deserve that."

"It happens to be true."

There was a silence; we did not need to seek each other's hands or even to turn to each other.

ABOUT THE AUTHOR

FRANCIS KING was born in 1923 in Switzerland and spent his
childhood in India, where his father was a senior government
official. He first visited England, where he was educated, at the
age of nine. After having travelled to many parts of the world for
the British Council, he eventually resigned from that organisation
to dedicate himself entirely to writing. Despite his now advanced
age, he continues to write acclaimed novels and to review books.
He is a past winner of the Somerset Maugham Prize and the
Katherine Mansfield Short Story Prize. A President Emeritus of
International PEN and a Fellow of the Royal Society of Literature,
he is a recipient of the honour CBE (Commander of the British
Empire), awarded by Queen Elizabeth II.